DAWN O'PORTER lives in Los Angeles with her husband Chris, her two boys Art and Valentine, and her cat Lilu and dog Potato.

Dawn started out in TV production but quickly landed in front of the camera, making numerous documentaries for the BBC and Channel 4, the most famous being her immersive investigations of polygamy, size zero, childbirth, free love, breast cancer and the movie *Dirty Dancing*. Further TV work included *This Old Thing*, a prime-time Channel 4 show celebrating the wonders of vintage clothing.

Dawn's journalism has appeared in multiple UK publications and she was the monthly columnist for *Glamour* magazine. She is now a full-time writer of six books – although she would probably have written sixteen if it weren't for her addiction to Instagram Stories.

Most recently, Dawn has written the script for *Especially for You*, a jukebox musical using the infamous Stock Aitken Waterman back catalogue. She is also interviewing a variety of guests for her new 'So Lucky' podcast series.

www.dawnoporter.co.uk
@hotpatooties
/DawnOF

Also by Dawn O'Porter

The Cows

SO LUCKY

DAWN O'PORTER

HarperCollins*Publishers*

HarperCollins*Publishers* Ltd
1 London Bridge Street,
London SE1 9GF

www.harpercollins.co.uk

This paperback edition 2020

1

First published by HarperCollins*Publishers* 2019

Copyright © Dawn O'Porter 2019

'Luck' definition © Lexico.com / powered by Oxford

Dawn O'Porter asserts the moral right to
be identified as the author of this work

A catalogue record for this book is available from the British Library

ISBN: 978-0-00-812610-0

This novel is entirely a work of fiction.
The names, characters and incidents portrayed in it are
the work of the author's imagination. Any resemblance to
actual persons, living or dead, events or localities is
entirely coincidental.

Set in Berling LT Std by Palimpsest Book Production Ltd,
Falkirk, Stirlingshire

Printed and bound in the UK by CPI Group (UK) Ltd, Croydon CR0 4YY

All rights reserved. No part of this publication may be
reproduced, stored in a retrieval system, or transmitted,
in any form or by any means, electronic, mechanical,
photocopying, recording or otherwise, without the prior
permission of the publishers.

MIX
Paper from
responsible sources
FSC™ C007454
www.fsc.org

This book is produced from independently certified FSC™ paper
to ensure responsible forest management.

For more information visit: www.harpercollins.co.uk/green

Dedicated to Caroline

LANCASHIRE COUNTY LIBRARY	
3011814022344 1	
Askews & Holts	24-Aug-2020
AF	£8.99
NST	

LUCK [n] /lʌk/:

Success or failure apparently brought by
chance rather than through one's own actions.

Everyone else is OK

Everyone else's life is perfect

Everyone is talking about me

Everyone has this figured out except me

Everyone knows I can't do this

We are all SO LUCKY.
What could we possibly have to complain about?

Everyone has their shit

Everyone needs to be kinder to themselves

Everyone's in the struggle together

Everyone isn't me

Everyone is fighting a battle you know nothing
about . . .

1

Ruby

My kid moved out the day she was born. For someone like me, becoming a mother was when I thought I'd finally give my whole self to another human without being constrained by the limitations of my condition. I thought my undying love for this little person would be met by her needing me in a way I had never been needed before. But as it turns out, I'm not sure my kid has ever needed me other than in a physical capacity to keep her alive. Being a mother hasn't been the sweet experience I imagined it to be. In fact, my kid is an asshole. Some might say she gets it from me.

It's 7.05 a.m. I am lying on my bed and she's screaming like she's being attacked in the next room. She isn't being attacked, she is fine. She doesn't sleep in a cot, she knows how to get up. But still, she shouts and screams until I go into her room. Only to tell me to get away from her when I do.

I didn't want a girl. I wanted a boy. I have no idea how to

teach a girl to love herself. I thought, if I had a boy, then Liam could just take care of that side of things. I also don't like how manipulative women are. I didn't realise it started so early.

I reach for my dressing gown that I keep on the other side of the bed. It's no substitute for a husband, but at least it's something to wrap around my body when I wake up in the morning. My dressing gown is one of the few things I adore. It's a 1970s terry-towelling, full-length, high-necked, long-sleeved Victorian-looking thing that hides almost every inch of my body other than my face and neck. I spent ages looking for the perfect one, nothing modern had the same coverage. It means I can answer the door before I get dressed, should someone come knocking. I often wonder who the woman who owned it before me was, as it came with certain signs of wear and tear. Did she also feel the need to hide herself in her own home? Did she have children who loved her? Did she live a life of self-inflicted solitude? Liam hated this dressing gown, but I saw it as my only option after what he did to me on our wedding day.

Getting Bonnie dressed every morning is on a par with being in one of those shark cages, and the shark getting into it with you. She kicks me directly in the chest and stomach. She's bitten me a number of times. She tries to get away, and I have to pull her back and hope to God I don't dislocate a shoulder or hip.

I love her, of course. But I don't love parenting. People tell you not to wish it away. They say I'll miss her being small. I won't. I will never miss this. Living with a toddler is like living with someone with a complete lack of empathy. Something I swore I wouldn't do again, when I moved out of home, and moved away from my mother.

Monday mornings are always the hardest, especially after she has spent the weekend with her dad. Liam doesn't bother with the boring stuff. He lets her eat what she wants, he lets her stay up late watching TV until she falls asleep. He doesn't bother bathing her or brushing her teeth. Which means that when Bonnie comes back to me she is sticky to the touch, with a yellow smile and dreadlocks in her hair. I am the one who then has to force her into the bath. The one who has to brush out the knots. The one who has to scrape the fur from her teeth. The one who ruins the fun.

I put the TV on for her while I make her breakfast. I don't like preparing food, even if it is for my child. I hate a lot of things I am supposed to like – especially when it comes to being a mother, but also just life in general. I don't like self-help, self-care, the 'mum scene' or social media. I hate politics, and the way it divides people. I hate football for the way it brings people together, but still puts them on opposite teams. I hate how a woman with her top off is more likely to sell a packet of mints than a woman with her top on. I hate how the male gaze is still more powerful than a woman's self-worth.

I hate how the male gaze so rarely comes in my direction. I hate how when it does I bat it away like a bug that might sting me.

I hate so many things. I hate that after my appointment I'll spend the day making a young girl look thinner and smoother when there was nothing wrong with her in the first place. I hate that my job has become this. I hate that I am part of the problem I am so upset about, but keep doing it because I am too afraid to try anything else.

My daughter calls me from the other room where she is watching TV. She tells me she hates the programme she is watching and wants something else. I change it and tell her she shouldn't use the word hate. I remind her that she has many more options in her lexicon that she can use to describe how she feels about something, and that she should be more clever with her choice of them.

I hate that I talk to her like that when she is only three and a half.

I call Bonnie into the kitchen for breakfast. She says she isn't hungry and doesn't feel well. I put my hand on her forehead; she's fine. I put *Octonauts* on and give her a bowl of dry cereal to eat on the sofa while I go and get dressed. I hate that I am not the kind of mother who puts my arms around my child and tells her everything is going to be OK.

My appointment is at eleven. After that, things will feel better.

There is only one dress to wear when I am at this stage of the cycle – my burgundy velvet maxi dress with high neck and long bell sleeves with elasticated wristbands. I made it myself when I was at university and it still fits perfectly. I'm the same size at forty-three as I was at twenty-one. That takes a certain amount of effort. When you have a condition like mine, you do what you can to keep the symptoms minimal.

Low weight is key. I eat like a bird and exercise for at least an hour a day. But in the privacy of my own home, of course. Someone like me can't go to a gym. I purchased myself an exercise bike with a computer screen attached to it, so I can do classes with real-time instructors. I noticed a little camera at the top of the screen. It is disabled, but I put some gaffer tape over it just in case. I kept imagining someone being able to see me on my bike. I couldn't take the risk that maybe they could. That is quite possibly the most horrifying thing I can imagine.

My burgundy dress says a lot about who I am. It all came together for me when a guy I'd had dinner with a couple of times once described me as an 'Amish Virginia Woolf'. He wasn't being kind. But, I actually loved the description. I feel a deep connection to Virginia Woolf. It's comforting to know that genius can lie in the socially impaired.

'Amish Chic' became my look. I make most of my own clothes now. Long, gothic velvet gowns. High necks, long sleeves, frills down each breast, a pinched-in waist and long, heavy skirts. I wear black pointy boots with a low heel that lace up the front and finish just above the ankle. My skin is pale, I wear a lick of mascara, some heavy blusher and try to match my lips to my dress whenever I can, usually burgundy. I may or not wear tights, depending on where I'm at in the cycle. But the uniform remains the same. I made a number of thick cotton versions of the dress for the summer months. Pale blue, a floral, but nothing too bold. Vintage Laura Ashley fabrics are my style, I buy them on eBay. The boots remain the same, no matter the dress or weather. I have repulsive feet. If someone wanted to torture me they would abandon me on a packed beach with a bikini and flip-flops on. I'd likely get into the sea and swim as far away from the shore as I could, hoping to one day reach a deserted island, where I would make a thick dress out of sheets of seaweed and hide in caves at the very hint of life on the horizon. I'm not a summer person. It is now June in London and some days are sweltering. If it's really hot I tend to stay at home as much as I can. One of the reasons I am so locked into my job is that it gives me very little reason to leave the house. I invested in an air conditioning unit last year, which has made the hot summer months much more bearable. Other than getting Bonnie to and from nursery, I have very little reason to go out unless it's social, which is a rare occurrence in itself, but of course I do have friends. To be fair to myself, I am very consistent and I offer very comforting advice to people when they need it. I'm quite proud of that.

Loading Bonnie into her buggy takes a moderate amount of strength on my part. I have to press her down just below her belly button, so that I can get the straps on her and secure her properly. She is particularly unpleasant this morning. I say her name over and over – 'Bonnie, get in now. Bonnie. Bonnie, sit down!' – all the while regretting it. It has never felt natural for me to call her Bonnie. It's a curse of a name, meaning beautiful. An unfair pressure to put on a young girl. It was Liam's grandmother's name, and it meant a lot to him to pass it on. I agreed, but only if she had my surname. Liam didn't argue with that bit at all. I hate how progressive he was about so many things.

She is quite small for her age, but very strong. It takes a minute, but soon enough I have her in. I give her a box of raisins to distract her and somehow we manage to get out of the house.

When she finishes the raisins she throws the box onto the street and demands more. I don't have any, so I ignore her and keep pushing. It's a ten-minute walk to her nursery and I walk fast to burn off the toast and Marmite I had for breakfast. Bonnie gets more and more upset, eventually becoming physical. She launches herself backwards and forwards in the buggy, then from side to side too, trying to get herself free.

'I want to walk,' she yells between long, ear-splitting screams. It's the same every morning.

'There's nothing wrong with her,' I say to a mother who looks at my child pitifully. 'If I let her out we will never get there.' She makes some stupid face that implies I am being cruel, then walks off. Her snotty little brat following in tow. The self-righteousness of parenting is what grates on me the most. I avoid other mums as much as I can.

'She's fine,' I bark at someone else who thinks coming over and saying, 'Ahhhhhh,' and smiling at my crazy child is in some way the right thing to do. It is patronising and insincere. There is nothing to 'Ahhhhhh' about when a toddler is being a level ten.

'Maybe she's hungry,' says an old lady waiting at a crossing next to us. I was doing OK until she weighed in.

'Oh, you think maybe I should consider feeding my child?' I ask. She doesn't get my sarcasm.

'Yes, the poor little thing is probably starving.'

'Oh, well silly me. Forgetting to feed my child.' I could stop there, but why would I do that? 'There was me, listening to her delicate little screams, wondering what on earth could be the matter when all the while all I had to do was feed her. How could I have been so thick?'

The old woman looks at me with fear in her eyes. To be fair, I have gotten quite close to her face. I don't like old ladies and the way they act like they've got all the answers.

'Up yours,' I say, crossing the road. It's a retro phrase I use a lot. Firm, offensive but not sweary enough for people to ring an alarm. I find it very useful. I occasionally add a finger.

Lauren Pearce – Instagram post
@OfficialLP

The image is of Lauren in her kitchen holding a large glass filled with something green. She is wearing jeans and a tight pink shirt. She is fully made-up with perfectly highlighted blonde hair.

The caption reads:
Keeping healthy is so important to me. Feeling good in my body helps my mind feel better. I love my new #GreenMachineQT juicer. I get at least 3 of my 5 a day in one drink. Happy body, happy brain. #AD #selflove #love #together #women #acceptyourself #beyourself #knowyourtruth #womensupportingwomen #vegan

@florecent360: Why do Ads when you're about to marry one of the richest men in the country? Give your fee to charity??

@missiondone123 to @florecent360: She is her own person! Would it be better to live off her husband? I have so much respect for a woman paying her own way. OWN IT Lauren, I love you!!!

@MineAintYours: AD? SELL OUT. GET A REAL JOB that doesn't involve you only wearing pants.

@MatyMooMelly: I love you so much. Everything you say is what I need to hear. Thanks for being you

@pigeontoe: #relatable NOT.

@fabouty: Remember to love yourself. You are such an inspiration to me.

@Hartherlodge: Srsly, get a grip. Rich, thin, fit. What the fuck else do you need? That smoothie looks like when a dog eats grass then pukes it up.

@seveneh: I wish I had your figure.

Beth

I think to myself, right in the middle of it. If I am going to have all of this sex, with all of these strange men, I have to get some enjoyment out of it for me. I pull myself on top of him, and rub myself on his thigh. I forget about his pleasure, and just focus on my own. I'm bringing myself to the most phenomenal orgasm when I hear . . .

'Beth? Beth?' His voice is breathy and gentle. 'Beth? Beth?'

My eyes open.

'Were you having another one of your dreams?'

Shit.

'Yes I was,' I say. He thinks that the dreams I have, the ones that cause me to writhe around moaning in my sleep, are recurring dreams of me ballroom dancing. Because that is what I told him. I said that ballroom dancing is an unrequited ambition of mine. He got me classes for my last birthday. I am yet to use the vouchers.

'I was doing the waltz, with you. We were going to win I reckon,' I tell him, sleepily. Thinking it best not to mention the hot builder who was just paying more attention to my fanny than my foxtrot.

'You'd have been a beautiful dancer,' he says, smiling. 'Here, he's ready for you.' He passes me my four-month-old baby,

11

Tommy. I sit up, unclip my bra, and put my nipple in his mouth. Michael looks away. 'Let me know when you're done,' he says. 'I'll come get him and you can get some more sleep.'

'It's OK, I better work. What time is it?'

'Nine.'

'Wow, thanks. That's a legit lie-in.'

'Well, you've pumped enough to feed an entire baby army. He took his bottle happily at seven, there was no need to wake you,' he says, kissing my head gently.

'Thank you. I'm very lucky to have you as my husband.'

'And Tommy and I are very lucky to have you. Call me when you're done.'

Michael leaves the room. I hold my baby to my breast with one arm and use the other to reach for my phone.

As expected, my inbox is bulging already. The caterers, the florists, the cake maker, the PRs. This job is extremely demanding. I'd hoped to get six months' maternity leave when I got pregnant, but this came in a few months ago and I couldn't turn it down. That's the trouble when you run your own business, no one pays you for your time off. So I ordered the tablecloths when I was in the labour ward. I sacked a florist while my stitches were being done. I'm everyone's best friend, but I can be a boss when I need to be.

Michael managed to negotiate three months' paternity leave because he works for a start-up that sees itself as entirely modern in its approach to absolutely everything. Which is an ironic place for him to work. He is forty-four and not modern. Unlike me – I'm thirty-six but sit in an office with a twenty-six-year-old every day who gives a masterclass on how to be a millennial. But I am grateful for Michael's random modern job, because it's meant that I've been able to keep up with the level of attention needed to organise the celebrity wedding of the year. And I'm grateful I didn't have to sacrifice my work, although having to be 'grateful' towards my husband hasn't gotten me any closer to resolving our problem.

I was really enjoying that dream. I put down my phone and slip my hand between my legs. As if he knows what I'm thinking, my baby gurgles and pulls back from my nipple, giving me a judgemental side eye. He's probably right.

I swap him onto the other boob and stroke his head. It's a miracle I have him at all, and I *am* so grateful. Not because there is anything wrong with me. I'm thirty-six and apparently a 'geriatric' when it comes to making babies, but the doctor said I have the ovaries of a twenty-year-old. Michael is perfectly fertile too, despite his age. Men are so lucky in that way; they can be fathers once they're well past their 'peak'. We have to do it at the most inconvenient time in our lives, when our careers should really be all we have to think about. He took all of the tests as a distraction from the act of actually having sex. It was awkward in the appointments with the fertility doctor; he'd say he'd do what he could to get to the bottom of why I wasn't getting pregnant, and all the while I wanted to scream the reason directly into my husband's face.

'IT'S BECAUSE YOU WON'T HAVE SEX WITH ME. YOU NEVER FUCK ME. THAT IS WHY I AM NOT PREGNANT.' I felt like if I ever got pregnant from the once a month I managed to get him to come inside me, it would be a miracle. But I did. And then I was. And now I have my baby, so at least I got that out of this marriage.

I love my husband, I do. He is kind and fun in pretty much every area of life other than sex. His mother is the battle-axe of all battle-axes and their relationship is weird and loaded with sexual context. They, of course, don't see it, but I do. Is it really normal for a grown man to pop over to his mum's house for a foot massage? Is it? No, it isn't. Is it also normal to call your mother every morning, or to ask her to go to dentist appointments with you because you are scared? I want my little boy to know that I am always there for him, but I also want him to have healthy sexual relationships with other women, and not insist that I come on all their family holidays. I will also do my best not to make his future lovers feel like their relationship with him is second place. As long as he always comes home for Christmas.

Michael is always 'tired'. He says it's his age.

We had a lot of sex when we got together, which was fun while it was happening but often ended strangely. He'd say things like, 'It's natural for a man to want to flee after sex.' Or, 'You didn't come, I don't mind if you finish yourself off.' Funnily enough I rarely did – a comment like that can send a clitoris sailing to the ground like an unopened parachute. Thud.

It wasn't that he was cruel, just weird about sex. But we did it lots, so the romantic in me always presumed that all we needed was time. Practice. I put his issues down to the lack of wedlock at the time. He's kind of traditional and maybe marriage meant a lot to him? I presumed he'd be in his element from our wedding night on. But no, it was as if he had sullied his bride. When we got back to our suite he said, 'It's a shame you've slept with people before.' I walked out of the room, took off the sexy underwear I had on under my dress, changed it for my normal stuff and went back in to discover him asleep, or pretending to be asleep to get out of having sex with his whore of a wife.

There were always subtle undertones of blame. And as his sex drive has dwindled, his challenged machismo likes to make me feel that it's all my fault. A few weeks ago he said sex was off the cards because my breath smelt. I cleaned my teeth. To which he responded with, 'Mint makes me nauseous. You always get the toothpaste I don't like.' The dentist told me two days later that there were no signs of halitosis or anything dying underneath my tongue. But even still, I covered my mouth whenever I spoke to him for about a week after that.

Even during childbirth my body seemed to bother him. He stayed up by my head and kept giving me a really annoying head massage. The midwife asked him if he wanted to watch as Tommy was crowning, and Michael said, 'God no, that's not something I need to see.' I remember thinking, 'We just created a miracle and you're too disgusted by my body to watch it enter the world?' He also insisted that I wore a t-shirt while I was in labour. I hadn't packed one, so he gave me the one he had under his shirt. It was so tight on my big belly and felt uncomfortable. Also there was a strong smell of BO that made me feel sick. When I tried to take it off he said, 'You'll regret that. I was going to take a photo.'

15

My nudity makes him uncomfortable.

It's not like my new stretch marks and flabby belly are going to help with that, is it?

'You must have as much sex as you want,' I say to Tommy, as he suckles. 'Just make sure he or she is up for it, use a condom, and always say thank you.' He looks up at me, and I think he understands.

'Michael,' I call, getting out of bed and laying the baby down.

'You done?' he asks, peeping his head around the door.

'Yes, and I better get to work.'

He picks the baby up right away and burps him on his shoulder.

'Cool,' he says, leaving the room. 'I'll leave you to get dressed.'

God forbid he sees me naked.

Ruby

Arriving at the nursery, Bonnie yells at me like I'm a wild bear she needs to scare away. I unstrap her from the hell of her pushchair. Almost as soon as she is free, she runs inside with a huge smile on her face, and straight over to a teacher. She hugs her. I have to look away.

'They're always hardest on their mums,' says Miss Tabitha behind me. I had no idea she was there. I try to collapse the buggy, but something is stuck in the wheel and it won't fold properly.

'She's good as gold when she's here,' she continues, twisting the knife further into my heart. I carried her in my belly. My body was sliced open to get her out. I've kept her alive for three and a half years. I sacrificed my work, I lost a husband. How does she think it is reassuring to hear that I am the only person to whom she expresses hate?

The buggy won't close. I want to get out of this nursery and away from Miss Tabitha's nonchalant and unhelpful support. I am so hot in this heavy velvet and the extra layer of insulation that lies beneath it. My stress levels are not something I can hide.

'Can I help?' she asks, infuriating me further.

'No,' I reply, sweat appearing on my forehead and dripping

down my nose. I wipe it away with my billowing velvet sleeve.

'Are you sure I can't help?' she says again, as if I'm an idiot. If she went away I'd be able to do this but she is standing over me like a teacher assessing my work. I am really struggling now. I know my rage is against me, and that if I stopped banging the bloody thing, took a breath and went at it a bit easier it would do what it normally does and just fold. But I'm annoyed, I am making a point and backing down isn't part of my DNA.

'DAMN IT,' I shout, slamming the buggy down and kicking it with my foot. I try not to swear, even in times of high stress. There is a moment of stillness before I realise a few of the other teachers have joined Miss Tabitha, and that one of them has shut the door into the nursery to shield the children from my aggression. They presume I am about to apologise. I am not.

'What are you looking at?' I say, my top lip curling over my teeth like a wild cat's. Something about the way I say this makes them all take a step back. A brave one starts walking slowly towards me with an extended hand.

'Don't touch me,' I bark.

'I'm not going to touch you,' she says gently. 'I'm going to collapse the buggy for you. There's no need to be so angry.'

'No need to be angry?' She has no idea! I feel a hand on my back. 'Leave me alone, please,' I screech, launching myself forward and landing on top of the pushchair. With me lying across it, it shoots about four feet down the corridor and crashes into the wall. The skirt of my dress gets caught in the wheel. An ear-splitting ripping sound fills the hallway, and my dress is torn open from the hem to just above the knee. I'm left lying across the pushchair with my legs exposed. They can see my legs. I could react with tears or anger. I, as usual, choose the latter to mask the former.

'Now look what you made me do!' I yell, jumping to my feet, desperately gathering my torn skirt so I can hold it shut with my hands. They say nothing but look at me with as much disdain as their job description will allow.

I have to get out of here. I can't face these women again. Not now they have seen my legs.

'You know what? I've been unhappy with this place for a while. You feed them too many snacks. Bonnie never eats her dinner,' I say, charging toward the closed nursery door.

'Ruby, the children are about to start their music class. Let's leave them to it, shall we?'

I ignore Miss Tabitha. I have to get out of here. They saw my legs. Oh God, they saw my legs. I open the door to the nursery, all of the children turning to look. I walk over to Bonnie and tell her to come with me.

'No,' she stomps.

'Bonnie, come with Mummy please. It's time to go.'

'No. No,' she screams, lying down flat on the floor.

'Come on!' I say, calm but stern, acting like I have a total grip of this situation. I am her mother. She can behave this way, but ultimately has to do what I say. I try again.

'Up now please, Bonnie. We have to go.'

She is now cataclysmic. Screeching and writhing, desperate to be saved from the horror of more time with me. I feel the same agony, but I cannot back down. I keep hold of my skirt with one hand, not allowing the split to open again.

'Right, Bonnie, enough!' I say, as I pick her up with my spare hand. I don't know how I manage it, sheer desperation maybe, but soon she is up and on my hip. She kicks and pulls but I hold her as tight as I can and I storm out of the room. Teachers try to stop me, but I need to get out of here. And I can't come back. Not now they have seen my legs.

I pick the stroller up with my left hand and carry both Bonnie and it out of the door and on to the street. The split wide open. Why oh why would this happen on the day I didn't wear tights?

I call Liam. The phone rings out. I call again. No answer. He texts immediately.

Sorry, in Amsterdam at this conference. Everything OK?

Damn it, I forgot he's away this week. I tell him nothing is wrong. He replies again with a picture of a very unattractive dog he said he saw.

Can you show this to Bonnie? She loves a dog!

I don't reply.

My phone rings out twice, then rings again. I'd put it back in my bag and am desperately trying to retrieve it while Bonnie screams in her buggy.

'I want to go back to nursery,' she chants. I want her to go back too, but I am too distressed to turn around. They think I'm crazy. They saw my legs. I can never go back. Ever.

By the time I find my phone I see that I have three missed calls from my mother. She hasn't called me in around three months. Why now? It's like she knows. I am having a disastrous parenting moment and she is right there to rub it in.

I struggle on for a while and we come to the entrance of a park. I push Bonnie in, and let her out of her buggy. She immediately runs off and starts collecting sticks and leaves, happy. I take a seat on a bench and call my mother back, taking in a long slow breath before I do.

'Who is this?' she asks when she answers. She is drunk, I can tell.

'Hello, Mum, I saw that you called.'

'What do you want?'

'I'm in a park with Bonnie,' I tell her, knowing this mood well, and knowing that detailed responses are pointless. 'Just calling back to check you're alive.'

'Like you care, you little beast,' she says, followed by a cackle so loud I put my hand over my phone to make sure no one else in the park hears it.

'Don't be unkind, Mother.'

'What did you say?' she asks, her tone instantly snapping into defence mode.

'I said, please don't be unkind. I don't like it when you call me that.'

'Oooo, she doesn't like it when I call her that. She gets all upset. The poor ugly beast.'

'Mother, did you want something specific because if not I am going to go.'

'I'm going to kill myself,' she says. Suddenly deadpan.

'Don't do that,' I tell her, as I have done so many times over the years.

'You can't stop me. I'm going to do it tonight.'

'No you won't,' I say.

'Yes I will.'

'Why?' I ask her, wondering if this might be the one miraculous time I get an answer.

'Shut up. It's not like you care about me—'

I hold the phone away from my ear while she continues to rant abuse.

'Are you done?' I ask, after a minute or so. She seems to be and goes quiet. 'Mum, I've got to go.' I brace myself for the next stab.

'Go on then. Piss off. If your own mother doesn't love you, who will?' she says, before hanging up.

I feel tears begin to well in my eyes as I watch Bonnie play happily without me. I know the second I tell her we need to leave, she will act just like my mother does towards me. Screaming, kicking, yelling, telling me she doesn't love me, acting like my very presence in her life is unbearable. I never imagined that becoming a parent would be like reliving my adolescence. Minus the cruel name at least. Mum has called me 'The Beast' ever since she burst in on me in the shower when I was sixteen. It's why I never dare risk my own child seeing me naked. Who only knows what cruel salutations a toddler might come up with.

How does everyone else make parenting look so easy?

'Move please,' says a man who is standing in front of me, blocking my view of Bonnie.

'Excuse me?' I reply, with a certain amount of attitude.

'Please move from the bench,' he repeats. 'Please.'

'I absolutely will not move from this bench. I was here first. I'm watching my daughter.'

'Look, I'd really appreciate it if you would go and sit over there. Please,' he says calmly, still laden with something heavy. 'You don't understand. Please, just move.'

He points to an empty bench a few metres away. I can't be bothered to fight him – I have had enough conflict for one morning and need a break. I gather my bag and the buggy and move a few benches down. Making sure he hears me say 'Up yours' as I go.

As I settle onto my new seat, I have one eye on him, and one eye on Bonnie. She is playing happily, so I concentrate most of my attention on the man. Is he trying to watch Bonnie play? He's now revealed that he is carrying a packet of baby wipes. It's very odd. I cautiously start to move towards my daughter, just in case.

But then he stands up and faces the bench. Using the wet wipes he cleans the bird poo and any other dirt off the slats. Scrubbing hard in places, polishing others. It is meticulous work. By the time he has finished, it is gleaming like the day it was painted. Satisfied, he sits on it and looks out at the park. I can see a million thoughts passing behind his eyes. I wonder what they are. Eventually, he stands up slowly and walks away; somehow, a little less upset than he was before. What an extraordinary show to witness.

I head straight over to the bench. A silver plaque is attached to the middle of it that I hadn't noticed before.

Verity, loving daughter and sister. Gone too soon, forever missed and loved. Your spirit will always live in these gardens. 1989–1996

I sit on the bench and look over at Bonnie. Could the man be Verity's father? I try to imagine losing Bonnie. Wondering how I would feel if all I had left were my memories and a bench.

I need to work harder at those memories.

My assistant, 'Risky' (youngest of three, her parents let her siblings name her) emails me, despite sitting less than three metres away. She doesn't remember a time when people didn't have computers to communicate on their behalf. It's like she forgets she can just talk to me. Sometimes, she even sends me an email, hears it ping into my inbox, watches me read it, then asks me what I think. It's really extraordinary. I email back. I'm not the one who's going to tell the future it's wrong.

Tell her she can have whatever she wants. I'll meet with her after ROD

ROD is the code we use for Lauren Pearce and Gavin Riley's wedding. We tell them it stands for 'Riley Order of Day'. But actually we call it 'ROD' because when we first got the job Risky said, 'I'd love Gavin Riley to hot rod me.' It made me laugh so much we named the project after it. It makes us chuckle, but if anyone realised what it really stood for they would probably get all offended. There isn't much of a sense of humour in the serious world of celebrity. A lot of the time it's like we are organising a political dinner. Lauren Pearce is so famous she thinks the government is bugging her phone. I've been sent more NDAs for this wedding than Trump's cabinet give to their female staff.

Risky is beside herself about the entire wedding. She follows Lauren's every move. She says she is her favourite 'influencer'. If Lauren posts about a face cream, Risky buys it. If Lauren posts about anxiety, Risky eats a CBD gummy. This morning I had to sit through around forty seconds of Lauren pouting into the camera on her Instagram Stories. She was talking about some granola brand she has every morning. She did the whole thing with fake bunny ears and a twitchy bunny nose. There were also some love hearts floating across her face. She said this granola has helped her stay full until lunch time, and all the other advertising rhetoric breakfast brands rely on. I know it's a lie, because I spent three months testing menus with Lauren and she doesn't even eat breakfast.

I like Lauren though, I think. I mean, it's not like I get much out of her. Considering her Instagram feed is largely posts about happiness, self-confidence and being grateful, she's quite unassuming in person. I've not really had much alone time with her – her mother Mayra is usually with us. I get the impression their relationship is a little tense. I've worked with a lot of brides, and generally mothers are supporting figures who are just excited for their daughter's big day. I'm sure Mayra is excited for Lauren, but she is very bossy. Some days it feels like it's her wedding that I am organising. She's the kind of woman I can imagine slapping me in the face if I forget to tell her she looks nice.

'I'm getting that granola. It's got dark chocolate in it, and that can boost your mood,' Risky says, obviously back on Instagram and abandoning all work.

'But don't you think she's only saying it's good because she's getting paid to say it's good?'

'No boss, Lauren only posts about products she believes in. That's her promise to us.'

'"Us"?'

'Her fans.'

'Oh, I see,' I reply, pleased there is a clause in Risky's contract that essentially says she isn't allowed to lose her shit around celebrity clients. Risky has met Lauren twice, and both times this extremely effervescent, connected, confident and cool young woman has turned into a mute. She thinks Lauren is the Jesus of the social networks.

'She understands mental health,' Risky tells me often. 'Her anxiety isn't taboo. It's inspiring. We have to talk about mental health more.'

'Well, you are certainly flying the flag for that,' I'd say, to which she looks proud of herself. She talks about her anxiety like it's her pet cat. Something she needs to handle with care or it will scratch her eyes out. Something that is always tapping on her shoulder when she is trying to sleep. Something she has to keep under careful observation until it dies.

I don't know what sounds worse, anxiety or marriage. I am glad I only suffer from one of them.

'It's OK for her to monetise her Instagram feed,' Risky says, now applying some bright pink lipstick. 'Why should she give so much of herself to us for nothing? And at least she isn't just living off her rich husband. She's paying her own way, I respect that. She's a businesswoman really, showing us all that we shouldn't be taken for granted.'

'Yes, I suppose that's one way to look at it,' I say, putting on some mango-flavoured lip balm. Some of our chats make me feel so old. It's strange to think of myself as a grown-up, but around Risky I feel positively ancient. When I was a teenager we had posters of celebrities we liked on our bedroom walls. They felt like untouchable gods. Now these people expose every inch of their lives on Instagram and reply to their fans. If Madonna had replied to a message I sent her in the Nineties, I might have imploded. I'm not sure how healthy all this direct access to famous people is, for either them or their fans. Risky is obsessed.

'Well, I am grateful for her brand partnerships, because this wedding is going to cost more than North West's fourth birthday party,' I say, delighted with my cultural reference.

'Um, boss. North West is already six,' Risky says. I let the conversation dissipate naturally.

Lauren rather publicly turned down £600k from OK magazine, saying she didn't want her big day to be about that. She then quietly signed a million-pound deal with Veuve Clicquot to live-post the wedding on her Instagram feed. I suppose she will be in more control of it now, but it all boils down to the same thing – an absolute abuse of privacy that you willingly sign up for, leaving you powerless to tell the press to back off. It's not my job to judge, and I am making a fortune out of this wedding. I take twenty per cent of the whole cost, and the budget seems to increase every day. But I do think relationships are hard enough, without the public being involved. It can't be easy when everyone wants to know all of your business.

A few years ago I did weddings for budgets of £30k or less. It took one influential guest at a wedding breakfast to think the beef pies were a revelation to book me for her daughter's wedding (an IT girl, already divorced twice; third time lucky, I suppose) and that was that, I was catapulted into the world of high-budget nuptials.

While Risky pretends to work but actually tries to take

surreptitious selfies 'at work'/'feeling hungry'/'hoping today is a good day', I sit at my desk and try to look like I'm concentrating whilst scanning porn sites, to give my neglected clitoris a tiny thrill. I'm worried it might go into panic mode, break free from my cumbersome body and throw itself at random strangers if this drought carries on.

I think being starved of intimacy is why I currently have horn levels that seem impossible to control. I realise I only had a baby four months ago, and that my libido probably shouldn't be this high. But it's all I can think about. An obsession. It would be the same if I went on a vegan diet to lose weight; I would crave beef burgers and fantasise about dinner at Korean BBQ joints, where I'd get to dribble over the preparation of food as well as the joy of eating it at the end. The ultimate food experience, surely? My husband has put me on a brutal sex diet, and I am gagging for a three-course (at least) romp.

It's been so long since we did it. Last time was right at the beginning of the pregnancy. As soon as my body started to change, Michael pulled back even more than usual. When this job came in, Lauren and her mother wanted to test menus from around fifteen caterers. I joined them, of course. I ended up trying everything on their behalf, as neither of them seem to eat anything apart from kale and tofu, and maybe granola if they are being paid. I was never exactly a slip of a thing, but two stone later (and no that wasn't just the baby), I was pleased when they finally decided on a chef.

Michael suggested I employed a 'food taster' to do that job in future. To stop 'this happening again'. By 'this' he obviously meant me putting on weight. I didn't think it was a problem, really. All anyone else said to me when I was pregnant was that I was so lucky to be able to eat what I wanted. That I was eating for two. That I needed the calories.

Everyone except Michael. It gave him even more of a reason not to have sex with me. And then there was the pregnancy itself.

'The baby, the baby, I don't want to hurt the baby,' he would say. I don't know if that was genuine or not, but even our doctor's assurance that the baby wouldn't be damaged by his penis wasn't enough to help. He just couldn't do it. I'm not pregnant anymore, but he still acts like my vagina has teeth.

My nipples release some milk, as they seem to every time I think about sex.

'Risky, where is my pump?'

'Oh, I washed it for you,' she says. She's excellent like that.

Risky goes into the kitchen and returns with my electric breast pump. She is wearing an Eighties crop top today and high-waisted jeans. She is tall, slim, and loves neon. She's not pretty, exactly. She has quite a big nose and her hair is damaged from over-dyeing. Her skin isn't great, which is why she hangs off every recommendation Lauren and her filtered face make. Risky is attractive in her own magical way. Her style, quirks and personality are gorgeous. I quite like millennials, I've decided. I think maybe they will make the world a better place. Risky is certainly going to try.

She plugs in the pump, screws the bottles into place and gets it ready while I take off my top and bra – one of the benefits of being the boss at an all-female workplace. Before I was lactating, I'd often get to my desk in the morning and take my bra off right away. Heaven. I put on the weird elastic bra thingy I got that holds the bottles in place, so that I can pump whilst being hands free and getting on with work. Hardly any point in coming to the office at all, if I have to spend up to three hours of the day holding breast milk bottles into place.

'I feel so hot right now,' I laugh. Half naked at my desk. My tummy rolls hanging over my trouser waistband, my big boobs being sucked on by plastic funnels.

'You're amazing. A powerhouse. Nailing motherhood and running a business, it's very inspiring,' Risky says. She's endlessly searching for role models to guide her, despite always reminding everyone of her independence. She is in a constant state of anticipation, waiting for someone she admires to say the thing that lifts her through her day. Some days, apparently, it's me. Risky fantasises about a perfect future full of love and success, she believes in romance and is a true woman's woman. 'I'm from a generation of women who were born feminists,' she likes to tell me. 'Your generation had to learn to be.' I often have to remind her that I am only thirty-six. She talks about her thirties like an event that will happen so far in the future, it is impossible to imagine.

'Let me know when you're done, I'll get the milk in the fridge right away,' she says, heading back to her desk. Just before she reaches it, she turns back and says, 'It's so great, you know. For you to have a husband who takes care of the baby while you go to work. I hope I find someone like that one day. I think both parents should make sacrifices for their children. That's what we believe.'

'We?' I ask, unsure.

'Feminists. Women, like us, who are in control of their lives. I'm going to talk about it on my podcast tonight.'

'You have a podcast?' I ask her. This is news to me. If I'm honest, I'm not even really sure what a podcast is, or why everyone suddenly has one. I don't have high hopes for Risky's. She is very sweet, and I know her heart is in the right place. But she generally has a lot to say about nothing. Her version of feminism is well-meaning, but quite innocent and inexperienced. She has absolute faith in all women.

'Yup. I've done three episodes. My last one has had nearly eighty listeners.'

'Wow, that's huge,' I say, offering nothing but encouragement.

'Yup, I'm really brave with my subject matter. I say it like it is and I'm all about female empowerment and women supporting women, and all that stuff. And you're such a big part of why I feel like one day I could have it all. A career, and baby, a marriage in which I am respected. You're so lucky.'

To the sound of the low hum of my breast pump, I let those words linger in the air for a moment or two. She looks at me, love hearts and protest posters flashing in her eyes. A sparkling twenty-six-year-old whose dream it was to work for a wedding planning company, who thinks that one day her own marriage will be everything she ever dreamed of. Equal. I'm not going to be the one who tells her otherwise.

'I sure am,' I say. 'Lucky, lucky me!'

Ruby

'I have an eleven a.m. with Vera,' I say to the receptionist, out of breath. I feel like I've climbed a mountain to get here this morning. I just need to get this done, and then I can calm down. I let Bonnie out of her buggy and tell her to sit on the sofa. I give her a bag of gummy bears to keep her busy. I ducked into a shop on the way here and bought nearly all of their confectionary to bribe her with for the next few hours. I need her to sit still.

'Your name?' the receptionist asks, even though I am here every five weeks and she damn well should know it. I put my Balmain handbag onto the desk. I find expensive handbags are a great distraction and a good way to gain status. I often present them to people when I don't want the focus to be on me. She barely even looks at it, demonstrating a distinct lack of taste.

'Ruby,' I tell her, tapping my fingers on the counter. She's wearing a very tight top and looks ridiculous. Her cleavage is staring me in the face. What is the point in dressing like that when you're coming to work in a space where you'll essentially only encounter women? Is it just so, on the off chance a man walks in, she is sex ready? I have half a mind to tell her she's overexposing herself.

'And your surname?'

'For God's sake, Blake,' I say, with agitation. 'Ruby Blake. Eleven a.m. with Vera.'

'Oh yeah, there you are,' she says, raising her eyebrows at my stress levels. 'Vera left, I'm afraid. So you'll be with Maron today.'

She has no idea of the impact of what she's just said.

'What do you mean, Vera left?' Vera has been my technician for eight years. Only the second in my life. I trust Vera. Vera is the only thing that makes this process bearable. She is Russian and commutes from Wapping, there is no chance of me bumping into her outside of our sessions. That is very important to me.

'Yup, our boss offered her a job in our Birmingham salon and she took it. Good for her. I'd have turned it down. I don't know why anyone would choose Birmingham over London. All those motorways . . . '

'Who is the Moron person?' I ask, cutting her off. I couldn't give a flying wax strip about how she feels about the traffic system in the West Midlands.

'It's Maron,' she says, correcting me. I hadn't actually meant to say Moron. I realise she thinks I'm horrible. I soften a little, trying to explain myself a bit better.

'I would have appreciated being told about this before I arrived. I've been seeing Vera for years.'

'Er, well, she only left a couple of days ago and we have a new technician who can do it for you.'

'I had hoped that my loyalty would be treated in kind, do you understand that?'

'Yeah, sorry,' she says, absolutely not sorry but wanting me to shut up. 'Take a seat please. Maron will be with you in a minute.'

She is petulant. It annoys me. I revert back to my angry mode as I think this situation deserves it.

'Do you understand why I'm annoyed?' I ask.

'No, we have someone who can do the procedure for you.'

'It's not about some random person, it's about years of building a relationship with someone and not wanting to have to start all over again.'

I feel like a man who fell in love with his prostitute and asked her to go steady. Of course Vera didn't care about me. She was just working.

'I don't know what to say, look into trains to Birmingham?' the receptionist says, as if that is a reasonable suggestion. I need to get this done today. I will meet Maron, and try to cope. I look over to Bonnie. She is quietly eating her sweets. Sticking her finger into the bag, fishing one out, rolling it around her mouth then swallowing it, savouring every single one like it's a bag of white truffles.

I sit next to her, take four Nurofen Plus, and wait. My heart is racing. Part rage, part fear. But I have no choice. Vera moved to Birmingham. I need to get this done.

'Ruby?' calls a tall blonde woman, who meets all the clichés of what a person who works in a beauty salon should look like.

'Yes,' I snarl, wishing I wasn't so desperate. But knowing if I wake up like this again tomorrow I'll smash my house to pieces.

'Hi, I'm Maron. I'll be taking care of you today.' She holds out a hand for me to shake. It is soft and well-manicured. My hard, bony fingers rattle in her palm. 'Want to follow me?'

I hate her instantly. I liked Vera. She was fat. When you live with a condition like mine, there is a lot of comfort to be had in spending time with other people who push the boundaries of what is considered attractive.

'OK,' I say, standing up, being brave. 'Right, Bonnie. You wait here.' I find an episode of *Peppa Pig* that I've downloaded onto my phone and give it to her. I leave the bag of snacks next to her, telling her she can have whatever she wants. 'I might be a while, but I'm just in there and I'll be right back. If the video stops, you press the triangle, OK?'

Bonnie isn't listening to me, she is too engrossed. This feels stupid and weird and wrong. But I have to get this done today. I need it done. I follow Maron.

'Um, excuse me,' the receptionist calls after me. 'You can't leave her there.'

'Why not? She's fine,' I say, knowing it's not fine. Of course it's not fine, I could be a couple of hours. I'm so stupid.

'If we don't accept responsibility for lost property, we surely don't take responsibility for children. She'll have to go in with you.'

That can't happen.

'Oh come on,' I say, softly, knowing that she already hates me and no amount of sweet talk will help.

'I can rearrange your appointment?'

I really need to get this done now. I can't cope with it. I hate it. It's making so feel horrible. I don't want to feel this ugly. I don't want to be this angry. But Bonnie is with me. This isn't OK.

'Can you get me in tomorrow?' I ask, thinking that gives me twenty-four hours to find some childcare.

'Sorry, the earliest I have is next Thursday.'

'FUCK,' I yell. Maron and the one with the chest look immediately over to Bonnie to see how much damage I did to her by swearing.

'OK, OK, Bonnie, come with me please.'

She doesn't move.

'Bonnie, here, NOW.'

She still doesn't move. So, muttering more swear words under my breath, I pick up all of the treats and my phone and drag her kicking and screaming into the treatment room. Maron points to a chair she can sit on. I face it towards the wall, sit her in it, load her up with snacks, give her back the phone, and ask Maron to leave so I can get undressed.

She does.

This is all wrong.

I take off all of my clothes except my underwear and lie on the bed, placing the pointless and tiny towel over my crotch. Vera always knew to give me a bigger one. I look at the back of my daughter's head, begging her not to turn around. She can't see this. She can't know. A bad smell fills the room.

'Ready?' asks Maron, tapping on the door and opening it a crack before coming in. I brace myself for the inevitable reaction to the sight she's greeted with, but she doesn't even flinch when she looks at me. I don't know what to do with that. There is no point in being in attack mode if no one is trying to attack you.

'Oh dear, it smells like someone has had a little accident,' Maron says, acknowledging the smell radiating from Bonnie. I realise I have no nappies; in a rush this morning, I've left the nappy bag at home.

'She'll have to wait now,' I say, lying back, submissively giving my body to Maron. She's seen it now, there is no point in me resisting her.

'Oh it's OK, you don't need to leave her with a poo in her nappy. I can wait,' she says, making me feel like the cruellest mother imaginable for making my child sit in a dirty nappy while I get what is, essentially, a beauty treatment. But I insist she must just get on with it.

'OK, let's get going, shall we, so you can freshen her up.' Maron lights a candle, which helps with the smell. My torture is about to begin.

'Please go as quickly as you can,' I ask her.

I lay my head to the side, away from Maron. She gets the things she needs to start the procedure.

'So is she your only one?' Maron asks, nodding in Bonnie's direction.

'Yes,' I reply in my blandest voice. I don't want to talk. Vera understood that.

'How old is she?'

'Three and a half.' Is she serious, she thinks I am here to make friends?

'Do you think you'll have another one?'

'No,' I say, sharply. Why do women always presume that other women want to talk? And why, when you only have one kid, do people always ask if you want more? As if having one isn't enough, that having siblings would be better for them. As an only child, I resent this question, as the subtext is that I myself missed out on something and that I am damaged as a consequence.

'She's such a good girl, what's her name?'

'Bonnie,' I reply, as monotone as I can. Not wanting to invite more chat. Maron stirs the wax, and loads it onto a wooden spatula. 'It's a little hot, give me just a second.' She says, dragging out my misery. 'That's such a pretty name.'

I regret it more and more every time someone says that.

'You're lucky,' she says. Which makes me want to stick a wax strip on her face, yank it off, and see how lucky she feels.

'Lucky?' I ask. Fascinated by whatever stupid logic she has for such a statement.

'Yes. You're lucky. My cousin has this condition too. She's how I got into waxing. I used to get rid of her hair for her in school. I got pretty good at it quite quickly. She's married now and can't get pregnant. And look at you with your beautiful daughter. You're lucky.'

'Sounds like she dodged a bullet,' I say, turning away.

Maron doesn't have a comeback for that. She takes a few moments to think of another deeply personal question. I don't know why beauty therapists, hairdressers, dentists or anyone at all who is being paid to do a service think that women come to these appointments to have their lives interrogated. It drives me mad.

'So how was the birth? I looove talking about birth,' she says excitedly.

'Why, have you done it?'

'No, but I can't wait to.'

I sometimes find the best way to end a conversation is to say something unpleasant.

'Birth was awful. The worst experience of my life, and that's saying something.' I hope that will shut her up, but if there is one thing I have learned about Maron in the few moments I have known her, she doesn't shut up.

'Oh no, why?'

'Really? You want to know?'

'Yes, I think it's important to hear all birth stories, it's research. If I know all eventualities then I won't be scared if they happen, right?'

'OK, well I'd been hoping to have her naturally.'

'Wow, good for you.'

'Yeah, well I'm terrified of medical intervention, so I didn't think I had much choice.'

'OK, and did you do it?' she asks, stirring the wax and testing it on her hand. She seems more satisfied with the temperature now.

'No, I had to have a C-section in the end,' I say, flashing back to the trauma. Seeing myself, naked, surrounded by strangers. Humiliation crippling me.

I'd booked a full body wax for two weeks and one day before my due date. After a treatment I have around two and a half weeks of being hair-free before it starts to grow back. So if Bonnie was on time, I'd be good. If she was late, even by two weeks, I would be hairy, but it wouldn't be its maximum thickness. It was the best I could do.

Bonnie came two weeks and two days early. I was fully hirsute. Thick, black, bear-like hair all over my body. Between my breasts, around my nipples, all over my abdomen, my back. My pubic hair thick down to my knees, heavy fur toward my ankles. When I went into labour I cried. I knew countless people were about to see my body and I panicked. My cervix did too, clamming up so tight Bonnie had no chance of getting out. I tried for hours, but she wouldn't come. The hospital lights were bright, I begged for them to go down. They insisted they needed to see. Liam did his best to comfort me, but I screamed at him and made him feel as redundant as I did ugly. I heard a nurse say, 'This is the most primal birth I have ever seen.' Meaning it was like watching an actual ape give birth. I felt repulsive. So self-aware. Everything you shouldn't have to feel in that moment. I wanted to be alone. To disappear into a dark corner and get my baby out by myself. I swear if I had been in the wild, it would have been OK. But there were people everywhere and no matter how much I screamed at them to leave me they wouldn't. After fifteen hours of active labour, the doctor insisted I had a C-section. I was wheeled down the corridor. More bright lights. They had to shave my belly to get her out.

'Well, at least you got her out safe,' Maron says, snapping me out of my memory. 'Well done you, birth is beautiful no matter how it happens,' she continues, her young, ignorant mind speaking on her behalf.

Beautiful is not a word I would use to describe any aspect

of my birth experience. I have never felt so ugly as I did in the hours that followed, either. My stomach was covered in stubble. I couldn't breast feed Bonnie because I worried it would scratch her on the back of the head. They wanted to shave my nipples so she could latch on. I couldn't cope with getting my boobs out in front of people anymore. The hair between them thick, the hair on them thicker. So I stopped, and asked for a bottle. Liam gave her the first feed. I just stared and watched, feeling like my entire world had been shattered. All that, just to hand her to someone else. I had already failed her in the first few hours of her life. It would only be downhill from there. My mother always liked to tell me I destroyed her body during childbirth. I don't plan to ever inform Bonnie of the destruction she caused. There is no need to lay that guilt on an innocent child who didn't ask to be born.

Maron lays the warm wax on my lower calf, presses the fabric down onto it, then rips the hair out of me. It's not too bad. I know that the further up my leg she gets, the worse it will be.

She clearly cannot work in silence.

'You OK there, Bonnie, can I get you anything?'

'Don't talk to her,' I snap. 'I don't want her to—'

Bonnie turns around.

'NO,' I shout, leaping off the bed and trying to hide behind it. 'NO, stay where you are.'

Bonnie drops my phone and when she picks it up *Peppa Pig* has disappeared. She screams and demands it is put back on. I can't reach the phone. The smell is worse now she is moving around. I don't want to come out from the other end of the bed. I can't let Bonnie see my body. She ramps the tantrum right up, chucking my phone at the wall. It lands on the floor and I see that it is cracked. Bonnie falls to the floor and starts hammering her fists. It's a tiny room, there are three of us in it, it's so hot.

'Give me a robe,' I scream at Maron, who pulls one off from behind the door and throws it at me. I put it on, come out from behind the bed and get *Peppa Pig* back on my phone. Bonnie goes back into her trance. I feel ugly and ridiculous.

'Shall we carry on?' Maron asks softly, her awkwardness hanging in the air. But the reality hits me. I could be here for hours. Bonnie will never sit here for that long. Not with a dirty nappy. She should be potty trained, it's my fault she isn't. I tried a few months ago but it was awful. I don't know when I'll be able to face it again. I'm sure Maron is judging me for that.

'Please get out,' I say to her. 'I need to get dressed.' She does as I ask. I turn Bonnie back to face the wall and put my torn dress and thick black tights back on. One stupid wax strip's worth of hair missing.

'You ruined that for me,' I snap at my child. My poor child, who didn't ask to be here. Who is off her head on sugar, her bottom probably starting to sting. 'Come on.'

Bonnie and I go back to reception. I strap her into her buggy, and with as much attitude as I can muster, I ask the receptionist how much I owe, accepting that I took up a reasonable amount of their time.

'Oh, don't worry,' says Maron, with a look of sympathy on her face. Sympathy that I do not want.

'Do you want me to reschedule your appointment?' the receptionist asks.

'Is Vera coming back?' I snap, making a point of being dissatisfied with the service.

'No,' she tells me.

'Then no, absolutely not. I will take my loyalty elsewhere.'

I turn and push Bonnie out onto the street. I am still hairy and I have no childcare. This is so unbearably awful.

As I get down the street I wonder, how must that have looked? To be so afraid of my daughter seeing me without my clothes on that I tried to hide behind a bed?

Maron must think I am a lunatic.

Yet it isn't her opinion that matters. Bonnie thinks I am cruel. I shout at her. I tell her not to look at me. I push her away emotionally, sometimes even physically, and all so I can hide inside the prison of my own body.

How is that any different to what my own mother did to me?

I'm not sure it is.

Beth

I read on the *Cosmo* website that love and desire are two separate things in a marriage. That love is the easy bit, but desire is the challenge when you spend a lot of time with someone. The trick is to keep desire going, and to do that you have to reinstate some mystery. A distraction from the thing they have become accustomed to. Something new that makes them see your body in a new and exciting way.

Right now, all my body is to Michael is a car crash after childbirth and a milk machine keeping our baby alive. I am functional, not sexual. Maybe all I have to do is make him look twice?

While Risky is in the toilet, I use my arms to push my boobs together and create a cleavage. I take a selfie with a seductive pout. It does not turn out how I expect it would. My boobs look lop-sided and my eyes deranged. Risky takes selfies at her desk all the time, she makes it look so easy. I try again. Even worse. My lips don't look sexy. I look like I'm trying to scratch my nose with my mouth. I go for more of a smile, but that's just weird. How do people make this look so natural?

'Boss, what are you doing?' Risky asks, coming out of the toilet. I hadn't heard her flush. Did I miss it? Weird. Anyway, I put my phone down and give up.

'Were you taking a selfie?' Risky almost whispers it, like she's discovered my dark secret.

'I may have been.'

'Wow, I've never seen you take a selfie, ever. Were you going to post it?'

'No, I was going to send it to Michael,' I say, sounding ridiculous. 'But I look like a deformed butternut squash in them so let's just move on.'

'No way. I am the selfie queen. I'm going to teach you.'

This is ridiculous.

'Risky, we have a high profile wedding in under three weeks. We do not have the time for a selfie masterclass,' I say, actually really wanting to know how to make myself look sexy in a photo.

'Tough. It's happening.' Risky sits at her desk and holds her phone in her hands. 'OK, copy everything I do. Hold your phone up a bit, you'll look thinner.'

I do as she says, and hold the camera around twelve inches higher than my face.

'OK, now look at it like it's just caught you masturbating but you don't mind because you kind of want it to join in.'

'What? Risky, come on!'

'What? There is nothing wrong with masturbating. I just masturbated in the bathroom. So don't be ashamed of pretending to masturbate, that's just crazy.'

I put my phone down.

'I'm sorry, you just what?'

'I just masturbated in the bathroom. I do it loads at work.

It gives me a burst of energy in the afternoon. It's better than a Mars Bar, isn't it?'

'Better than a Mars Bar?' Sometimes I think Risky is another species.

'I guess so,' I say, and I must look a little disgusted because she somehow feels the need to continue talking about masturbation.

'Seriously, boss, we're two women who share an office. If we can't be open about self-pleasure here, where can we be? We need to abolish the stigma surrounding female masturbation. The silence around it has gone on long enough. I take my vibrator everywhere with me, just in case.'

'Just in case of what?'

'Just in case I need it. You know when you become so consumed with the need to come that you have to duck into the nearest room and bring yourself off just to get through the rest of your day?'

I do know that feeling. I feel it almost every day. The difference between me and Risky is that I have attached so much of my sexuality to my husband that I forget I have the power to satisfy myself sometimes. Rather than tell my assistant that, though, I try to bring the focus back to our job.

'OK, anyway, we should do some work.'

'Not before we nail this photo. Phone up, channel your inner Princess Diana – is that a better reference for you, she was big in the Eighties, right?' I nod and do as she says. It might make me feel old, but I know exactly what she means in terms of the bashful but slightly suggestive look Diana would probably have given her phone, should they have existed when she was alive. 'Now drop your head more to the left. Give a little smile, like you're thinking naughty thoughts, and take the photo.'

I do it. And have to admit, the photo is really nice.

'Wow, I look hot,' I say. Risky rushes over to look. When she sees it she makes all sorts of 'Look at you, you saucy minx' type comments, before snatching the phone from me.

'OK, we need a filter. And a slight tone change. Let me just . . . and . . . yup . . . that's it . . . Oh my God, look at it in black and white.' She hands it back to me. I really do look amazing in black and white.

'Cor, thanks, Risky. I look so hot even I'd masturbate to that pic.'

'Yes boss!!!'

I send it immediately to Michael. After a minute or so, a speech bubble pops up and I am excited to read his response.

Nice. Hey, can you grab some milk on the way home? We are out.

3

Ruby

After the wax disaster, Bonnie and I made an emergency detour to Boots to get some nappies and I sorted her out in a horrible cafe toilet about four streets from the salon. Far enough so that I didn't have to worry about Maron or the receptionist popping in to get their lunch.

I get Bonnie a slice of chocolate cake the size of her head and tell her to eat it. She doesn't need much persuading.

'Mummy needs to work,' I explain. I search for train times and prices to Birmingham. I'm not ready to give up on seeing Vera again for my treatments. But I'm looking at anything from fifty to a hundred pounds to get there. Plus the cost of the wax, which is generally in the hundreds for what I need. It would be an entire day, with travel and my appointment. This is not a reasonable option. I need to find another salon in London. And I need to find Bonnie another nursery. I'm never going back there either. I take a sip of black coffee and try not to think about the amount of sugar Bonnie has eaten today. More than I have in around four years. But I don't see what else I could have done.

I see that I have an email from Rebecca Crossly about a job.

Hey Ruby, any chance of those images by end of play today? Editor is onto me about not touching up too much, the mag is under fire again for retouching. But if we don't I'll get blacklisted by the PRs. So, basically, rework but keep it natural, let's try to get away with as much as we can. Just make sure you get rid of that scar. R x

Oh and make her less orange, she looks like an Oompa Loompa.

I tell her yes. Even though it will probably be tomorrow now. I'm the only retoucher Rebecca uses, so she has no choice but to wait. Rebecca is a photographer who is in high demand. I started working for her when she shot brochures for hotels around ten years ago. The level of hotel was very high-end – five-star resorts all across the world. I enjoyed it, making the sky bluer and the grass greener. She started getting work for magazines and kept throwing the work in my direction. A lot of food at first, some landscapes, but the jobs soon turned into people. I was excellent at retouching people because I had years of practice of making photographs of myself look nicer. I have a secret file on my computer – I named it 'MENSTRUAL DIARY' in case I die and someone gets into my computer and is tempted to look at them. The file is full of pictures of me that people took before I had the self-assurance to say no. They are hard to come by, but of course they exist. At university

51

people used disposable cameras; I was lucky to be a student before the advent of camera phones and social media. I might not have survived that. I have a little shoe box – something I also hide – full of photographs. I scanned them all into my computer and worked them up into images I wouldn't mind the world seeing. Of course I'd never show them to anyone, I couldn't live that lie. Ironically, this doctoring is now exactly what I do for models and celebrities, who don't have the same issue with dishonesty.

Rebecca now shoots for *Vogue*, *Elle*, *Cosmo* and any other publications that print photos of beautiful women who need to look even more beautiful. It's a lot of work that's kept coming my way. It's hard to turn that down when you're a single mother and need to pay for your three-bedroom Victorian terrace in Kentish Town, a love of antique furniture and a penchant for expensive handbags.

My job and my moral compass battle with each other every day. I know how much a negative body image can ruin a woman's life, and here I am perpetuating the problem and giving that complex to millions of other women every single day. I get away with it because my name never appears anywhere. I am the silent partner in crime. The hidden face behind other people's fake perception of beauty. I am the source of the problem.

As I am replying to Rebecca, Bonnie happily laughing into her wedge of cake, a surge of warm blood fills my knickers. Another devastating side-effect of my condition. Extremely sudden, heavy periods. I'm forty-three years old and I still have absolutely no grip on my menstrual situation. For someone who needs to feel control as much as I do, this is particularly punishing. It's so hard for me to be positive about anything to do with the female condition.

'Bonnie, come with me please.'

'No.'

'Bonnie, come on, you can finish your cake in a minute. Mummy needs to go to the toilet.'

'NO,' she says, not even looking up at me. Why can't she just do as I ask, just once? Everything is always such a battle.

I pick up her plate, gathering my bags too. She goes to a level eight immediately. I walk backwards with the cake and she follows it like a horse chasing a carrot. Tears spouting from her eyes like a cartoon baby. When I reach the door I grab her by the hand and drag her in. I am past the point of caring what people think of me today.

In the cubicle, our third confined space of the day, I turn her around and give her the plate. She sits on the floor, and tucks back into her cake. It's disgusting but she has stopped shouting. I can't win at everything.

This is all so wrong. I hitch up my skirt, blood already escaping from my underwear. It's always the same. An unpredictable tidal wave of horror.

Rooting around in my bag, I realise I have no sanitary towels with me. I don't have the kind of flow any amount of scrunched-up toilet paper can deal with. I sit for a moment, thinking the unthinkable.

What choice do I have?

I put on one of Bonnie's nappies.

Lauren Pearce – Instagram post
@OfficialLP

The image is of Lauren in front of a full-length mirror, her opulent bedroom in the background. Her clothes are on the bed; she chose not to wear them for this photo. Her pose isn't particularly natural, suggesting it took a few goes to get it right. The angle of her body compliments her best bits.

The caption reads:
Aren't women's bodies amazing? Whether you love or hate the body you were born with we have to appreciate what they can do. I hope that one day this belly grows a baby, that these breasts feed it. Sometimes I forget that I am one of the most powerful things on this earth. Made to feel better with this gorgeous lingerie by #AllTheFrills. Underwear for women who want to feel their power. What makes you feel powerful? #AD #loveyourself #bodypositive #womensupportingwomen

@Hanngfer1: I WISH I WAS YOU

@peachybell2: Easy for you to say with a bod like that. If I wore those pants I'd look like a hippo at a fancy dress party.

@nevergonnabutimight: You've got no idea about power. You're marrying power. Go get your botox redone and shut up.

@jessicachimesin: Thank you for being you. So inspiring to see a woman loving herself. You are everything I want to be.

@quertyflop: FAKE NEWS

Beth

After receiving Michael's text, I slump into my chair. Risky clocks it.

'Oh no, he didn't like it?' she asks, obviously seeing the heartbreak pouring out of my eyes.

'No, he loved it. Yeah, I'm just nearly out of battery.' She comes over to me with a charger and plugs in my phone. She has my back on so many levels. As she walks to her desk, I blur the lines of boss and employee as casually as I can.

'So . . . ' I say, trying to be all blasé about it . . . 'What kinda vibrator ya got?'

I nonchalantly start to finger some paperwork, and then *bam*, a small, pink-silicone, bullet-shaped battery-powered device is waved under my nose.

'It's the best!' Risky says, testing its various speed levels. I am hoping she washed it. It is very close to my face.

'Oh cool,' I say. Choosing not to tell her I have never actually owned one.

'Yeah, it's small enough to fit in a clutch bag. I can take it everywhere.'

Seriously, how often does this woman need to orgasm?

'Lovely. What brand is it?' I ask, pretending not to care very much.

'Oh, I don't know. I got it on Amazon. I'll send you the link.' She skips back to her desk, but just before she sits down, she says, 'Actually, you know what? I have another two at home. You have this one.'

She holds it out for me to take. I just stare at it.

'Come on, have it.'

I pull my sleeve down over my hand and take the vibrator.

'Thank you,' I say, awkwardly.

'Great. You'll love it. Let me know when you've had a go.'

'I absolutely will not.'

'Beth, being a woman is hard enough, the least we can do for ourselves is make the most of the precious gift we were given.'

'The precious gift?' I ask nervously.

'Yes, our clitoris.'

'Ah yes, of course.'

She hasn't finished.

'So much of society is geared towards empowering the male sexual experience. The penis is overexposed. Figuratively and literally. The penis is unavoidable, therefore it gains power simply because of its literal presence in the room. Our vaginas are hidden away inside of us. They need to be released into the room. And that starts with us.'

She is standing up, looking thoughtfully into the middle distance like a footballer at the beginning of a game while the national anthem plays.

'With us?' I ask.

'Yes, with us Beth. With "The Woman".' She comes to my desk and rests her elbows on it, her face quite close to mine.

She continues with her manifesto. 'We need to get the vagina out there, release it, and put it on the stage it deserves to be on. Squat over a mirror boss, squat right down and look directly into your vagina and say—'

'OK, Risky, we really should—'

'And say,' she isn't done yet, '"This is your stage, Queen." And then give yourself a beautiful, stunning, full-body, full-throttle, full-*vagina* orgasm.'

'OK, shall we crack on?' I say, feeling quite uncomfortable now. I don't think my assistant imagining me squatting over a mirror is going to create the ideal work dynamic. She finally snaps herself out of masturbation mode.

'OK, I'm just going for a wee and then I'll get back to the wedding of the year.' She heads off towards the toilet. I watch her inquisitively.

'I'm genuinely going for a wee this time!' she says, clearing up any doubt.

I drop the vibrator into my bag.

Ruby

As I am walking Bonnie home, my phone rings in a strange way. When I get it out of my bag, my face is on the screen as though I am taking a photograph. I look revolting. Liam is calling me on FaceTime. He has never done this. I do not use FaceTime. This sends me into such a tizz that I accidentally answer it, the camera shooting directly up my nose. I immediately panic about stray hairs on my chin. I plan to hang up but he yells 'Hello!' loud enough for Bonnie to hear him, and now I am forced to keep the conversation going.

'Liam, why are you calling me in this way?' I ask, holding the phone above my face and as far away as I can. One benefit of my job is I know which camera angles are flattering. Not that any camera angles are flattering on my face. I photograph like a dying horse. Why the hell would he FaceTime me, has he lost his mind? I turn so the sun isn't shining directly on my face, that is a sure fire way to highlight any hair.

'I miss you guys,' he says in his usual bouncy and chipper way. He said 'you guys' for Bonnie's benefit – we do try to sound affectionate in front of her.

'Liam, this really isn't a good time,' I lie. We have no plans, we are heading home to watch TV; it's actually a great time for him to call.

'Give the phone to Bonnie,' he asks, realising I am a lost cause for conversation. I do as he asks. They chat for a few moments about his travelling. He makes multiple stupid faces, which she thinks are hilarious. He asks her questions about what she is up to, and she says she misses him and my heart thumps, because I know she would never say that to me. I stand impatiently waiting for them to end their sweet and emotional chat. A part of me pleased she has him to encourage that side of her, the other part of me wishing I was better at all this.

'OK, I love you Bon Bon, give the phone back to Mummy.'

Bonnie shoots her hand up into the air and I take my phone back, quickly holding it at an angle that does not involve a close-up of my chin.

'OK, done?' I ask him, unnecessarily sternly.

'Actually, one of the guys at this conference invested in that new animated movie, *Forever Never*. He's given me tickets for the premiere this weekend. He gave me three, I thought you might like to come with me and Bonnie?'

He keeps doing this. Asking me to go on little jollies with him and Bonnie. He is trying to make up for what he did, I know it. Like going to watch a movie together will take away the pain and humiliation of my wedding day. The day he ruined my life. It won't work.

'A cartoon? I can't, sorry.'

'OK, are you sure? I mean, it's a movie. You wouldn't have to talk to me. Come on Ruby, it would be nice for Bonnie to have us all together,' he says, speaking more quietly, so I have to bring the camera closer to my face, which I hate.

'No, Liam, I can't. I have Bonnie all week, I need a break at the weekend, OK? It's what we agreed.'

'Actually, it's what you agreed, but OK,' he says, raising his eyebrows. 'I just thought it would be nice.'

'Well like I said, I can't. OK? Anything else?'

'No, other than, you look nice.' He smiles; it's confusing. I don't like it. I catch sight of my face on my phone, I look horrible.

'OK, well if you're done then have a safe trip back and we'll see you on Friday at six p.m., on the dot. Wave goodbye to Daddy, Bonnie.' I turn the phone back to her, let Bonnie wave, then cut Liam off half way through him telling her he loves her. Which makes me feel nasty.

When we arrive home, Bonnie is coming down off the additives and sugar she's eaten today. She's falling asleep in her buggy. It's one p.m., I'll stick her in front of the TV, and I'll get some time off to work on the images Rebecca sent through. Then I'll feed Bonnie some fish fingers and vegetables.

I unstrap her and carry her to the sofa. She's too tired to fight me. I put her head on a cushion, get *Peppa Pig* on, lay a blanket over her and let her be. I should get an hour of peace, maybe two if she goes back to sleep. I haven't spent an afternoon with her in so long, I'm not even entirely sure if she naps anymore. It strikes me that that is terrible.

In the kitchen, I take off the tights. It's a hot day, I'm sweating and plan to get my dressing gown on now I don't intend to leave the house again today. I put both hands on the edge of the sink and take a second to think and breathe.

Today has been awful. So the last thing, and I mean the absolute last thing, I need to see right now is a mouse run across my counter top, fall off it, land on the floor and disappear into a hole smaller than my finger.

'NO!' I yelp.

My fear of rodents is a close second to my fear of anyone seeing me naked. I cannot cope with them. I hate them. I hate them so much. I run to the dining table and clamber up onto one of the chairs. The mouse runs across the floor again. It disappears and I convince myself it's crawling up my dress. I feel like I'm covered in mice. I pull my dress up over my head, getting stuck in it because I forgot to unzip. I'm trapped inside metres of thick velvet. My hands are fighting to get me free. The chair starts to wobble, I can't steady myself. I fall, crashing to the ground, smacking myself on the floor, my dress coming over my head.

'Mummy?'

Bonnie's voice becomes clearer as my hearing returns. I must have been knocked out for a second because I hardly know where I am. I rummage around with my dress until I find a gap for me to look through. Nothing is broken, I don't think. I pat my thigh with my hand and realise my dress is around my neck and my body is completely exposed. My arm hurts. I can't cover myself. Instead, I freeze.

'Mummy?' Bonnie says again, looking at me with something between disgust and fascination on her face. For the first time in her life she gets to see what I have been hiding. My thin, skeletal frame, covered with thick black hair, starting at my chest and covering my stomach and my back and going all the way down to my ankles. Today, as if to add insult to injury, there's the addition of a Pampers Baby Dry, heaving with blood.

I lie still, surrendering to the shame as my daughter takes it all in. I remember my mother's face the time she burst in on me in the shower when I was sixteen. At first she looked disgusted, then pleased. Pleased she had discovered something she could taunt me with for the rest of my life.

Bonnie has an unidentifiable look on her face. I've hidden my naked body from her for three and a half years. Even when she was a tiny baby I turned her bouncer to face the wall when I was getting dressed. I didn't want to frighten her or give her a complex about what she might become. I established a no-nudity clause when I became a parent, and I have never, ever broken it. Until this moment.

'Bonnie, sitting room, now.'

She stares at me. What do I see in return? Shock? Disgust? It's hard to tell.

'Please, Bonnie. Mummy will be in in a minute.'

She doesn't move. Her eyes water a little, she is pale. I think of the mouse. I have to get off the floor. It isn't easy, my arm is starting to throb. Just as I get myself to a seating position, Bonnie's mouth opens, and a stream of hot vomit shoots all over me. Chunks of undigested chocolate cake and half-chewed Percy Pigs cling to the hair on my stomach and shoulders, pooling into my lap and resting on the blood-soaked nappy.

I poisoned her with sugar.

Beth

I have been relentlessly googling how to reinstate some magic into a marriage, and it seems one of the answers is to spend more time together, one-on-one. That makes sense. I don't remember the last time Michael and I went out for a meal. We fell into a TV dinner hole when I was pregnant and watched a series on Netflix until we passed out. It was time together, but not really. Our conversations now centre entirely around Tommy, and that is hardly going to help us work out our issues, is it? I send another text just before I leave work. This time a less humiliating one, requiring a straight answer, rather than any kind of compliment.

Do you think your mum would babysit tonight? After I put Tommy down? He won't need feeding again until 11 and maybe if we stay local we could grab a nice dinner somewhere?

Nice idea, let me ask.

Mum says that's fine. See, I told you it would be handy living so close to her. Bye.

This is literally the first time I have ever associated anything positive with living so close to my mother-in-law, Janet. She is interfering and obsessed with her children. She is one of those women who probably had sex three times in her entire life, each of which resulted in a child. All of whom are a bit weird. Michael's brother has been married and divorced four times and not one of his ex-wives will speak to him. I've met him seven times and on at least three of those occasions he has hit on me or offended me in some way. Their sister is single at forty-eight. She lives in a house share in Canary Wharf and is obsessed with conspiracy theories. I can't handle more than a thirty-second conversation with her. When I had Tommy, she turned up to the hospital high on ecstasy and told me that she thinks Tommy is the reincarnation of Benedict Cumberbatch. I reminded her that he isn't even dead, to which she answered, 'Yes, but how do you know?' Luckily, she hasn't come to see us since.

My mother-in-law will, however, speak of her children like they are perfect and as if she did a sensational job of raising them. I just nod and smile. Janet is prim, thin and neurotic. I am informal, fleshy and balanced. If his mother and I met in any other capacity, we would very likely scratch each other's eyes out. But because of Michael, we somehow keep our claws in. I am willing to restrain myself even more knowing that her hideous proximity to our house means that she will be available for regular babysitting in the future. This is OK with me, because I will be out, far away from her.

She arrives at 6.30 p.m. as requested and insists that she puts Tommy to bed. My evenings with him are precious and I look forward to his bedtime every day, but I sacrifice this one to get a night out with my husband. It's OK, it will be worth it. I get changed. I have a pretty standard uniform for work at the moment: my skinny maternity jeans – I know it's been four months, but they are soooo comfy – and a long shirt that I can open easily for breast feeding. I wear low-heeled boots and subtle make-up. It works for both sitting alone with Risky all day, and popping out for occasional meetings. But tonight, I want to spice it up a bit.

I try on a few pairs of my pre-pregnancy trousers. None of them fit, which is OK, I haven't even tried to shift the weight yet so there is no point getting upset about it until I do. I try on a black pencil skirt, but it won't get past my bottom. I try on a few of my favourite dresses, but none of them do up. I then remember a black body-con dress that I bought online around three years ago but have never worn. I'm not sure what mood I was in when I decided to get it, because it really isn't my style. It only fits now because it is ninety-eight per cent elastane, but who cares, it's on. I put on some three-and-a-half-inch stilettos that I haven't worn in around ten years and totter downstairs. Michael is wearing a grey t-shirt and a pair of blue jeans with trainers.

'My goodness,' Janet breathes. 'Is that the underwear that's supposed to make you look thin?'

'No, it's a dress,' I tell her.

'Well have you got any of the underwear that makes you look thin?'

I ignore that.

'OK, so you don't need to bath him. At six fifty take him up, put him in his sleeping bag, give him the bottle and lay him down. The white noise is already on. If he wakes up before we come home please don't bring him out of his room or give him more milk. Just rub his belly to soothe him if he gets really upset.'

'So cruel,' Janet says, putting her empty cup on the table. 'Poor baby.'

'Pardon?' I ask gently, as Michael ducks into the kitchen. He hates it when his mother and I are in the same room. He thinks I will cause problems.

'All this leaving the babies to cry, it's so cruel. If a baby cries, you cuddle them. Those terrible parenting books telling mothers to neglect their children.'

'It's important to have a schedule. And of course we cuddle him, but we also want him to sleep well and not be afraid of being alone,' I say. I don't want to talk about parenting with Janet. 'Michael, shall we go?'

As he comes out of the kitchen, I hold my tummy in and stand up straight. I am waiting for a compliment.

'You'll be cold,' is all I get, and he passes me my ugliest and biggest coat from the cupboard. I swap it for a black leather jacket, which I regret instantly but pretend to wear with pride. I look like Kim Kardashian's horny aunt. Although I am sure she would at least have had a manicure.

I pick up my bag and walk over to Tommy to give him a kiss. As I do, my heel gets stuck in the floorboards and I go flying across the living room. I land splat on my tummy and the contents of my bag empty all over the floor. Risky's pink vibrator rolls slowly towards Janet's foot.

'Oh, what is this?' she asks, picking it up. She turns over the bottom of it and realises it has three settings. 'Oh Tommy, look!' she says, gently running it over his face and body, at which he smiles and giggles. 'He loves it,' she says, joyfully. 'Isn't Mummy clever, I've never seen a toy like it.'

'No, Janet. That isn't a toy,' I say, imagining Risky's vagina juice rubbing all over my baby's face.

'What is it then?' she asks, holding it up.

'Yeah, what is it?' Michael asks, going over and taking a closer look. Horror drenches his face as the realisation comes.

'I'll take that,' he says, snatching it from his mother's hand, stomping with it into the kitchen and throwing it in the bin.

'What on earth was that about?' Janet asks, before slowly catching up. 'Oh my goodness,' she says, rubbing her hands on her clothes, then running into the kitchen and holding them under the hot tap, applying endless soap, as if she just picked up dog shit with her bare hands. 'Well I never!' she exclaims. 'Shocking!'

Michael is now standing in the middle of the living room staring at me. I pick up all of my things and put them back in my bag. Although embarrassment courses through every inch of my body, I do what any sensible woman would do and pretend absolutely nothing has happened.

'Bye Tommy,' I say, kissing him. 'Shall we go?'

Michael follows me out of the door.

We walk in silence down the street, Michael so cross he is breathing like a wild boar that is about to charge and murder a threatening female, and me trying to keep up with him in my stupid shoes. I feel like a fat tart chasing a man who isn't interested in her. I mean, maybe that is actually exactly what I am.

'Michael, please, slow down.'

He stops suddenly, giving me a chance to catch up. A few

blocks down we come to a little cafe that is open quite late and he ducks in. This was not what I had in mind for dinner.

'Still serving?' he asks a lady behind the counter. She is packing everything up but asks a man who looks to be the manager if it's OK. He says it's fine, and she starts putting the trays of sandwich fillers back out for display.

'We'll stay open for a bit for you,' the man says, unashamedly giving me the once-over. Michael takes a seat and I totter up to the table. The bright cafe lights are glaring, making me ashamed of all my make-up. My fat, wobbly arms feeling like jelly, my tight dress doing nothing for me, other than showing off all the things I suddenly feel very self-conscious of. I sit down.

'What do you want?' Michael asks me, throwing the menu in my direction. He gets up before I have chance to speak.

'I'll get the prawn Marie Rose on brown, please,' he tells the man. 'And a glass of milk. Beth?'

I get up again, the dress feeling tighter now, the shoes even higher. I look at all the food.

'Can I have the chicken mayonnaise with avocado on white please?'

'Brown,' Michael interjects, correcting my order. It startles me so much I forget to order a drink.

We sit back down. There is no music. The two people who work here are now making our order together to get it out quickly so they can close. I hate everything about what I am wearing.

'It's not like she saw me using it,' I say, needing to break the ice.

Michael leans forward. 'What is the matter with you?' he says, through a tight mouth.

'Nothing is the matter with me.' I pause, knowing he needs an explanation, but I'm not quite able to rationalise it's a second-hand one! 'I just treated myself to a sex toy. Lots of women have them, it's not a big deal.'

'You think seeing my mother rub my wife's vibrator on my child's face isn't a big deal?'

I spare another thought for Risky's vagina juice. Please, please, let her have washed it.

'It was clean,' I say, as two sandwiches are put in front of us.

'And here's a complimentary bowl of crisps,' the lady says, putting them in the middle. Michael pulls them towards him and starts layering them into his sandwich.

'Mum will be so upset,' he says, through a mouthful of prawns and mayonnaise. He often talks to me like I am gross, when his table manners are actually horrible.

'It's very unfortunate that it happened, but it was in my bag and I tripped. It was an accident.'

'Dressing like that wasn't an accident though, was it?'

'No,' I say, dropping my head. 'No, I did this on purpose hoping you would like it.'

'You know I like you in jeans.'

We sit in silence for a while and eat our sandwiches in the very bright cafe on what was supposed to be our date night. He can hardly bring himself to look at me. I have no idea what to say. I just want things to be better. So eventually I give in.

'Michael, I'm really sorry for what happened tonight. I wish it hadn't. But I've been so excited to have dinner with you and I hope we can still have a nice time?' I take a small, delicate bite of my sandwich and make sure my mouth doesn't open as I eat it. He takes his time, but eventually backs down.

'OK. Thank you for saying sorry. And please, no more of that . . . nonsense. OK?'

By 'nonsense' I presume he means sex toys. I nod my head and smile.

'So how cute was that picture you sent me of Tommy in the park? That squirrel was so close to him, amazing how tame they are.'

He cheers right up.

'I know, and if Tommy was any bigger I'm sure he would have grabbed it.'

We sit in the cafe for a further fifteen minutes, talking about nothing but our baby, because when we talk about anything else, we realise we have nothing to say. When we get home – we were gone just over one hour – Janet is watching *EastEnders* and barely looks at me as she leaves. Michael walks her home. I go straight to the kitchen to retrieve my vibrator, but she must have taken out the bins, and rooting around in the outside rubbish looking for a sex toy is not a low I am willing to reach right now.

Upstairs, I take off the body-con dress and put it in a bag ready to take to a charity shop. I rub cream into my sore feet and set my alarm for eleven p.m., when I will give Tommy a dream feed.

Tonight didn't exactly go to plan. I have zero chance of getting laid. And what a waste of a perfectly good vibrator.

Lauren Pearce – Instagram post
@OfficialLP

The image is of Lauren, she is lying on her front on a bed, her body reflected in a large gold-framed mirror. She's reaching forward, holding the phone to take a selfie. The angle is just right, so you can see the curve of her hip and the top of her bottom. Her feet are raised and cutely hooked together. She is looking seductively into the camera, as if it is a lover. She is alone. There is a carton of coconut water next to the bed.

The caption reads:
Happiness and hydration go hand in hand. I don't feel myself if I don't drink enough (and no, I don't mean vodka LOL). Taking care of my body and my skin helps me to feel good. I start every day with a #FRESHCoconutWater #AD #Cocofresh #selflove #reachout #mentalillness #hydrate #vegan #women

@turningup286872: Thank you for being you

@kellyheap: Is all you do drink drinks? Smoothies, coconut water? Can we see you eat a bloody meal please?

@HowdyMunchBrain: Twat. You have the perfect life. Get over yourself.

@Flickerlights-off: Queen.

@PatreonofLorralites: You're so lucky. I wish I was you. I'd do anything to be you.

@gellyjeellybelly: That shit tastes like feet. What's Gav like in bed, I reckon he likes a blowie, amiriiight?

@YUMMIETUMMY: I find you so inspiring. The best example of how to live your best life . . . keep posting, keep being you.

4

Ruby

Bonnie was ill for most of the night. Neither of us have slept. She watched TV from six a.m., but five hours later she's bored and walking around the house moaning like a handmaid, as if forced to stay by a cruel regime she is desperate to overthrow. I have a number of errands to run. I see mothers all the time, taking their children out and about: food shopping, clothes shopping, going into restaurants . . . they make it look so easy. I don't do things like that with Bonnie because she screams at me whenever I try. I get most of my chores done while she is at nursery, or while she is with Liam at the weekend. I see those other mothers just getting on with their lives in the company of their children and wonder if maybe they have drugged them? Or if they share some secret to keeping toddlers under control that I don't know? Maybe today I will discover it, because I have no childcare and I simply must get on with my day. I have urgent things to do, like buying mousetraps, tights and a new bra.

I wouldn't usually force myself to try on new bras in a bright changing room, especially before a wax, but the under-wire came out of my only one this morning, and it's been so long since I got a new one that I have no idea what size I am. My body shape has barely changed in twenty years, but my boobs have never been the same size the day I got pregnant. I'm almost sure I've dropped a cup size.

I tend to do this with things that bring me comfort, like bras. I wear one until it literally falls off my body, hand-washing it most nights in the bathroom sink. This one has been going for five years.

'Bonnie, you're going to come with Mummy to the shops.'

'NO, shops are boring. I want to go to nursery.' She crosses her arms, stamps her foot and pushes out her lower lip.

'Bonnie, if you're good I'll buy you some sweets.' She is in her buggy in under thirty seconds and waits patiently as I put on her shoes. Are sweet bribes how the other mothers control their kids? I think of all Bonnie's vomiting last night and groan. But she does seem a lot better.

We finally get walking and I push her buggy into the Marks and Spencer's food hall, letting her choose a few different items of confectionary to keep her occupied.

'Take four things,' I tell her. 'If you're good, you can have it all.'

We then head over to the hosiery department where I pick up six pairs of eighty-denier black tights, the ones that apparently regulate my temperature, and a few bras that look about the right size. In the dressing room I leave Bonnie on the other side of a curtain eating a Rocky Road bar so I can try them on. But as soon as I shut the curtain, she goes apeshit.

'Mummy, Mummy!' she screams, drawing the attention of all the old women trying on bras. About four grey hairdos poke out of changing rooms to witness the child screaming in distress.

'Bonnie, stop it,' I say firmly. 'I'll be twenty seconds.' I shut the curtain quickly, and she screams again. I have no idea why she suddenly has separation anxiety; usually she kicks me until I leave her alone.

'Mummy! Mummy, no!'

I tear open the curtain.

'Bonnie, please pack it in. I need to try these on.'

I hear a 'tut' from the cubicle next door. A little old lady pokes her head out and looks at Bonnie sympathetically.

'Poor girl, she's frightened,' she says, in that annoying way that old people do. They were parents to toddlers so long ago that they have forgotten how awful it is. They remember the sweet bits, the cuddles, the playfulness, the stories. Mother Nature has rid their memories of the turbulent mood swings, violent meltdowns, sleepless nights and their own stress-induced outbursts. Of course that is what happens – if all adults and old people were like me then we would horrify younger generations into never reproducing. It is imperative that humans forget the turmoil of birth and parenting small children for the evolution of the human race, but dearie me, when you come face to face with it in a Marks and Spencer's changing room, it's hard to accept it as natural.

'She's not frightened, she's being silly.'

'Ahhhh, give her a cuddle,' says another of the set-and-perm brigade.

'She doesn't need a cuddle,' I say, whipping the curtain shut again. I just need to try on some bras, then we can leave.

'Oh dear, is your mummy very angry?' one of them asks, seriously testing my tolerance levels.

'MUMMY. MUMMY,' Bonnie screams. What the hell is she playing at? She never does this.

'Bonnie, wait,' I say, sternly. She has to be patient. And I peep my head through the gap so she can see me whilst I try to blindly to put on a bra on the other side of the curtain.

'Ahhhh, poor baby,' the first old lady says, bending down to Bonnie. She is only wearing a bra. It's weird and creepy and Bonnie doesn't like it any more than I do. I rip a bra off its hanger. I just need to try them on.

'Oh dear,' the old lady says. 'Do I smell poo poo?' Bonnie screams louder as the old lady invades her personal space by putting her hand on her crotch and giving it a very hard squeeze. What the hell does she think she is doing?

'I feel a poo poo,' she says, as Bonnie kicks her right in the face. I only have one boob in the bra when the old lady falls through the curtain and into my dressing room.

'NO!' I yell, as I see blood pouring from her nose.

'Help me, help me,' the old lady screams. I look at her on the floor. Despite my half naked state, I feel a surprising lack of self-awareness. I'd take my body over her decrepit old one any day. It's unusual for me to feel one-upmanship on anything involving my physical appearance. I rather like the feeling. I cover myself before multiple other old ladies rush to her aid.

I get myself dressed, grab all the bras and tights and quickly leave the changing room. I'll pay for them all, and try them on at home.

'You need to teach that child some respect,' one of the grannies shouts after me. I turn around and march straight back over to the cubicle.

'Some respect?' I repeat, to the three-strong gaggle of geriatrics nursing the perverted one's nose. 'You grabbed my daughter's crotch and she quite rightly kicked you in the face.'

'I was checking her nappy,' she says, all breathy, hurt and offended in that way old people get when they are out of order but think everyone should let them off because they're ancient. Well not me.

'I've told her since she was old enough to understand me, that if anyone she doesn't know or likes goes anywhere near her crotch she is to do whatever it takes to get them off. Old men, young boys and nosey old bags included. You deserve that bloody nose and I hope you're sorry,' I say firmly. The women stare at me as if I am a dinosaur and running for their lives is pointless.

'SECURITY,' calls one of them, like a damsel in distress who can't fight her own battles. Stupid old ladies.

'I didn't touch you,' I say confidently. 'You touched my daughter and she defended herself. What are you going to do, have them arrest her? Or will I tell them that you grabbed my little girl's vagina?'

'How dare you,' the bloody-nosed old witch says to me.

'No, lady, how dare you! Up yours!' I say.

79

When we eventually get in the queue to pay, a pungent smell of poo lingering around us, Bonnie has calmed down. I kneel down to her level.

'Bonnie, I am proud of you for kicking that woman in the face. If anyone ever tries to touch your vagina and you don't want them to, that is exactly what you do, OK?'

She looks at me as if she has no idea what I am talking about.

Then she kicks me in the face.

Lauren Pearce – Instagram post
@OfficialLP

The image is of Lauren sitting on the edge of a bath, one leg lifted and her foot beside her. One hand has a razor in it, the other is holding her phone. She has a black silk robe on.

The comment reads:
Body hair, why do we even have it? I mean, I know it was supposed to keep us warm when we lived in caves, but we have clothes now. I love having silky legs (Gavin likes it too;). Did you know that if you run out of shaving foam you can just use your conditioner? Oh, I know . . . such a good beauty hack. You're welcome. #beauty #selflove #nohairylegsthanks #LaurenPearce #womensupportingwomen

@jemmajubes: No way?? Doing that tonight

@garflib: GENIUS. I don't know how he is the one with the empire when you are this brilliant (eye roll)

@daveyodavey: Take that robe off next time.

@betterthangoodfor: I bet your mum is so proud, seeing you half naked on Instagram. I bet its all she ever wanted for you. #Getarealjob

@sesememe3: Your skin is like china. You're perfect, keep being you.

@mellisaheart: Has Gavin got a big dick?

Ruby

Small victories are all you can cling onto when you are as terrible at parenting as I am. I sometimes wonder if I have any positive impact on Bonnie at all, but I'm experiencing a rare moment of elation at the thought that maybe one of the things I have told her has gone in. It's a terrible shame I have to enjoy this triumph with a black eye of my own, but it is what it is.

When we leave Marks and Spencer I take her back to the park. It's a lot easier than having her at home, and if we spend an hour or so here, then I won't have to feel so bad about her watching TV for the rest of the day while I work in my office, hiding from the mouse. When we arrive, I see the man again. He is sitting on the bench holding a packet of baby wipes. The bench is pristine.

I find comfort in knowing other people are hurting. I have a habit of telling myself that I am worse off than everyone else. When I meet someone else with a physical or emotional defect, I feel connected to them. I guess that makes sense.

Bonnie is playing happily alone, kicking leaves and running in circles around a tree. I sit next to the man. He doesn't seem to have a problem with me being on the bench now that he has cleaned it. His hands are clasped together, his elbows resting on his knees. He is looking out into the park, those memories replaying for him again. As if stumbling on a particular moment, he smiles to himself. It brings him out of his trance and he notices me beside him.

'Your daughter?' he asks, pointing towards her.

'Yes. Her name is Bonnie,' I tell him.

'That's a beautiful name.'

'Thank you.' I don't tell him I regret it, he doesn't need to know. 'I've seen you here before,' I say. He could shut this conversation down if he wants to, I almost certainly would.

'Yes, I'm here every day.' He turns to acknowledge the plaque. 'This bench is dedicated to my daughter, Verity. She died when she was seven. We used to come here all the time.'

'I'm so sorry.'

'Yeah. Thank you.'

We sit for a few moments and watch Bonnie. Her sweet, innocent energy captivating us both.

'How old is she?' he asks me.

'Three and a half.'

'Ah, that was my favourite age.'

I have a feeling that I could have said Bonnie was any number of years, and that this man would have said it was his favourite age. But if anyone has the right to romanticise about parenting, it is him.

'Lovely that you're with her during the week. My wife insisted Verity went to a nursery even though she didn't work. Then she went to school. If I could go back I'd quit my job and be a house husband, but you never think like that when they're alive.'

'I guess you don't,' I say, choosing not to tell him the truth: that I spend very little time with Bonnie, and that I am finding these few days of having no childcare incredibly challenging.

'I have a bench dedicated to my dad in Cornwall,' I say, wanting him to know I have a little understanding of grief. 'He died when I was a teenager. I know we're designed to outlive our parents, and I'm not comparing what happened to me to what happened to you, but it's nice to have a place to go to remember him because his death really tore me apart.'

'This bench is a vital part of my survival. We spread some ashes here too. I'm as close to her as I could possibly get when I sit on this bench. Do you get to your dad's bench very often?'

'No. No, unfortunately my mother and I don't get along and trips to Cornwall have become quite rare.'

'I'm sorry to hear that. Not all mothers are good to their children. Bonnie is very lucky to have you.'

I want to tell him that she isn't. That I am not a good or nice mother. If I were to be honest with him, I would tell him that some nights I lie in bed dreading the morning because my interactions with her are often so distressing. Some days I stand outside her nursery and take long, deep breaths to try to stop the tears consuming me as I prepare myself for the two hours of childcare I need to get through before I put her to bed. I could tell him how I don't really know what she likes, because I rarely ask her. Or that when she cries, I tell her off instead of cuddling her. I could tell him all of those things because he is a stranger and it wouldn't matter. But I don't.

'Yes,' I say, instead of all of that truth. 'I feel very lucky to have her too.'

'Well, cherish every moment,' he says, getting up. 'It was nice to meet you.'

'You too,' I say, smiling as he walks away. I wait until he's gone before I try to get Bonnie home. He doesn't need to be reminded how hard parenting can be.

Beth

Sometimes, because there are only two of us and we can work remotely, Risky and I work in a lovely café around the corner from the office. We cover the table in paper and talk to people on the phone – probably to the huge annoyance of the people around us. I always have the full English breakfast, a smoothie and a decaf coffee, aka the most pointless drink on the planet. But I love the taste and I have to watch my caffeine levels because of breast feeding Tommy. Risky always gets the avocado on toast, but only eats half of it. She washes it down with around three large lattes. If Risky was around in the Eighties, she'd definitely have been a chain smoker.

'Look, it's awful and I'm really sorry it happened, but it wasn't anyone here. OK? I hope you get to the bottom of it. And yes, tomorrow is fine,' I say to Lauren's PR, Jenny, on the phone, whilst rolling my eyes at Risky and trying to eat a piece of sausage as quietly as I can. Someone leaked a wedding invite and she's obviously calling everyone on her contacts list and having a go at them. This is quite typical of Jenny. PR around Lauren and Gavin is impossible to control; she likes to make herself feel useful by yelling at people on their behalf.

'OK, what do we need for the meeting with Lauren and Gavin tomorrow?' I ask Risky.

'Oh my God, I can't believe I'm going to meet Gavin,' she says, fanning herself with a menu.

'Risky, do I need to worry about you getting overexcited?'

'No, no boss, I'll be OK. I probably won't be able to get a single word out. Gavin fucking Riley. My mother is going to have kittens, she's obsessed,' she says, beginning to perspire.

'He seems nice enough,' I say, calmly. I've met Gavin a few times now. He's very handsome. Charming. Everything you would expect from a young, hot millionaire businessman from perfect stock. He's definitely got a glint in his eye, which is a little suspicious, I think.

'Poor Gavin,' Risky says, calming a little, talking like he is an old friend.

'Poor Gavin? For his business genius, perfect wife and couple of hundred million?' I ask facetiously. Risky's need to sympathise with everyone on the planet is really perplexing sometimes.

'No, poor him for all that sex stuff.'

Ah, she is referring to the enormous sex scandal he was involved in a few years back. Totally guilty, I think.

'That woman had clearly made up the whole thing,' she says, stepping down from her feminist pedestal for just a minute. 'As if he'd shag her with a champagne bottle. So clichéd and fake. Lauren handled it amazingly, she stood by her man. They must be so strong as a couple. Getting through something like that. I mean, I'm always for believing women, obviously. But she was so blatantly lying.'

'Or maybe he did it?' I suggest, daring to fuel her fire.

'Beth, Gavin donated three million pounds to a women's refuge charity last year. Plus, he just paid for a girls' only soccer school. Not to mention the way he sacked his old CEO publicly when an employee accused him of sexual misconduct. He put out a statement saying his company, and him, have a zero-tolerance policy when it comes to sexual harassment. Gavin Riley is more of a feminist than most feminists, there's no way he'd cheat on his wife by sticking a champagne bottle up some slapper's fanny.'

Turns out women supporting women is really hard when hot rich men get in the way. I keep that to myself.

'OK, have we got everything we need for the meeting? You have their file?'

'Check!' she says, pulling it out of her bag.

'You have some self-control?'

'I think so!' she says, with a strong exhale. 'Oh, there was one thing. Lauren booked a photographer, Rebecca Crossly? Apparently, they just did a shoot together and she liked her, so that's taken care of. Lauren posted about her this morning. Look at this amazing photo.' Risky shoves her phone under my nose. I see a photo of Lauren, naked, as usual. Her modesty is protected by a strategically placed blanket. She looks every bit like she just got caught masturbating. 'The photos are coming out after the wedding. Doesn't she look amazing?'

'Yes, she does,' I say, turning away from the screen. I actually feel OK about my body until I look at pictures of thin and beautiful people on Instagram. It's the main reason I don't really go on it. I see it as a form of torture. It's like being skint but walking around the Selfridges' food hall. Don't put yourself through it.

'Rebecca Crossly,' I mutter, typing her name into Google. A lot of heavily Photoshopped photos of naked women come up – it seems to be her thing. No weddings. But if Lauren booked her, then I guess that is fine. She fired the original photographer two days ago but her mother refused everyone I suggested. So now it's not my problem. 'OK, cool.'

My phone vibrates and it's Michael calling on FaceTime. I answer and see my face appear in the corner of the screen. I've definitely gained a chin in recent months.

'Hey, Mummy, I just wanted to say I miss you,' he says in a baby voice, holding the phone to Tommy's face. A woman on the table next to me smiles and Risky looks like she might ejaculate.

'Oh, hey little man, Mummy misses you too!' I say back, his gorgeous face making my breasts swell and my heart thump. It's just another few weeks, then I'll be with him full time. I can do this. 'How are you guys doing today?'

'We're good,' says Michael, holding the phone in front of his face now. 'We just had a walk, and now we'll have a bottle and bed. Your stash is running low, maybe we should be thinking about formula soon?'

'No. No, we have loads of breast milk here, I'll bring it home,' I say, a little desperately. Breast feeding is my way of dealing with being back at work so soon after having Tommy. I might not be doing the day-to-day with my baby, but I'm keeping him alive with my boobs and that is really important to me right now.

'OK, well we just wanted to tell you we love you,' Michael says, squashing his face close to Tommy's. He blows me a kiss, and we say goodbye. He's always so sweet on the phone. Maybe it's because he knows we can't physically touch.

I realise that Risky has gone into a daze. She is resting her hand in her palm and smiling at me. 'The dream,' she says, sweetly. 'You're married to the perfect man.'

I smile and nod.

'Boss, can I ask you something? Woman to woman?' she says, looking pensive, turning inwards from the table next to us. I am expecting a question involving place settings, or suchlike, so nearly choke on a fried mushroom when she says, 'Do you think it's weird that the guy I'm seeing only wants to do me up the bum?'

'Pardon?'

'It's just that we've been seeing each other for a few weeks now and he's all about anal. It's like my vagina doesn't exist to him. That's not right, is it?'

I often worry that I don't set enough boundaries as a boss, or make the line between work and friendship clear enough. What is apparent here is that I have absolutely not nailed that. I wipe the corners of my mouth with a napkin and do my best to say the right thing.

'Have you done the anal?' I ask, like a grandma trying to be cool.

'Yeah, obviously,' she says, as if I am stupid.

'Oh yeah, I mean totally, obviously,' I say. Followed by some strange faces and little *pfffttt* noises to reiterate that I think anal is completely normal.

91

'I mean, I don't mind it. I like it, actually. It's probably my fault for asking him to do it in the first place. But I just wonder what his deal is, why he isn't interested in my vagina.'

'You asked him to do it?' I ask, casually. It's been so long since I've felt able to behave like a vixen that I had forgotten some young women make their own sexual demands. I used to.

'Yes, I asked him on, like, our third date. So not too bad.'

'Not too bad?' I ask, unsure what she means by that.

'Yeah, not so early that he might think I was slutty. Anyway, it's all he wants now, I wondered what you thought? I respect your opinion on healthy relationships.'

I clear my throat, drink some cold coffee, close my computer, and try desperately to think of something to say.

'Maybe he's gay?' I say, eventually, regretting it instantly.

'That is a little closed-minded, Beth. Just because a man likes anal, it doesn't mean he is gay. And anyway, I've got lots of LGTB+ friends, and sexual orientations don't bother me. I'm not exactly a hundred per cent straight,' she says, proudly. Risky adores men; she is the most romantic and traditional woman I know. But her 'generation' wants to believe they have choices, and so she loves to tell me about the one time she kissed a girl at school. 'My friend Casey and I once kissed for ten minutes. She even tried to finger me.' She tells me the same story again, and I nod and smile because if I started asking questions about it, I'd probably never stop. I am thirsty for sex talk. It's a shame I only have my assistant to do it with.

'I just want to establish that my vagina needs love too, you know? I'm going to tell him tonight.'

'You are? What will you say?' I ask, hoping to learn a few things about how to communicate sexual issues within a relationship.

'Oh, I probably won't *say* anything. I was thinking about just using a dildo on myself at the same time. You know, just to remind him that the other hole is there.' She looks pretty proud of herself for this idea, and nods a few times. 'Yeah, I think that's what I'll do. Great advice, thanks.' And then she gets back to work. The woman on the next table has gone the colour of ketchup.

Risky and I sit quietly at our table getting on with our work, our little conversational interlude hanging in the air like a fantasy I could reach and grab if I let myself. I take a huge intake of breath and blow it out quickly and loudly.

'You OK, boss?' she asks me.

'Ah yes. Absolutely. Just working out what to do next,' I say, getting up and stretching my arms in the air, as if I have nothing on my mind at all. I then walk slowly to the toilet where I masturbate furiously, before coming back to the table, ordering the bill, and suggesting we better get going.

Ruby

I saw the mouse in the kitchen again this morning, and nearly went into a full-on meltdown. I went to two shops and both of them had run out of mousetraps, although one had the kind that are just a sticky strip. The guy told me casually, 'The mouse sticks to the strip and can't get off.'

'What? So it's stuck there? Alive?' I asked him, so horrified I could barely speak.

'Yes,' he replied, as if to say, 'Isn't that genius?'

I had to get out of the shop immediately because I had the sensation that mice were all over me. I tried to get to a third shop but Bonnie was getting impatient, so we are home again. She is watching TV and I am Googling ways to get rid of rodents from your house.

As advised, I stuff every hole in my kitchen with steel wool. I then pour peppermint oil all over everything and create a barricade across the entrance to the kitchen with suitcases, box files and shoe boxes. I finally settle into my office, which is also the spare room, and try to breathe.

I can't stop thinking about the man on the bench. I can't deny I feel a little lighter having shared a moment with someone who is worse off than me. Usually, my only solace is talking to strangers on the Internet.

When I was a teenager and the hair started to appear, the World Wide Web wasn't a resource I could use as it didn't exist yet. And besides, it should have been my mother who comforted me. But she was already on the path to self-destruction, and offered me little but stress and humiliation. Not being one to connect with strangers over a problem, I'd never have thought to ask around to find out if anyone else suffered from the same condition. Also, back then, I didn't even know I *had* a condition. I just thought I was a freak of nature. And my mother making jokes about it in front of other girls my age made it worse. I remember one time we were giving my friend Alison a lift home from hockey practice – an already traumatising experience for me as I'd insist on wearing a jumper and jogging bottoms while everyone else was in shorts and t-shirts. I'd get so hot I'd feel too faint to carry on, meaning that my hockey skills – which were actually pretty advanced – went unnoticed, because I was too busy trying to hide my body. When my mother picked Alison and me up on this particular day, she asked Alison if I had showered after the game.

'No, Ruby showers at home,' Alison said.

My mother then had a field day.

'No she doesn't. You mean she doesn't shower at school either? Oh no Ruby, you need to wash all of that hair on your back or it will get smelly. No one wants a smelly girl.'

Alison laughed. I don't know if it was out of awkwardness or because she and my mother were as bad as each other, but that laugh haunted me. The shower situation was far too

95

challenging, so to avoid rumours about me never washing, I gave group sport up altogether.

I committed to a life of hiding. Until a few years ago, after Liam and I split up and my despair was disabling me even more than usual, I finally took the time to search out forums where other women were experiencing some level of what I was going through. Of course, there were plenty. I have read countless accounts of how women hide themselves due to excess body hair. Relationships that have failed because of it. Childfree lives are a consequence of it. Self-hatred, self-harm all popular side-effects. There is reassurance in everything I read. Primarily to know that I am not alone, but most often the comfort comes in knowing that maybe my case isn't the worst. I don't mean that in the literal sense. The amount of body hair I have is extreme, that isn't up for debate. I've yet to see or hear about anyone who has it worse. The hair is thick and dark, it covers most of my body. It takes hours to remove and grows back within weeks. It's a terrible case of a horrible condition, but the comfort I take from the forums I visit is that, compared to a lot of people I read about, I am not depressed, despite the many challenges I have faced in my life.

My mother was my first. My father's death the next. My hormonal imbalance kicked in when I was a teenager and will be with me forever. It torments me, and pokes fun at me, keeps me up at night and tries to bring me down. But actually, when all is said and done, I don't hate myself. Not really.

My job helps. I'm really good at it. I mean, it's vile and

evil, and I am perpetuating beauty standards that I know are not real and that leave women – who don't have issues anywhere as bad as my own – believing that they are not good enough. But I'm good at it. And I know it. It is important to me that I am not failing at everything.

A lot of the blogs and posts by other women who have excess body hair are written by women who can't see beyond it in any aspect of their lives. Failed careers, such a lack of self-belief that they gave up on themselves entirely. I haven't done that. I make an effort with what I wear, I keep my weight down. I am excellent at my job. None of this changes much in terms of my self-esteem, but at least I still have the will to try.

One particular online post grabs my attention.

I cannot leave the house because of my facial hair. I am so ashamed, so embarrassed. My anxiety has gotten so bad because of it that I am no fun to be around. People hate me, I can tell. They don't know what to say, because my social skills have become so bad. I used to be fun.

My husband tries to get me out of the house. He is so loving and supportive, and we have a fairly stable marriage. I am very close to him, but no matter how much he reassures me, I can't help myself.

I have two children, aged six and four. I am very close to my children. I have talked to them about my problem and they understand how it makes me feel. They tell me they love me, and that I am a fun mummy. I find going out so hard that when I am home I do my best by my kids, I play with them, I read to them, I lie with them at night. It's the least I can do to make up for them not getting invited to other kids' parties, because the parents don't want to have to talk to me.

My husband and I are OK. I manage sex. He says he loves me and finds me beautiful, but how long will that last? I am a recluse. I can't force him to be too. I'm scared for a future where my kids leave home and my husband meets someone else.

I wish I could do better.

It's always so strange to read these posts. To know there are other women out there who have even a small clue about what I am going through. There we all are, being open and honest on the Internet. Sharing stories of how impossible the outside world feels. It's like we enter into a black hole and come out in another universe. But we have to leave it and survive in reality. I wonder if one day, generations from now, people like me will be able to live entirely happy lives, just online. Experiencing total physical solitude, yet with thousands of people for company, who never have to see your face. Food will be delivered, clothes unnecessary. You could exist in whatever state you were dealt, and never have to feel ashamed.

I click on 'Add a Comment'.

I just wanted to say that even though it might not feel like it, you are doing great. I am so like you, but in the process of self-punishing I managed to push away a man who loved me, and my relationship with my daughter is fraught. Feel good about the family you have created and hold onto them. I wish you all the best. Ruby x

As I am about to click 'POST', though, I change my mind and delete what I wrote. What difference would it make anyway?

I brought the baby monitor that I used when Bonnie was tiny into my office, so I can watch her in bed and make sure the mouse isn't crawling on her in her sleep. I have work to do. I read an email from Rebecca about a new retouching job.

The original photograph is of a young woman, an actress, apparently. Sara Jenkins. She had a baby last year and is posing naked to show off her 'post-baby body'. Her post-baby body, in reality, isn't great. There are stretch marks across her stomach, and a large red scar below her belly button. She has requested that I take away the stretch marks and the scar, thin her thighs, smooth her skin and give her a tan. All so she can lie to other women and make them feel like failures for not being perfect after the carnage of a C-section.

This woman, Sara Jenkins, is a fraud. I give her the tan she asked for and cover the scar. I move her belly button up, give her a more defined waist, smooth her bad complexion. I try to leave a few signs of motherhood, to keep it real. A natural crease above her pubic area, just poking out the top of her tiny briefs. A few dimples on her thighs. I fill them in and thin them down like Rebecca told me to, but I leave the pores visible. She isn't made of plastic after all.

I send the finished image off to Rebecca. She replies in under ten minutes with more instructions.

The PR went mental at this. Lose the crease above her vag. Smooth the thighs more. Hurry, please. They were supposed to be in yesterday.

A few minutes later:

Oh, and sort her chin out. I had to give her whisky to make her relax. She didn't want to get her kit off. FFS.

I do as I am paid to do and remove all signs of life. I am increasingly aware of the current culture, and how people are held accountable for terrible things they do or say on email or at work. I always try to write positive messages that exempt me from any future blacklisting or blame in this terrible world that I work in. My industry is under fire. A #MeToo equivalent is heading our way. I want to make sure I am not lampooned. I send the photos back with a note.

Here you go Rebecca, please find attached the retouched images. It's a shame so much work was requested as I thought the originals were lovely. I'm not sure she needed the whisky. Is there a less intoxicating method you could use? Taking some time? Talking? Clothing?

I know it's hard to work with a model and for an industry to whose beauty standards we are beholden, but as long as the requests are coming from those in the photo, then what are we to do? Ruby.

She writes back almost immediately:

Err, ok Ruby. Thanks for the lecture. Pictures look great. You made a tense bitch look hot AF. More soon.

I am right though. The instructions for the retouching nearly always come from the person in the photograph, despite everyone else getting the blame for it. There is a backlash now, with lots of celebrities saying they don't want to be retouched. And screaming about the attack on feminism if they are. Good for them, really. But as they attack the magazine editors on Instagram, and hammer an already dying industry for hating women, they don't see what I see. The women in the photographs themselves begging for perfection. Sending the pictures back to me again and again, until the image is so far from the original photograph that they are barely recognisable. They have to be held accountable too. So much of feminism leans towards breaking down the patriarchy. But every day I see that it is women who are damaging other women.

What I would do to have their skin, their confidence? But maybe they are no different from me. They hide the truth as much as I do. They just hide it from a bigger audience, and with a lot less velvet.

Lauren Pearce – Instagram post
@OfficialLP

The image is of Lauren and her fiancé, Gavin Riley. They are standing in a garden, he has a suit on, she is wearing a low-backed, black slinky dress. She is snuggled into him in an awkward embrace entirely set up for a photograph. He has his hands on her hips, she is turning to look at the camera, her left hand in full view. The enormous diamond engagement ring glistening in the sun.

The caption reads:
Love is the answer, always and forever. It's just weeks until I marry this man. My love, my hero. Maybe I am the luckiest girl alive? He's my scented candle, my relaxing bath, my CBD gummy . . . hahaha. You know what I'm saying don't you? Even my anxiety can't take me away from him. Who do you love this much? #PanteneFullVolumeShampoo? #Ad #loveistheanser #mentalhealth #findyourpeople Photo Credit @TheMayraPearce Hey mum;)

@helpmyfeetshine: He is your scented candle? YOUR SCENTED CANDLE? FFS.

@gogerritguuurrl: COUPLE GOALZ

@ChattyMacHatty: One day I'll find love like this and I will be this happy. For now, I'll just live it through you.

@Shawnty45: How do you always look so perfect?

@bethanybeetsit: I am so happy for you guys. Can't wait to see your dress.

@helenviceP: I heard Gav banged a couple of models in the bog while you ate a salad in the restaurant, is that true?

Beth

Risky and I are meeting Lauren, Gavin and the PR Jenny at the Marriott Hotel on Westminster Bridge. An entirely random location, booked at the last minute, under fake names, to avoid any press intrusion. Jenny organised everything, and it all feels a bit dramatic. The hotel is one of those huge buildings with long corridors and hundreds of rooms. These places fascinate me. Hotels this size feel like worlds unto their own. Who knows what is happening in this building at any one time. Sexual deviants upstairs, major celebrities downstairs, no one with any idea that the other is there. Risky and I walk down the long corridor looking for a door with 'Ralph Knott' written on it, as that is where the meeting with Lauren and Gavin is happening. Risky is practically panting with excitement; she hasn't met Gavin yet. She put make-up on for the entire cab ride and is acting as if she's about to walk a red carpet.

I knock on the door and after a few moments, Jenny comes to open it. When she sees us she rudely looks Risky up and down as if scanning her with some imbedded identification chip she has in her brain, then looks along the corridor like we have a team of investigative journalists behind us, before opening the door wide enough for us to get in. We have to duck under her arm. I am guessing this location is about Jenny trying to seem like she has control over the absolute mess that the privacy of this wedding has become. It doesn't really achieve that though; it's just given everyone a real ball-ache of a journey into central London during rush hour. I'd be a better PR than Jenny. Her lack of organisation and people skills is petrifying.

'Did you see any paps on the way in?' she asks me.

'Nope, I didn't notice any.'

'They're probably hiding,' she says, checking the corridor one more time. I suppose she has to at least try to make people think she is important and competent.

The room is big with wooden panels all over the walls. There are six chairs in a circle in the middle. It feels like we are a group of reprobates who are having a secret meeting. Maybe we are.

'Lauren, so good to see you,' I say, walking over to her confidently. I do my best to act nonchalant with any of my celebrity clients; I think it's important for the business.

'Hi, thanks for coming,' she says, nervously. Clinging onto Gavin like he is an intravenous drip filtering small amounts of confidence into her. 'How's the baby?'

'Oh, he's great. So sweet.'

Jenny lets out an uncomfortable sound and makes a strange gooey face. She is what the media would refer to as a hot mess. Previous conversations have revealed that she is single and childfree. She is about forty-five. She wears clothes that don't suit her, too trendy. The heels are too high. Middle-aged fashion victims rarely look good. If you're not dressing for yourself by forty-five then you need to have a major rethink.

My shirt and jeans might not be fashionable, but I am extremely comfortable. Jenny reeks of a woman who never worked herself out. I, on the other hand, know exactly who I am. Chubby, married and gagging for a shag.

'Oh my God, sorry,' pipes up Risky, not exercising my calm and collected skills. 'Sorry, I just . . . ' She doesn't finish her sentence, she just hugs Lauren awkwardly, then shakes Gavin's hand before giving him a kiss on the cheek and apologising around sixteen times for being so nervous. Jenny rolls her eyes at her. I smile and retain my cool.

Gavin is a huge name in British finance. Chairman of Riley Ltd, he inherited a multi-million-pound empire when his father died suddenly at fifty-three. Gavin is young, gorgeous and very rich. He's been renowned in the City ever since he was old enough to work, but he became a household name when he appeared as a 'Dragon' on the TV show *Dragons' Den*. Now every woman in the UK's fantasy, he is as famous for being sexy as he is rich. Through some family connection, I presume, he met the lesser-known Lauren Pearce, an underwear model. They are getting married, and now Lauren has been catapulted into the world of major celebrity. I get the impression she doesn't really know what to do with it. For now, her unique selling point is definitely her body.

'Massive fan of the show,' Risky says to Gavin. 'My mum is obsessed. For Christmas she got me one of those reading lights with the speakers that you invested in.'

'Oh, that's great. Yes, View-Voice is a great company, people love them,' Gavin says, obviously quite used to these interactions.

'You should make a video for your mum,' Lauren says, seem-ingly very comfortable with Risky's worshipping of her husband.

'What? You would do that?' I don't know if I'm . . . '

'Of course, what's your name?' Gavin asks.

'Risky.'

'Risky? That's cute,' Gavin says, causing Risky to buckle at the knees and blush like she's had a bowl of tomatoes squashed into her face. I have noticed that celebrities call their fans 'cute' a lot. It's endearing but establishes rank. You would never call someone you admire cute, would you? Risky is delighted with it.

'Yes, my brother and sister named me,' Risky says. 'I think my mum regrets not saving that idea for our new dog.' Everyone laughs, she is very good. I feel a bit proud of my assistant, especially for acknowledging her name makes her sound like a Cocker Spaniel.

Jenny isn't comfortable with this casual conversation and suggests we get on with it. I try to get the visual of Gavin doing Risky up the bum out of my head. I'm not sure where that came from.

Risky looks at me for approval to pose with Gavin. There is a bold line in her contract that says she isn't allowed to hassle famous clients for photos, but I say it's OK. Everyone seems happy. I let it pass.

'Hey Marion, I'm here with Risky and just wanted to say . . . ' Gavin pauses, and looks into the lens, his arm around Risky. 'I'm out!'

Risky almost collapses when he performs the show's catch-phrase. 'Mum's going to die when she sees that.'

Gavin, Lauren and Risky all watch the video back together and give it their mutual approval. 'It would look great with the Aden filter if you post it. Make sure you tag me,' Lauren says, suddenly in her element. Risky promises she will. It's like they are talking in code.

'Right, shall we kick this off then?' I say, realising we could be here all day doing social media posts. 'OK, who's going first, shall I? My name is Beth and I'm addicted to weddings,' I say, regretting it immediately. Risky bursts out laughing, as if her contract says she must support my comedy.

Despite just agreeing to start the meeting, Lauren picks up her phone and checks it quickly. She leans over to Jenny and whispers, 'That post about the wedding shoes got 156k likes.'

Jenny looks thrilled. 'You tagged Jimmy Choo, didn't you?'

'Yeah, I'd never not do that again, not after last time.'

They both make a face that suggests Jimmy Choo himself was quite upset, and we finally crack on with the meeting.

'OK, so we have lots to go through,' I say, pulling a bunch of papers out of a plastic folder and resting them on my lap. 'Shall we start with the order of the day?'

'Yes, or maybe the music?' Lauren suggests, in her gentle voice. She's very pretty but nothing mind-blowing in real life. She has a sweet face, and a friendly smile. She looks as natural as a twenty-eight-year-old with bleached hair and a fake tan can look. I've noticed she often looks to someone else for confirmation after she has said something, as if her decisions always need to be backed up to make them valid. This time she looks to Gavin, who puts his hand on her thigh and says, 'Whatever baby.'

I look at his hand on her leg and it sends a shiver up my body. It landed so confidently on her. So solid and firm. He leaves it there and rubs it up and down. She shuffles her chair along so it's closer to his, and he puts his arm around her as if she is cold, even though it's very hot in this weird room. Lauren is childlike, I decide. Not the confident, bubbly person she puts on display on her Instagram feed. From what I have seen, there is always someone, or something, supporting her. Whether it be physical contact from Gav, emotional propping from her mother or reassurance from Jenny, someone is always egging Lauren on. She's not the person you would expect to meet, the one who takes her clothes off a lot, who talks about happiness and confidence like they come naturally to her. To me she seems quite lost. Or maybe I am just projecting.

The hand on the leg is causing me distress. I can't imagine easy breezy affection like that. It's so rare that Michael makes any physical connection with me at all. The concept of my husband touching me should not feel so alien.

'OK, so music,' I say, snapping myself back to reality. 'I have the DJ booked for later on. And I spoke to Bastille's manager, they are absolutely up for doing the first dance as well as the later set. All they've asked for are snacks and a few bottles of champagne, which is no problem. Would you like me to invite the band to the wedding breakfast?'

'For sure,' Gavin says, squeezing Lauren towards him. He is so tactile with his wife-to-be. The rumours of infidelity that surround him are hard to believe when he seems incapable of taking his hands off her.

Lauren smiles, shyly. Gavin runs his hand up her leg and it

takes a hard push of professionalism from me to keep my focus on the job. I once heard that he shagged Felicity Smithe, a model, in the toilet of a restaurant during a lunch sitting while Lauren was waiting at the table. Apparently one of the waiters saw them walk in together and leave a few minutes later. It's one of those whispered celebrity gossip stories that everyone seems to know, but never made it into the papers. In fact there are a number of those rumours floating around about Gavin. It's not impossible to imagine that they might be true. Physically he is little short of perfect. And then of course there is the money and power. Women must throw themselves at him all the time. But yet, he chooses to marry Lauren Pearce. I have so many questions that I plan never to ask.

But I always wonder: if I know of his infidelity, surely she must too? But who would tell her about the rumours? I get the impression she doesn't have many real friends; every time I asked her about bridesmaids she was never sure who, or how many, she would have. Eventually she settled on a couple of models who are her 'besties' according to her Instagram feed. I heard one particular rumour that Gavin had a three-some with both of them.

Suddenly the door crashes open.

'I hope you didn't start without me?' says Mayra, Lauren's mother, striding into the room. She is a tall, stunning blonde, probably in her early fifties, but really she could be any age and I wouldn't be surprised. She's had a lot of work done, her clothes are always stunning, and she is vegan.

'Hey Mum,' Lauren says, with a light tone of sarcasm, hinting that Mayra might have actually acknowledged her.

'Sit up straight, Lauren,' she says, raising her eyebrows to the rest of us. 'My goodness, twenty-eight years old, the future wife of a tycoon and she still needs her mother to correct her posture.'

She takes a seat on the sixth chair and gets out a notepad. Every time Mayra arrives at our meetings everyone snaps into action. She is like Lauren's manager, and clearly has a strong hold over her and her career. She micro-managed the menu selections, forcing me to try multiple desserts that she wouldn't eat herself. I happily obliged.

'I'm pregnant,' I'd say. 'If I can't indulge now, when can I?' Over twenty pounds of excess later, I think I maybe should have stood my ground.

'Oh my goodness, how could I have been so stupid,' Mayra says, walking over to Gavin. She places a hand on each of his cheeks and kisses him on both sides of his face. 'My darling, looking dashing as always.'

Gavin seems used to it. Mayra doesn't apply the same affection to her daughter and sits back down. I think I catch Lauren rolling her eyes.

It's quite awkward.

'OK, shall we crack on?' I suggest. Risky nods enthusiastically, she's still quivering with excitement.

As the meetings gets underway, I'm sure I catch Mayra adjusting her cleavage and winking at Gavin.

I probably just imagined it.

Ruby

I still haven't found Bonnie a new nursery. I meant to email around after finishing the Sara Jenkins retouching job yesterday evening, but it took a lot longer than planned to meet Rebecca's exacting standards, so Bonnie's on the sofa watching TV, again. She will probably watch it all day. Which makes me feel bad, but I'm not sure what else I am supposed to do. I have a lot of work to do.

I thought about the mouse all night. I was certain it would crawl on me in my sleep. Have babies on my pillow, or nibble at my toes. I really shouldn't have googled, 'What is the worst thing that can happen when you have a mouse in your house?' The results were on a par with going camping and watching *The Blair Witch Project* on your way there. I am jittery to say the least.

I carefully moved the suitcases, box files and shoe boxes so that I can enter the kitchen. I am wearing tight black leggings with my boots and a tight black polo neck. I don't usually wear tight clothes at this stage in the cycle as the hair pokes through the fabric, which is the single most disgusting thing I can imagine, other than a mouse getting stuck in my skirt or sleeve. Which is why I am basically wearing a cat suit. No entry points into my outfit. A mouse touching me is my worst fear.

I edge cautiously into the kitchen. There is no sign of the mouse. I pop some bread in the toaster. What happens next is the single most traumatic experience of my entire life.

The mouse leaps out of the toaster. Like a bouncy ball on the way back up it flies into the air then lands with a splat on the kitchen floor. I scream as if a murderer wielding a machete has just jumped out of my toaster, and climb back onto a chair. My heart is racing, and my breath almost impossible to catch. I watch as the mouse lies deathly still on the floor. I wonder if it's dead. It is probably wondering the same thing. Then it gathers itself and darts towards its usual escape route. It runs at it over and over again, headbutting it, desperate to break through the steel wool but it can't get through it, no matter how hard it tries. It bolts around the perimeter of the room then disappears up and underneath the drawer in which I keep all of my plates.

I realise Bonnie is standing at the entrance to the kitchen. She gives me such a start that I scream at her face. Of course, this sends her running off and balling as she climbs the stairs.

'Bonnie,' I call after her. 'Bonnie, I'm sorry.' But she is in her room and it's probably best she stays there for a minute. This mouse means business.

I google 'homemade mouse traps'. According to the Internet, I need a bucket, a stick, and some peanut butter. I have access to all of those things. I put the bucket in the middle of the kitchen floor. As per the instructions, I smear the peanut butter heavily around the inside of it. I then put the 'optional' four inches of water into the bucket. The stick is resting between the floor and the rim. Apparently the mouse will run up the stick, following the smell of peanut butter, fall into the bucket and drown. If I don't put the water in, it will get stuck in the bucket and be unable to escape. Both methods catch the mouse. So I guess it's just down to me and how much I want the little sod to die.

I stare at the water and imagine the dead mouse floating in it. Why is that so unbearable?

I jump when I realise Bonnie is standing by the kitchen table. This time I manage not to scream at her.

'What are you doing?' she asks me.

'Go back to the sofa please,' I tell her. She doesn't move.

'What are you doing?'

'Bonnie, there is a mouse in the kitchen and I am trying to catch it.'

'A mouse?' she asks, excitedly.

I carry on building.

'What's that?' she asks.

'It's a trap.'

'Why is it a trap?'

'So I can catch the mouse.'

'Why is there water in it?'

'So it . . . because when it falls into the bucket . . . because if there is no water then it won't . . . '

I empty the water out again. I have no idea how I will cope if I find a live mouse in the bucket, but for some reason the idea of a drowned one is even worse. If Bonnie saw it first she'd be quite upset by it. If I catch a live one and it can't get out maybe I can put a bread board over it and Liam can get rid of it when he picks Bonnie up on Friday. Whatever, I probably won't even catch it. This trap is ridiculous.

'Can I keep it?' Bonnie asks, coming closer.

'No.'

'Why?'

'Because it's a mouse and they're dirty and I hate them.'

'You shouldn't say hate. You have so many words, why do you say hate?'

'It's not that you can't say hate, it's that you should reserve it for the things you actually hate. Like, I really do hate mice. They scare me.'

'Scare you, why?'

Oh for God's sake.

'They scare me because they're tiny, and so quick. And they make horrid scratchy noises and wee all over everything. They spread disease and they're furry and . . . ' I shiver, I need to stop talking about them. I feel like they are all over me again.

'But I like furry things,' she says, confused as to why I wouldn't. 'And you're furry.'

I freeze. So she did notice it before she was sick on me. I wait for her to say something else, something cruel, but her focus is entirely on the mouse.

I grab the bucket and put it in the corner of the kitchen.

'Come on, Bonnie. Let's get out of here,' I say. 'The mouse will never go in if we are standing near it.'

Together we rebuild the barricade, and then head back to the TV.

Lauren Pearce – Instagram post
@OfficialLP

The image is of Lauren cuddling a little dog. She is on a sofa laughing, as if the dog is tickling her. Both physically and figuratively. It is unclear who is taking the photo.

The caption reads:
Being mummy to this guy is everything. How is it possible to love something this small so much? As long as I've got this guy, everything will be OK . . . who is feeling me with the #petlove #selflove #selfcare #dogsofinstagram #womensupportingwomen #LOVE #happiness #happy #AD #CuteyCollars

@heliumhater: That dog looks like a pair of slippers.

@didshereallydoit: Ahhh, he's so cute. I love how much you love him. You'll be an amazing Mummy one day

@flippeditthreetimes: More posts with Gavin more posts with Gavin

@soletrader: have you had your tits done?

@queerearforthehateguy: do you actually work?

@helenofOhBoy: YOUR LIFE IS PERFECT

Beth

There is no better feeling than my baby's actual lips on my nipples. Pumping is exhausting and makes me feel like a milk machine, but I have to keep it going. I don't always have time for these moments.

When I get home from work I give Tommy his last feed before bed; my body feels relieved and my boobs are gloriously empty. It's a feeling no pump can achieve. The endorphin rush of being where I am supposed to be makes me emotional, but I bank it. There is no need to be upset, I'll get my time with Tommy when this job is done. Until then, I won't complain about the night feeds, I'll cherish them. Adrenalin is keeping me going. I actually feel pretty good about everything, other than my husband finding me repulsive, of course.

'So how was your day?' I ask Michael, as I come back down and into the kitchen. I have my dressing gown on, and I slipped on a nice bra and some pretty knickers but he doesn't know about them yet. They are cutting into me a little, but I think I still look hot enough. I hadn't realised he was on the phone; he puts his finger over his mouth as if to tell me to 'shhh'.

'OK Mum, dinner is almost ready so I'd better go. Bye,

119

chat tomorrow,' he says, bringing his call to an end and looking at me as if I should wait. 'Right, sorry about that,' he says, giving me the all-clear to speak again. I'm not sure why my presence at home would be so terrible for his mother to know about. 'Tommy had a good day today. He finished his bottles, did two poos, one went all the way up his back and took half a packet of wipes to sort out. The other was nice and hard,' he says, filling me in. He knows I like all the details.

'I love it when you talk dirty,' I say, flirtatiously. He looks at me curiously as he hands me a glass of wine, then turns away.

'What are you cooking?' I ask. It smells delicious.

'Spaghetti bolognaise. You need to keep your protein levels up if you're going to keep breast feeding,' he says, stirring his beef sauce.

'Yes doctor.'

He cares about me. I know that much.

I watch him, his back to me. He is thicker around the middle than he used to be. His brown hair is now almost completely grey. He has a tea-towel tucked into his jeans pocket, another over his left shoulder. He tastes the sauce, adds a little salt and tastes again. I move a little closer and put my arms around his waist. I feel his body stiffen as though he just died and rigor mortis has kicked in.

'I love you,' I whisper in his ear, holding a little tighter.

'Love you too,' he says back, sweetly. 'And I'm proud of you. You've taken on a lot in a time when you should be a big blob in front of the TV for a few months. Who says women can't do it all?'

'Thanks. Having a house husband helps.'

'Having a progressive employer helps,' he says, reminding me he will be going back to work as soon as this wedding is done.

I hold a little tighter, pushing my body into his back. He strokes my forearm like it's a guinea pig at a petting zoo. Gently, as if it might bite, or give him fleas. Kind words flow out of him so easily, yet physical affection seems to get stuck just under the surface.

'What are you doing?' he says, elongating the 'iiiiing' in a fake playful tone.

'I dunno,' I whisper, undoing my dressing gown and turning him around. I hold it open, so he can see my underwear. I know my body has seen better days, but I still feel sexual. And if I feel sexual, then why should my body matter? My mother was a really open woman. When I was an insecure teenager, she told me that men find confidence the sexiest thing of all. I've let those words drive me for most of my life. It's only now that I am starting to doubt them. Doubt myself.

'Beth, come on now,' he says, pulling my dressing gown back together. 'Not here.'

'Not here? In our house?'

'Beth, please. I'm cooking.'

'Turn it off. Come on, let's do it, here, on the chopping board.' I pull myself up onto the kitchen island and open my legs. I've got underwear on so it's hardly an X-rated image, but he can't cope with it anyway.

'Beth, please. Come on now, don't be . . . Don't be . . . '

'Don't be . . .? Come on, say it,' I press, presuming he is about to say something like 'silly'.

'Don't be gross.'

'Gross?' I repeat, my eyes unable to blink. 'You think I am gross?'

'No, you're not gross, but all this . . . ' He flicks his hand around, gesturing to my body. 'It's just a bit . . . '

'Gross. Yes, you said.'

'I was just on the phone with my mum, you can't come in and beg for sex when I've just been talking to my mother.'

'This isn't begging, this is offering, Michael. There's a big difference. I'm offering my husband my body because I'd enjoy it if he took it.'

'Either way, it's all a bit . . . desperate. Isn't it?' He's turned around now, back to his bolognaise.

Desperate?

After a few moments of him stirring, and me not knowing what the hell to do next, he breaks the silence.

'What shall we watch with dinner then?'

Really? He's going to move on, just like that?

'I don't mind,' I say, trying not to sound upset.

I tie up my dressing gown and go plonk myself on the sofa, upset and despondent. As I search through Netflix for something good enough to distract me from the disaster that is my sex life, he lays my food on the coffee table in front of me.

'It's brown rice pasta,' he tells me. 'Healthy.'

'OK,' I say, not really hungry.

'Yes, I thought few healthier choices wouldn't do any harm. Love you,' he says, heading back to get his own plate.

I eat the entire bowl.

Ruby

'I think you learn by example when it comes to parenting, don't you?' I say to the man on the bench. I've brought Bonnie back to the park, hoping he would be here. He is. I was pleased to see him. I've been thinking about him a lot.

'I guess, but also, I hope not. I think, more importantly, we take our experiences with our own parents and adjust it for ourselves. At the end of the day, we all just do our best, don't we?' he says.

I look at Bonnie and realise that that's exactly what I am not doing when it comes to her. My best.

'My mother is a horrible woman. She was a horrible mother,' I say, forgetting myself a little. Just telling this man the solid facts. 'She was cruel to me, she still is.'

'That's terrible. And unfair. But you say parents lead by example? Clearly you don't.'

'I try.'

'She's adorable.'

I'm not cruel to Bonnie like Mum is to me. I don't call her mean names or taunt her. I wouldn't do those things. I'm not nice though. And most of the time she's angry with me or scared of me. One of the two. And that is entirely my fault.

'So what was Verity like?' I ask him, not knowing what the right questions are.

123

'Oh, she was very sweet. Calm, kind. I like to think she was like me, she didn't want to be the centre of attention. The exact opposite to my other daughter, who is much more like her mother. They are both quite hard to manage at times.'

'Isn't parenting just hard to manage at times?'

'Yes, that is true. I'd say the hardest thing about parenting is sharing yourself. When you're hurting, having to love another person is tough. Having to hold yourself together for them, and not letting your pain become their problem. That's the hard stuff. It takes a lifetime to learn, and when you finally do, it's too late. They are either grown up, or . . . ' He seems lost for words, staring into the distance as though I'm no longer sitting by his side.

'It's OK,' I say. 'You don't need to finish that sentence.'

'No. OK, well, I have to go, nice to see you again.' He stands up and extends a hand. 'Ross.'

'Ruby.'

'Have a good day,' he says as he walks away.

'You too,' I tell him, wondering if a 'good day' is possible when you've been through what he's been through.

'Bonnie, we better go too,' I say as I approach her, bracing myself for a meltdown that doesn't come. She climbs into her buggy.

'Mummy?' she says, as we walk. 'Can we go to the park together more often?'

'That should be fine,' I tell her. 'Yes, I mean. Yes, that will be fine.'

I am trying to do better.

5

Ruby

I have a bottle of Elnett on my desk, which I plan to spray directly onto the mouse should it come into my office. I realise this might have a traumatic outcome, but I don't know what else I can do. Before I look at another email from Rebecca, I need to sort this childcare situation out. I search for local nurseries and send the same email to all of them.

Hello, I recently moved to the area and would love to find a nursery for my lovely little girl, Bonnie (3.5). I have heard wonderful things about your place and wondered if you have any spaces available?
 Looking forward to hearing from you, Ruby Blake!

Next, salons. There are so many, it's impossible to know where to choose. Yelp is very useful for this kind of thing, but I will never understand why people leave reviews. Why would you bother if it wasn't a complaint? I can't imagine that, at any point in my life, I will be tempted to leave compliments on Yelp about a service I paid for. These people must be so bored.

I was very happy with the service here. Kaitlin was lovely and it was the first time I've had a bikini wax and it didn't hurt. I'll definitely go back, especially after seeing the look on my boyfriend's face when he saw my wax ;)

Why would you write that? What does she want? A high five for getting her vagina shaped like a porn star's?

Amazing place. Love the products they use. My legs are gorgeous and silky and smell amazing.

Why would she want smelly legs?

This was my first wax. I know, I know, I'm 39 and have always shaved but I'm getting married next week (yey) so treated myself. Loved it. Hooked.

That's how I felt the week before my wedding. Freshly waxed, excited. Most out of character. Maybe her new husband will humiliate her too.

Just completed my third lasering session on my bikini line. Hurts, but so worth it. No more razors!!!

Well isn't she brave. I tried lasering. You can't get it done unless the hair is grown out, so with the twenty-plus sessions

I would have needed I'd have been forced to remain hairy for months on end. I just couldn't face it. Not only that, it was more painful than childbirth. I thought the pain was going to kill me. It was like she was holding a Bunsen burner to my skin. When I imagined that on my nipples I knew I couldn't take it. Vera got as far as my left ankle before I told her to stop.

When I met Liam, I'd found a boyfriend who understood he couldn't see my body for three weeks at a time and he was happy for our sex life to exist only in the window after a wax. I made sure I was hair-free when I was ovulating, and somehow we managed to conceive a baby. I can't imagine feeling that way anymore, it was like a moment of madness that I fully submitted myself to. They say love is a drug – well, it certainly made me crazy.

My phone vibrates . . . for a heartstopping moment I think it's the mouse and spray some Elnett on it.

'Ruby, it's Bec.'

'Hello Rebecca. Everything OK with the pictures?' I ask, as I pluck my chin using the tweezers and small vanity mirror I keep on my desk. I keep them in various positions around the house; there is always hair to remove.

'Yes, all good. So, look, have you checked your email yet?'

I make an excuse about just getting home from the doctors and say I'm about to get to it.

'OK, well I've just done a huge cover shoot with Lauren Pearce, you know who she is?'

'No,' I say, even though I do. I take very little notice of celebrities and I'm quite proud of that. I'm not interested in their narcissistic, attention-seeking lives. However, it's impossible to not know about Lauren Pearce, she is on everything and in everything. But to establish that I don't care I say no anyway. Rebecca doesn't sound impressed, she sounds annoyed.

'She's a model, um, influencer kind of person. Marrying Gavin Riley, the *Dragons' Den* millionaire, in two weeks and she's just sacked her photographer because she thinks he was leaking stuff to the press about the wedding. I did a shoot with her this week, she was happy and asked me to do the wedding too. She's turned down *OK!* magazine and done some deal with a champagne brand who will pay for the wedding if she includes them in the social posts that go out over the course of the day. That means we need you on site to work on the images with me and get them out. You in?'

'She wants me at her wedding?'

'Yeah, I mean not as a guest. You should probably bring a sandwich, but yeah, you'd be at the wedding. I'd suggest you set up in a back room and I'll run the cards into you when I'm done. She wants to approve them then post on the day.'

'She wants to approve pictures on her wedding day?'

'Yes,' Rebecca says, as if she doesn't have time for such questions, and I should be just saying yes. But I don't want to go to a wedding, especially one of someone I don't know. I don't feel comfortable at large events like that and I can only imagine the stress of it all on the day. I don't want to be bossed around and surrounded by people. I like working alone. In my house. Weddings give me nightmares. Well they would, after how mine turned out.

'She's paying really well, offered four grand above your normal fee to be present on the day.'

'Oh.'

'Come on, Ruby, that's a new handbag if nothing else. I know how you love a handbag.'

She knows this because I used to carry very impressive bags with me when I worked in advertising. Leather ones. To tone down all the velvet.

'I mean, I'd ask someone else, it's a good gig,' she says, impatiently.

'No, it's OK, I'll do it. Presuming it's on a weekend?' I ask, logging onto Net-a-Porter and having a look at the new season Chloé totes.

'The weekend after next. How could you not know that? It's all anyone is talking about.'

'Not the people I talk to,' I tell her, proudly. Realising that I don't really talk to anyone.

'OK. Email me the details,' I add.

'I will. Also, I've emailed over the pics from the shoot I just did with her, they need a lot of work. She's given me a list, I sent that too. Can you get them to me by tomorrow? Thursday latest?'

'I'll do my best. My child is home sick so I . . . '

'Ruby, do I need to ask someone else?'

'No. No, I'll get it done.'

'OK,' she replies, as if I should count myself lucky. I think Rebecca thinks I should thank her for all the work she gives me. That would make me feel incredibly inferior, when I know that in her line of work my job is more important than hers. Anyone can take a good picture on an iPhone now, it's me that makes the magic happen. She should really be thanking me. I'm always available, I work weekends, and my work is impeccable. I hang up the call.

The photos of Lauren are of her in the nude. She is posing around her kitchen, living room and in her garden. Occasionally there is a picture of the loving couple together. Him, fully clothed, standing firm and looking handsome, her draped across him like a naked cat, or in something embarrassingly slinky. Apparently, these are to go in a magazine the week after the wedding. She has chosen to do a naked photo shoot to go alongside an interview about being in love. To me it reeks of claiming ownership; a warning to other women to stay away from her man.

Maybe going to their wedding will be an interesting experience. Even though Rebecca is planning on hiding me in a 'back room'.

I'll get to see how the other half live. Get a glimmer of the reality of these people. But one thing I know for sure is that the confidence Lauren Pearce pretends to exude about herself is an absolute lie. The list of changes she has requested to her body is ridiculous.

OK Ruby, here is the list from Lauren.
Bec

* sort roots out.
* Bronze all over
* Weird vein on foot, get rid of
* Eye bags
* plump lips
* Whiten eyes
* Bring out clavicle a bit
** Get rid of the peach fuzz.
*Remove Tattoo

I look at the pictures again. The tattoo is a simple 'V' on her hip. Probably some ex-boyfriend, she's trashy enough to do something like that. This 'peach fuzz' she is talking of, a thin layer of blonde fluff that lies on her forearms, upper thighs, a hint of it on her top lip. If that was all the body hair I had my life would be entirely different. I'd take that thin layer in black, over what I have to deal with. What a stupid, affected, vain, fake trollop this woman is. I find her despicable. It's women like this that set us all so far back, by promoting their bodies as their currency. I saw her on *Loose Women* defending herself against a *Daily Mail* article about how women who pose naked are not feminists. She said she is proud of her body and wants to show it off, that it makes her feel good and makes her feel powerful. She says she wants to encourage other women to feel the same way. To take ownership of their bodies and feel empowered by their sexuality.

'Empowered' is the most subjective word in the English dictionary. When women say nudity is empowering, they are diminishing millions of other women's fears to something stupid. My nudity is my worst nightmare. If I took my clothes off in public people would be repulsed. I look like an anorexic ape. If anyone ever told me to embrace my body and love myself, I'd tell them to spend a week dressed as a giant monkey and see how Zen they feel at the end of it.

If everyone just kept their clothes on, the world would be a happier place.

I go at the pictures of Lauren like she is a burger. I have to make her look as delicious as I can.

I can't exempt myself from the problem.

'Mummy!' Bonnie calls up the stairs. I ignore the first call, she doesn't sound desperate. 'MUMMY,' she shouts again, and this time it's impossible to not come running.

'What is it?' I say, going downstairs two at a time.

'The mouse is in the bucket!'

Beth

After I feed Tommy his morning boobs, Michael lies on the bed burping him on his shoulder. Usually he disappears downstairs while I get ready, so I see this as an opportunity to be subtly suggestive. I go into our bathroom but leave the door slightly ajar, so he can see me in the reflection in the mirror on the back of the door. I slowly take off my nightie. Pulling it over my head, sucking my tummy in, pushing my bottom out slightly to accentuate my waist. I let my hair fall down my back, and shake my head slowly from side to side, so that my hair tickles my skin, just like hot women in shampoo ads do. I carefully check that he is watching me get into the shower. He isn't.

I shower, and when I come out I realise he is still on the bed. I see this as progress and continue with my performance. I dry myself off. Pointing my toes, swishing my hair from side to side. I moisturise, rubbing body butter up and down my legs in slow, sensual, circular motions. I turn away to rub it on my tummy because that looks like I'm kneading bread, but I make sure he has a good view of my bottom, which is the best-looking part of me right now. I give it all I have, my hands swooping and swirling across my body, one foot on tiptoe to give me the best silhouette. I put on an unnecessary amount of cream, hoping he is enjoying watching my hands slide around onto my bum, on my shoulders, around my waist. I feel sexy as I do it. I've still got it, even after having a baby.

In the mirror I try to subtly see if he is watching, but he's disappeared from the bed. Maybe he is getting undressed, and is planning to come in? I lean back against the edge of the sink. I put one foot on the toilet. No, that's too much for Michael, I'll scare him off. I put it back on the floor. I pull some hair over my shoulder so it tickles my nipples. I bend one leg and push my foot into the pedestal. I suck in my tummy. I hear him walking towards the door. I'm going to get laid, I can feel it in the air. This is the moment my husband will ravish me. My heart is racing. I lick my lips. I'm so ready for this. Then SLAM. The bathroom door shuts so forcefully that the glass in the window rattles. I stay very still, partly waiting, partly too stunned to move. Surely, he didn't just slam the door on me?

'Michael?' I say, gently through the door. 'Are you OK?'

He slams the bedroom door too. The mirror falls off the wall.

Lauren Pearce – Instagram post
@OfficialLP

The image is of Lauren in expensive fitness gear doing a downward dog. It's a selfie; she is somehow managing the shot by taking a picture of her reflection in a mirror.

The caption reads:
Why is #lovingyourself so hard? Some days I struggle with what I see in the mirror, with what everyone else sees. You know those days? I get married in a few days. It will be the happiest day of my life, yet today I feel uneasy. Scared, even. Not of love, not of my choices, but of myself. Hmmmm, sorry, just thoughts going around in my head that I probably shouldn't share. How is your day? #questions #selflove #happiness #daysliketoday #baddays #anxiety

@regretmenog: You are so real. I #relate to this. Just focus on that gorgeous man and realise how lucky you are

@everymanforherself: Yeah, it must be really hard being a millionaire. Poor you. Can I send you a slap in the face to cheer you up?

@kellyannconwaynemiisis: The reason the world is run by men is because of women like you. JUST SAYING.

@gillyvanilli: babe, I feel you. I just can't #selflove today. I am a Dr and I prescribe a nap and some sex with that man of yours . . .

Beth

Lauren asked that I meet her at her house to discuss final details of the day. This nearly gave Jenny a breakdown, but there wasn't much she could do. It's a huge house in Highgate, just off a little square. This part of London is like another world.

Lauren and I are in her kitchen. She looks flawless with perfectly tonged hair and subtle make-up – always Instagram ready. The kitchen is huge, white, open-plan, modernly designed and magazine-shoot-worthy. There is a double oven and six-hob range, which she apologised for as soon as I arrived, saying the only things she knows how to work are the kettle and the toaster. She doesn't pretend to be a domestic goddess – a chef brings their low-carb, low-fat meals to the house every few days. Her only real care for the wedding breakfast was that there was a decent vegan option. She let Mayra choose the rest, via me.

'Can we do a selfie?' she asks me. 'We haven't done one yet.'

'Oh, OK,' I say. Not seeing any harm in that.

She stands next to me and puts her face close to mine. Her head lands perfectly to the left, her cheekbones pop out as she pouts, her eyes squint as if she is looking a lover in the eye. I don't know how she manages to make this photograph sexual, but she does. I wonder if she and Gavin are at it all the time. Two beautiful people, young, no kids. I bet if I went over this house with an infrared light there would be sperm everywhere.

'Are you on Instagram?' she asks me.

'Not really. I mean, we have a work account and I post lovely images from our events. And I do have a personal one but that's just for friends and family, I'm rarely on it.'

She isn't really listening, typing away into her phone. 'What's the handle?'

It takes me a second to remember it; Risky does most of our social posts. 'Um, @BFFWeddingConsultancy.'

'OK, found you. BFF, does that stand for Best Friends Forever?'

'Yes. When I started out people kept saying I was like their best friend, easy to talk to and to work with. I thought it was a nice title, to let people know it's a friendly service,' I tell her. I actually kind of regret the name of my business, it's a bit silly. Also, I used to like being everyone's best friend, but I didn't intend for my husband to see me that way too.

'It's cute,' Lauren says.

'Thanks.'

She concentrates extremely hard for a second or two. 'OK, tagged you. Let me know how many followers you get after that, I'm always interested to know. I posted about my friend Danny's dog and she got so many replies she set up a page for the dog and he already has 402k followers. You should follow him, he's at @DiggettyyDogetty. Funny.'

'Cool,' I say, 'OK if I sit here?'

'Sure.'

I take a seat at the twelve-seater table. There is a little dog asleep in a basket underneath it. Lauren takes another selfie, holding her left hand up and looking lovingly at her engagement ring.

'My fans like to know when I'm doing wedding stuff,' she says, typing something then bringing her phone over to the table where I'm sitting, and leaving it face up right in front of her. I notice that notifications from Instagram flood her home page. I only have seventy-three followers, but I had to turn the notifications off because they were driving me mad. Why wouldn't someone with 2.1 million do the same?

'So how is everything going with the sponsorship deal, is there anything I can do to help? Obviously it's quite a unique set-up?' I ask, referring to the million pounds Veuve Clicquot have offered her for posting Instagram posts throughout the day, featuring them heavily, and as many pictures of the happy couple as possible.

'It is. It's quite deliberate,' she says. I'm not quite sure what she means. It shows on my face. 'You know, to show I don't have an issue talking about champagne?'

'Ohhhhh,' I say, realising she is referring to the rumour about Gavin shoving a bottle of champagne up a girl's fanny.

'Also, I'm one of the first to do a deal like this. It's very exciting. Of course Gav said I didn't need to do it but I like to show people I don't rely solely on my husband. I'll have total control over the images. My photographer will bring a retoucher, so they can work on the pictures as they are taken,

I can approve them and then my mum will post them with a comment.'

'Are you sure your mum is happy to do that, won't she be wanting to enjoy the day?'

'You've met my mother?'

'I have indeed. She certainly knows what she wants for you.'

'Sure, that's one way to look at it. Anything to show the world how wonderful our lives are.' She drops her head, looking sad, and I can't tell whether or not it's an act as we sit in this huge, beautiful kitchen.

'I'm contracted to do twenty-five pictures on the day, but it might be more. We have to give my followers what they want.'

'You talk about them like they are your babies,' I say, jokingly.

'I think of them that way. I wouldn't exist without them.'

'You wouldn't exist without them? Of course you would.'

'No, I wouldn't. Not in any real sense.'

'In any real sense?'

'I wasn't exactly Bella Hadid when I met Gav. Suddenly I'm extremely famous, but for what? For marrying someone rich? My Instagram feed and my brand deals give me something to stand for other than just being Gavin Riley's fiancé. My followers mean a lot to me. You probably think that sounds stupid. You've got a baby, you don't need followers.'

'Having a baby doesn't mean you suddenly don't need anybody else. You want kids?'

'Desperately, I always have. Gavin does too. It's probably

why he's marrying me, he knows I want to start making a big family as quickly as possible. He needs someone to pass all this on to.' She smiles as she looks around her enormous kitchen. I can't work out if she's happy or not, there is always some pain behind the pleasure. She doesn't feel like the lady of a house like this.

'And of course, there are the likes. They feel good,' she says, snapping back to Instagram.

'Yes, that must be quite addictive. I got thirteen likes for a post I did about a plate of chips last week. It was electrifying.'

Lauren laughs. And I realise it's the first time I've seen that happen.

'Shall we see how our post is doing?' she says, picking up her phone again. She made it a whole two minutes without touching it.

'No, we don't have to, it's OK. I'm not famous. The only person's opinion I have to worry about is my husband's.'

'I bet your husband is lovely,' she says.

I lie and tell her he is.

'As is mine,' she confirms, and I wonder if she is telling the truth.

'Look, we already have 1,345 comments.'

'What? That's insane,' I say, genuinely taken aback. She shimmies up to me and we both look at her phone. The photo of me is terrible, I am quite red and my skin is shiny. My cheeks are a lot chubbier than they used to be, and I really need a haircut. I hadn't realised how long it had got. The caption says *Meet Beth, my wedding planner. The woman making all my dreams come true.*

141

'That was a very nice thing to say, thank you,' I say.

'You're welcome. Oh look, this guy always messages me. Same under every post: "*That Gav, I hope he knows what he's got.*" It's cute.' She keeps scrolling through endless compliments about how beautiful she looks, how perfect she is. How jealous everyone is, how much they wish they were her. There are a few about Gavin, people saying they love him.

'Your fans love you,' I say. 'I can see why you're on it a lot.'

'I block the haters. It's a bit like trying to kill flies though, you get one but as soon as it's dead another one appears. But mostly people are nice. Instagram is good . . . for someone like me,' she says, suddenly quite coy.

'Someone like you?' I ask, gently. Not wanting to overstep any marks here, but fascinated.

'Someone who's trying to fill a void,' she says, as if that isn't a huge answer that obviously leaves me wanting to know more. She stands next to me and scrolls through all the comments. There are a few mean ones, but they are mostly about how gorgeous she is, how sexy, how lucky. She smiles as she reads them, and I wonder if, for a moment, that void she mentioned narrows a little. Then we see a comment that ruins the mood.

Of course she's a wedding planner, looks like she loves a buffet #fatty

'Oh,' I say, wishing I had pretended not to notice it.

'Oh that idiot. Who is he anyway?' she says, getting up and putting her phone on the kitchen counter. 'People like him don't matter. Some lonely weirdo who has nothing better to do than post things on the Internet. Ignore it.'

I wonder if she sees the irony of what she just said.

I sit up straight, and suck in my tummy. Suddenly feeling like a massive blob of flab.

'It's all good,' I tell her. 'I absolutely do love a buffet, so he's not wrong.'

She thinks that is funny.

'I like you,' she says, as if she's thinking a thousand things but only saying one.

I smile awkwardly. 'Thanks, I like you too. Shall we get back to the wedding?'

'Yes, let's do this.'

'So, the leaked invite. Is there anything I can do to help with that?'

She rolls her eyes.

'"Leaked invite". Sure. If your mother handing an invite directly into the *Sun*'s showbiz editor's hand is a case of a "leaked invite". It's OK, it was inevitable.'

'Your mother did it?'

'My mother does whatever she can for attention.'

'And you're OK with that?' I ask. 'I mean, I had to sign a lot of NDAs but your mum just hands out the invite?'

'What do you think I should do, have her sign one?' she says, snapping at me a little. 'And maybe I'll get Gavin to sign one too, stop him . . . '

She trails off there. I say nothing, desperate for her to finish her sentence. She doesn't. 'How's the baby?' she asks me, moving on.

'He's fine, so sweet,' I say. 'Thanks for asking.'

'Do you like your nanny? I worry we will never find the

right person when the time comes. You hear so many terrible stories,' she says, as if that is the biggest concern of having children. 'I mean, it can't be easy having to live with another person – luckily we have the annex.' She points into the garden and at a little house.

'I don't actually have a nanny,' I say, feeling like a pleb. 'My husband is with him, he managed to get three months' paternity leave. I'll take a month or two off when your wedding is over, then I suppose we'll work out the childcare. But this is working for now.'

'Wow, your husband is looking after the baby? He took three months off work? Wow, Gavin would never do that. I mean, he'll be a good dad, I'm sure. But would he do that? No way. You're very lucky.'

By the sounds of things she doesn't plan to do much of it either. I don't know why I'm judging her for that, I'm the one sitting here all upset about some guy calling me fat on Instagram, while my tiny baby is at home drinking from a bottle instead of my boobs.

'Yes, so people keep saying,' I say, a little more sarcastically than I mean to.

'Oh? Is it not as perfect as it sounds?'

'Is anything?'

She smiles and shakes her head. 'Maybe never where men are concerned.'

'You are also very lucky, and I'm sure you'll find the perfect person to help you.'

Lauren smiles, and takes a sip of her water. 'Lucky?' she says, as if I need to explain myself from across the giant marble table, in her giant house, in one of the most sought-after squares in North London. 'I suppose it's about what you consider luck to be. None of this comes for free.'

'No, I'm sure you and Gavin work very hard. But you know, lucky to have a nice house, a gorgeous husband-to-be. A career. It may take work, but it still makes you lucky – not everyone who aims for this gets it.'

Our conversation is interrupted by Mayra bursting into the house.

'Beth, is this a wedding meeting without me? What's going on?'

'Hello Mayra, we were just going over a few things. Just over a week to go now, how exciting,' I say.

'Yeah, Mum, it's my wedding remember?'

As if Mayra is reminded she has company, she switches into nice person mode.

'Of course, it's so exciting. Everything looking good, Beth?'

'Great, yes. It's all coming together,' I say uncomfortably. She has a tendency to make you feel that way. 'I better be off, is it OK if I use your loo before I go?'

'Sure, down the hall, third door on the right,' Lauren tells me. It's quite exciting to pee on Gavin Riley's toilet.

As I come back up the corridor, I hear them talking quietly. It's obvious the conversation isn't very pleasant. I wait silently outside the kitchen, hoping they'll finish.

'It's my Instagram feed, Mum. I'll say what I want.'

'But all that stuff about feeling unhappy. And feeling scared. You mustn't talk like that publicly, it isn't good for the brand. You make us all look so unstable.'

'For the brand? Mum, it's how I feel. If it was down to you my entire life would be fake.'

'I think we should do a picture, the two of us, your hair's looking so beautiful. Let's give them something lovely to look at, shall we?'

'But why? It's fine to say it's not all perfect, I—'

I cough loudly to announce my return. Lauren looks visibly upset. Mayra looks as stony-faced as ever. But that could just be the Botox.

'Right, then, I'd better go,' I say awkwardly, picking up my bag. 'I'll see myself out. Call me if you need anything, OK Lauren?'

'She will,' answers Mayra, with a painfully fake smile.

As I walk down into Hampstead Heath I let the fresh air fill my lungs. I could do with some exercise, and it's so rare that I get to be fully alone. With Risky in the office, continuous phone calls, panic meetings and location visits, there is barely a second for myself. I tell my brides to look after themselves in the run-up to their weddings. To make sure they relax, to work on their 'self-care' regimes. Maybe it is advice I should take for myself, but when exactly am I supposed to do that? At home it's Tommy and Michael, the night feeds, the strained conversations, the awkwardness of bedtime. It's a lot. Wherever I am I always worry I'm giving one part of my life more attention than it deserves and neglecting the other. I need to find a better balance. Somewhere in this wild schedule there needs to be time for me and my own needs. Whatever they are. I don't even know anymore.

I get a bit lost, entering the park from a strange hill with multiple routes branching out at the end of it. Not really caring for a moment, and just wanting to walk, I take a left. It's a little spooky, but I know there are people close by if I were to scream. In a clearing just to my left I catch a glimpse of something that causes me to blink furiously, wondering if it's a figment of my imagination. Two naked bodies leaning against the bonnet of a rather sorry-looking Ford Fiesta. The car is parked in a tiny slipway, you'd need to know it was there to find it. Or just happen upon it, like me. I quickly dash behind a tree.

There is no one else around, this isn't one of the main routes into the park, but still they don't seem to be trying to hide. They are screwing silently but frantically. The woman is bent over the car, the man is thrashing into her from behind. I'm trying to go unnoticed, but I can't take my eyes off them. They are being so bold, they must know people will see? I watch subtly from as far away as I can. I should keep walking but for some reason I can't move. All of a sudden, I get a flurry of text messages to my phone.

Shit.

I get it out of my bag. It's Risky, something about the company Instagram page getting over 2000 new followers in five minutes. She keeps texting with higher and higher increments: 2040, 3200. I guess Lauren really does have all the pulling power, her post has made me famous. In a flap, I manage to put it on silent, and I put my phone back in my bag. The man looks up and sees me. I duck back but it is too late. I mouth that I am sorry, I bow my head as I back away.

I try to act like it doesn't matter, gesture that they should carry on. It's my bad for being here, not theirs. He doesn't seem worried. He gestures with his head for me to stay. He taps the woman on her backside, and points to me when she looks up. She smiles too, then closes her eyes as if my presence just increased her pleasure levels by double.

I now feel like it would be ruder to leave.

Still from behind the tree, I watch the couple as they continue to fuck like two animals in the wild. I am close enough to see the flesh on his buttocks shake as he slams into her thighs. Close enough to see her erect nipple in between his fingers as he rubs her breasts with his hands. Close enough to see the hairs in his hands as he pulls her ponytail. Close enough to see the fluff on her vagina as he pulls out, turns her around, goes down on her until she comes and then masturbates himself until he ejaculates all over her chest.

It's filthy. So real. Two normal people having genuine hot sex. The greatest porn. It's not very often you catch anything like this, and to see it in the flesh . . . I'm so turned on I barely know what to do with myself.

They get back into their car, where they put just their tops on and drive away. This is when I realise I am not the only one watching. I see a couple walk away from behind another bush, and a man whose face I don't see. It's weirdly unthreatening. It doesn't feel as strange as it should.

I am extremely aroused. Is that wrong? I think it is. Michael would not like this. But I did. I liked it a lot.

I hurry home, I need to put this sexual energy where it belongs. Because that will make the fact that I enjoyed it OK.

Ruby

As I edge into the kitchen, Bonnie is standing right over the bucket, looking into it. She's smiling. When she sees me, she points at it.

'A mouse!' she exclaims with total joy. Her bravery is astounding.

'Bonnie, away from the bucket,' I say, backing into the wall, scaling the perimeter of the kitchen in slow motion. In my heart of hearts I didn't think my trap would work, I just needed to feel that I was doing something. But it caught the bloody thing in less than a day. Now I suppose I have to deal with it.

'It's cute,' Bonnie says. Highlighting that cavernous gap between our characters. She reaches her hand towards it.

'NO, Bonnie, don't touch it,' I scream, terrifying her again. 'Bonnie. Mice might be sweet, but they are dirty. And it might bite you, OK? You have to be careful.'

She seems to understand and retracts her hand, she even takes a little step back, which is a huge relief to me. If the mouse jumped out and landed on her, I'm not sure I would be able to protect her. I'd probably run outside and leave her to deal with it herself. I hate them so much. Oh my God, when I see it, I nearly vomit from fear. Its long tail is disgusting, its little body and teeth, its pink eyes.

149

Breathing is impossible now, my heart is racing. I have to get it out of my kitchen.

'What shall we do with it?' Bonnie asks. She can't take her eyes off it.

The way it's running around in the bucket is awful. I should have drowned the bloody thing. Now it's stuck in there and terrorising me. I'd planned to leave it until Liam came to pick up Bonnie on Friday, but I can't have it in here. I just can't. I won't be able to come into my kitchen. I have to get it out of the house.

'We have to let it go,' I say to Bonnie. For a second or two, wondering how terrible it would really be to flush it down the loo.

'In the garden?' Bonnie asks.

'No, it will just come back into the house.'

'The park?'

'No Bonnie, it's too far.'

I'm going to flush it down the toilet.

'Where then?' She looks up at me. Her eyes desperate, her pretty little face so adorable I can barely take it. She so rarely looks at me like this; she is softened by the presence of another heartbeat in this house. It's just such a horrible shame it's a rodent.

'Please Mummy?'

I'm transfixed by her for a moment, the sweetness in her tone, the delicacy of her face. It makes me respond exactly how I should, rather than how my brittle nature has often decided is normal.

'OK,' I say, stepping up. 'Go and find your shoes. We'll take it to the park.'

I put on some Marigolds and get a roll of clingfilm out of the drawer. I remove the stick and throw it out of the kitchen window. I roll out some clingfilm to about twelve inches longer than the perimeter of the bucket, trickier than it looks whilst wearing rubber gloves, and lower it slowly. A wrong move from me and I could tip the bucket. My hands are in such terrifying proximity to the mouse that I want to close my eyes, but that could result in the mouse crawling into my clothes. I turn my head to the side, but stretch my eyes so I can just about see, and I lay the clingfilm over the top, pressing down the sides to seal it.

Exhale. That was round one. I then add layer upon layer of clingfilm, longer each time so it doesn't come away. I squash it to the sides, making it as tight as I can. I finish the whole thing off with a huge layer of kitchen foil that I scrunch into place and poke some tiny holes for air circulation with a pin. I now can't see the mouse. That is better.

I lift the bucket and put it into the bottom of the buggy. It miraculously fits.

'Bonnie, quick!' I yell. She comes running down the hallway. I sit her on the stairs and put on her shoes, her coat. I strap her into the buggy, and she doesn't resist me at all. I open the door and walk to the park as quickly as I can. All the while thinking it's going to jump out and land on my feet. But I hold it together, manage not to get us run over, and soon we are there.

'What about over there?' says Bonnie, pointing at an area of shrubbery. It's as good a place as any, I suppose. Bonnie sits calmly in her buggy until I've pushed her over to it. As I unclip her, she smiles at me. It's like she's someone else's child.

'OK, I'll get the bucket,' I say, putting my Marigolds back on. Bonnie waits patiently. Again, most unlike my child.

'I'm not scared of the mouse,' she exclaims. I could be wrong, but I maybe detect a hint of protectiveness in her voice. Is she telling me I shouldn't be either?

I carry the bucket from the buggy to the shrubbery like it's a bomb that will explode with any sudden movement. I lay it on the ground. Bonnie goes at it like a bar of chocolate.

'Wait, wait,' I tell her. 'We have to get this right.'

She does as I ask. I start to peel away the clingfilm. The mouse bolts around the base of the bucket when it sees the light pouring in. I want to kick it over and run away screaming. I hate it so much.

'Mummy, you're shaking,' Bonnie says, putting her hand on my arm. My knee-jerk reaction is to shake her off, but I manage to stop myself and allow her to rest her hand on the fabric of my dress, raised from my skin by the fur.

'I'm OK,' I tell her. 'I'm just cold.'

'But it's not cold?'

She looks at me in that way again. In a way that suggests she cares. She holds the look, and it sends a warm bolt of something soft inside of me, and I find myself not wanting to move on from this moment.

'I'm not really cold,' I tell her. 'I'm frightened.'

'What are you frightened of?'

It's haunting being asked that question, even if it is by your three-year-old daughter. It's hard not to list the things, to get them off my chest, just simply because someone, anyone, seems to care.

'Of the mouse,' I tell her.

'Don't be scared Mummy, it's just a mouse.'

It's just a mouse? You could say that about anything really, couldn't you? It's just a dead dad. It's just an unloving mother. It's just a failed marriage. It's just a job that makes you feel guilty. It's just a body covered in fur. It's just an existence without intimate connections. It's just dying alone.

'Shall we do it then?' I ask Bonnie, knowing what the answer will be. With my Marigolds on, I tip the bucket onto its side, facing away from me of course. The mouse doesn't come out for a minute or two, like maybe there is something comforting about the bucket. But then it appears, sniffing slowly as it discovers new ground. Looking here, looking there. Sniffing this, sniffing that. And then it gains the confidence it needs and runs quickly into a bush and disappears. Bonnie screeches with delight. I stand back and watch. Maybe, just maybe, the slightest smile appearing on my face too.

6

Lauren Pearce – Instagram post
@OfficialLP

The image is of Lauren and her mother. Both pretty, both
blonde. Both in jeans and nice tops, both fully made-up.
They are hugging, with enormous smiles on their faces. The
perfect mother/daughter combo.

The caption reads:
What would I be without this woman? Strong, funny, my
inspiration. Love you Mummy! #womensupportingwomen

@usertype: I'd bang you both, has Gavin?

@essenceturbo: Ahhhh, nothing like a mothers love. This is
so precious. She must be so proud.

@wednesdaydays: Go ladies! Looking gorgeous. I miss my
mum, enjoy every moment.

@isolatetheday: Gorgeous ladies. So excited for you both . . .

Ruby

Good morning Ruby, thank you so much for your kind words about our nursery. We are happy to say we have a space for Bonnie and can take her with immediate effect. You can bring her tomorrow if you like, for two hours, to ease her in. If that suits, we will see you then.

Please fill in the attached forms in advance. Maria x

Oh thank God. I finally get a reply from one of the nurseries I'd contacted. Hopefully this childcare mess will be sorted soon. I get back to Maria straight away.

Yes, wonderful, we will see you at 9am tomorrow. Thank you.

I'll drop her off and tell them I'll be back in two hours, but instead I'll call saying I am stuck in a meeting and they will say it's totally fine, and that she can stay the day. It's what I did with the last place. She didn't need any settling in, she couldn't wait to get away from me.

I get back on Yelp to look for a new salon. One has mostly five-star reviews and is right over the other side of London (good, as less chance of me bumping into anyone from it). I book a morning appointment through their online portal for next week, and hope that whoever does it has seen worse than what they will see when I take my clothes off.

I've developed an irritating interest in Lauren Pearce's Instagram page. The woman is ridiculous, shameful and captivating all at once. A recent post about not loving herself has really fuelled my judgement. She is in a yoga pose that looks as effortless as it does beautiful. She talks about not feeling good or happy yet looks sensational and Zen as hell in the photo. The entire purpose of the post is for mere mortals like me to write compliments underneath it. Well I won't be doing that. What on earth does a twenty-eight-year-old blonde, beautiful, thin, rich and engaged to a finance exec turned TV star, know about self-loathing? It makes a mockery out of people like me who have real reasons to dislike ourselves. Mental health is the latest zeitgeist. Celebrities using it as currency. Getting on the depression bandwagon, hoping to be called 'brave' for admitting to not being happy, whilst showing us nothing but examples of the perfect life.

Either Lauren Pearce is faking happiness and that post revealed a little of the truth, or she is faking self-doubt to gain attention. Either way, she's a fraud. But for some odd reason, I can't get enough of her.

'Mummy, come and play with me,' Bonnie calls up the stairs.

'Not now, Bonnie. Please! Mummy is very busy.'

'Ooooooooohh,' I hear, as the crash of a huge box of Lego hits the living room floor. It isn't followed by a scream.

I continue to trawl through Lauren's Instagram feed. It's worryingly addictive.

Beth

I find myself consumed with a strong need to orgasm. I am torn about whether what I experienced today was a form of cheating or not. Witnessing sex accidentally is not infidelity, but choosing not to walk away, is that? Finding yourself magnificently turned on as a result of it, is that the problem? We can't hide from sex, it's everywhere. Everywhere I look there is something that turns me on. And I am craving being desired, it's turning me into the person Michael thinks I am. Maybe he's right. Maybe I do have a problem?

I tell myself I will feel less deceitful if my husband is part of this. If he is the one who brings me to my climax, then what I saw was all for the good of our relationship, right?

When I walk into the house, Michael is on the armchair facing the door. His computer is on his lap, his head back, his eyes closed. He is exhausted from taking care of Tommy all day. It's unlike him but I guess he's having a quick nap before dinner. The house smells delicious. I tiptoe in, then realise he isn't asleep. He's moving. His arm is moving. Suddenly he opens his eyes and rolls them back to the computer screen. His lip curls and his arm gets faster.

'Oh my God, Michael, are you . . .?'

Sheer panic floods his face. He pushes his penis back into

his jeans, sits up straight, but keeps his computer on his lap to hide his crotch.

'Beth, what are you doing here so early?'

'I . . . I just . . . I finished . . . What were you watching?' I ask. Could this be the moment I have been waiting for? He is horny, I am horny? Could we do this together?

'Nothing. Work stuff,' he says, his penis obviously softening enough to risk getting up. He carries his computer in front of him into the kitchen, facing away from me, then subtly does up his flies. I know exactly what is happening.

'Michael, it's OK. What were you watching?'

'Work stuff, I told you.'

I look at his computer on the table. What's he into? If I knew, maybe I could do that for him?'

I come up behind him. I put my hands on his hips. He pulls away and starts tending to the saucepan on the stove. It's so strange to see him being sexual, but also it excites me. He has a sex drive, this is good. It is progress.

'How was your day?' he asks me. His body language and tone making it clear that he will not discuss his masturbation.

'Michael, it's OK. Turn around, I'm in the mood too.'

'Beth, please. Get your hands off me or I'll burn the dinner. Go and sit on the sofa, this is ready.'

I do as he asks, feeling like I've been sent to stand outside the headmistress' office. I daren't say another word. He lays my evening meal in front of me. It is chilli con carne. This time, no rice. Just a green salad.

We put on the TV and watch an episode of *Killing Eve* while we eat. I can barely concentrate. He masturbates but he won't have sex? What does that mean and what was he watching?

'Shall we do another episode?' he asks me when it ends. I say no, I'm tired, and I'd like to go to bed.

'Me too,' he says, clearing our plates away and putting them into the dishwasher. 'Tommy didn't nap today, I'm exhausted.'

He likes to tell me how tired he is before we get into bed together. It is Stage One in his sequence of excuses for getting away with no sex, and it happens every night. But maybe tonight he is horny? Maybe tonight will be different. Maybe he is trying to make this better too.

In the bedroom I get into bed, naked. He puts on his pyjamas after taking an unnecessary amount of time cleaning his teeth, probably in the hope that I will fall asleep.

Apparently a marriage is considered sexless when the couple do it less than ten times a year. We haven't done it since I was four months pregnant. Tommy is now four months old. I realise that birth is a good excuse for both of us not to want it, but I'm not giving birth anymore. It's time. The ice needs to be broken soon, and Michael knows it.

He gets into bed and immediately fluffs up his pillows and reaches for the parenting book he is reading. 'I'm going to read up on weaning onto formula, I think we should start,' he says, licking his finger and flicking through the pages until he finds the right bit.

'No, I'm not ready. You know that.'

'OK, well, it won't hurt to read up on it,' he says, pretending to read.

I shimmy closer to him.

'You're naked,' he says, as if that is as surprising as me wearing a clown costume.

'Yes, you like it?' I hold the covers up so he can see.

He glances quickly, before adding, 'Careful you don't leak on the sheets.'

'Leak out of what?' I say, trying to have a little fun.

'Don't be . . . ' he starts.

'Gross?'

'No, I didn't say that. Don't be . . . oh it doesn't matter. So, it says here we should mix breast milk with formula and introduce him to it that way. What do you think?'

'I can't have this conversation again. No,' I say, taking the book out of his hand and throwing it onto the floor. He remains in the same position, as if the book hasn't gone anywhere. I pull myself up on top of him. He is faced with my breasts. Full enough of milk to look fantastic, not full enough to squirt in his face. I fed Tommy before he went to bed; I'll be doing a feed at eleven p.m. It is the perfect time for sex. 'I miss you,' I whisper seductively.

'You miss me? What are you talking about, I see you every morning and every night.'

'I mean, I miss you inside me.' I start to move my pelvis backwards and forwards. He is looking at my belly button, the absolute last place I want him to be looking after I had a baby. I put his hands on my thighs and guide his head up. 'Look at me,' I tell him, as I smile softly. 'Look at my face.' He settles on my jaw.

I can feel his penis toying with the idea of getting hard. I am soaking his pyjamas bottoms with my vagina. I am proud of myself for waiting until I got into bed with my husband, despite being overwhelmed by horn since I saw those people in the park. This is exactly where my sexual energy should be directed. In my marital bed, with the man I love. I allow myself to move more freely. Images of what I saw in the park flashing into my mind. I use them only to increase this moment, and I stay present. My husband is the one getting me off. This is about me, and him. Michael's penis is getting harder and harder. His eyes start to roll, his hips start to move with mine. He's with me now, here we are. We can do this. I reach down and pull down his pyjamas enough for his dick to be free. It's a nice dick. I've always loved it. I have him now. I kiss him. My husband who I love. Our tongues swirl in each other's mouths, our breath bounces off each other's faces. I grind myself down onto him. My orgasm building like lava working itself up a volcano, ready to spout out and explode. I sit up straight, and the visuals from the park come back to me. I'm with them now. Watching that man bang his thighs against the woman's buttocks as he slammed his penis into her. The way he flipped her round, and ate her like the most delicious thing he'd ever tasted. I roll my hips as I imagine his tongue flapping over her clitoris, her swollen labia surrounding his mouth. The thrill of me watching, the juices flowing from her like a lemon being squeezed. My hand finds its way to my vagina and I rub it hard, my entire pussy closing in as it tenses up so it can release itself all over my husband's gorgeous penis that is swirling inside of me and feels so good. I come so hard it feels like I may have swallowed him inside of me forever. My legs spasm, my vagina throbs. My breath is short

'I'm tired,' he tells me, again. 'Looking after Tommy all day, it's a lot of work. And then for you to come home and demand that from me. It isn't fair.'

I say sorry again. Which upsets me more than any other part of this entire exchange. Does he not think I am tired? Working full time on this wedding, still doing night feeds? I could fall asleep standing up but I am trying so hard not to complain. I know I'm lucky, people keep telling me.

'I'm going to go downstairs,' I tell him. 'I'll come to bed after the eleven p.m. feed.'

'I do love you,' he tells me just before I leave the room. I torture him by not replying. It's the only power I have.

Downstairs in the kitchen I open Michael's computer.

EXTREME HARDCORE PORN. BANG THE MILF THEN COVER HER IN HOT JIZZ

And he thinks I'm the one with the problem.

Lauren Pearce – Instagram post
@OfficialLP

The image is of Lauren in her bathroom. It's a selfie of her looking in the mirror. She has lovely black underwear on and wet hair. She has a green face mask on. There is mascara on her eyelashes and she has shiny lips.

The caption reads:
Who knew happiness like this could exist? Not long now until I become Mrs Riley. Are my husband's deep blue eyes OK to be my something blue? Tell me Instagram! Also, I love this avocado and cucumber face mask by #BrighterYou. #AD #love #selflove #marriage #TheOne #pinchme

@kellykimes: SO HAPPY FOR YOU, you deserve it!

@hailysimms5: You have the perfect life.

@geraldy9: I would literally leave my husband tomorrow to marry Gavin Riley.

@feelitdealitownittwice: I'd wear Gav's eyes as a bra!

@pauldovey: why you rubbing salad on your face, love?

@hideousfacepalm: Is he making you sign a pre nup?????

Ruby

'My mother has threatened suicide since I was sixteen,' I tell him, as we watch Bonnie chase a little friend she has made around a tree. I'm back on the bench with my unlikely new confidante. I don't seem to be able to stay away. It's easier talking to someone whose agony is so deep that my problems feel like paper cuts.

'That's rough, not easy I'm sure?' the man says.

'No, not easy.'

'So how is she now?' he asks.

'She's a morbidly obese alcoholic who lives in Cornwall and communicates mostly via status updates on Facebook, which I am rarely on.'

'Hard not to take a suicide threat seriously though, I made that mistake.'

'You did?' I ask, wondering if he means his wife.

'My other daughter. The one my wife and I managed to neglect as we dealt with our grief around Verity. She reminded us she was still alive by trying to kill herself on what would have been Verity's twenty-first birthday. Luckily she didn't manage it, but it certainly woke me up to what she needed.'

'What did she need?'

'She needed us. All kids want is their parents to tell them

everything is going to be OK. But when you're a parent, and you don't know if everything will be OK, it's hard to pretend.'

'Yes,' I say, knowing I have made no effort to pretend to Bonnie that the world isn't a cruel and horrible place. 'Well, it sounds like she has you now. Don't underestimate that. I only had my dad until I was sixteen but that short amount of time with him is the only reason I have a soft side. His influence is inside me somewhere. He died just before my mother's weight gain turned her into an unthinkable cunt.'

'Woah, strong words,' he says, and I hope I haven't offended him.

'Sorry, I don't swear very often. Only when I really need the extra words.'

'Was your mother really so bad?' he asks me, as if maybe I'm bitter and exaggerating.

'Yup, even worse. She drank herself to sleep every night and spent the days exhibiting clear signs of a bipolar disorder that to this day remains undiagnosed. She was cruel and hateful. I know it's not always someone's "fault" when they are that way. Once when she was drunk she made a comment about how her granddad touched her up in the bath. She never mentioned it again, but I'm sure it was probably true.'

'God, that's terrible. Your poor mum,' he says. And of course, he is right, she didn't ask to be abused. But neither did I.

'I suffered as much at the hand of that abuse as she did. The only thing that ever connected us was our mutual need not to be seen. That doesn't offer much time for mother–daughter bonding.'

'Why would a woman as beautiful as you not want to be seen?'

'I . . . um . . . I . . . ' I can't think of a thing to say back to that. Part of me wants to slap him in the face, accuse him of being a pervert. Push his compliment away like it's a knife trying to stab me. The other part is so amazed that this man has the capacity to be kind after what he experienced that I feel like should accept his compliment and not make his day harder than it probably already is.

'That's very kind,' I say, eventually. 'I have a condition that affects my confidence. I'm a work-in-progress.'

'A condition?' he asks.

'Yes, it's mostly aesthetic. If you don't mind I won't go into the details of it.'

'Of course. Look, if your condition affects your confidence then that's one thing, but to turn that into your kid's problem, that's another. You've learned how damaging that can be. Everyone has something, but it isn't our kids' faults. Your mum failed you. That sucks.'

'Yes, it does.'

'I realised I was messing up my other daughter just in time. My ex-wife though, she's yet to adjust.'

'She isn't kind?'

'She isn't kind, she isn't supportive. She isn't all sorts of things. Her grief is complicated. She never wanted kids. Sometimes I think I forced her into it. Then one of her kids dies. She resents the grief for a person she didn't really want in the first place. She now obsesses over creating a world of perfection to mask her pain. That's a lot of pressure on my daughter – forced into stifling her real feelings. Count yourself lucky, you and Bonnie have each other. You're there for her, she'll be there for you. You're doing everything right.'

She'll be there for me? I think about that all the time. When it comes to me and my mum, she feels like the child and me the adult. I always wonder now if I should be trying to help her more. I've thought about going to Cornwall, gathering her things, bringing her back to London and having her live in my spare room. But history reminds me what a terrible idea that would be.

'Well, I better get going,' the man says. 'Have a good day.'

'I'll try,' I say as he walks away.

He really is very handsome.

7

Beth

I typed 'having sex in open spaces with people watching' into Google to see if other people enjoyed it too, and quickly discovered it's called 'dogging'. There are multiple websites listing locations for this activity, talking about it like it's a meeting spot for dog walkers to meet for a cup of tea. The language is so casual. Stuff like, 'Many doggers like to remain in their cars, others enjoy having sex on the bonnets or against a nearby tree.'

People all over the country are doing this in their lunch hours. Apparently, for married people who like to watch strangers have sex, it's the best time to get away with it as it doesn't eat into family time. Wow.

The 'doggers' drive to a known location and have sex in (or on) cars. Some just watch, others participate. Of course, I've heard of dogging, but it always sounded so much more sinister than what I experienced. Other than the act of having sex in an open public place, it didn't feel sinister. It felt exciting. I can't stop thinking about it. The way the man looked at me, the way she didn't want him to stop. They knew I was there. That was the whole point. Apparently by doing it in the open air like that they were potentially inviting others to join in. I can't stop wondering what it may have been like if I had.

'Beth, did you finalise the foyer arrangements?'

I'm looking at a website for a woman who says she travels the country dogging and likes sex with as many strangers as possible. Once she even got tied to a tree and was left there, so whoever was passing could give her a quick bang. There is no mention of how she got down.

That feels extreme.

'Beth, earth to Beth, the foyer arrangements. Did you finalise the flowers?'

'Pardon?'

'The flowers, for the foyer?' Risky says, a little impatiently.

'Oh, no. Can you please?'

She gets up from behind her desk and walks over to mine. She's wearing another crop top. I have half a mind to ask her to stop dressing so seductively at work. I realise that would not be OK.

I slam my computer shut.

'Beth, are you OK?' she asks, concerned.

'Yup, absolutely fine. Why?'

'You just seem a little distracted.'

'Me? No. Just busy. Busy busy busy.' I make a buzzing sound, like a bee. Risky's sympathetic look gets even more sympathetic, as if I am losing my mind.

'You know, I can totally hold the fort here if you need a day off. Go home, get some sleep, spend some time with Tommy and Michael.'

'Why?'

'Because it's a lot. Having a baby, working full time, breast feeding and pumping all day. You're exhausted and unfocused. When my sister had a baby she didn't realise she had a problem for months.'

'A problem? What problem, I don't have a problem,' I say, defensively. Can she somehow see my search history? Jesus, I only went dogging once, and that was an accident. I'm only googling it to see what it was called.

'You must miss Tommy and Michael so much, the timing of this wedding is very unfair on you. I really admire you for keeping going. You're an inspiration to me, you know.'

'An inspiration?' I ask. I wonder how inspiring she would find me if I told her I am fantasising about cheating on my husband. How I am so tired that I can't remember if I gave my son a middle name or not. And how all I can think about is that man's bottom smacking into that woman from behind. But sure, a total inspiration.

'You need to consider more self-care,' Risky says, crossing her arms and raising her eyebrows. 'I'll look on Groupon and see if I can get you a good spa deal, OK? You're so frantic. Have you thought about meditating?'

'No, I haven't.'

'OK, well maybe you should download these apps.' She slips me a Post-it note with the words 'Time for Me' and 'Get Away with Yourself' written on there. She obviously had them

175

written down for some time and was waiting for an opportunity to give them to me.

'You need a better work–life balance,' she says. 'If women are going to have it all, they're going to have to take better care of themselves.'

'You know what? Maybe I will go home today,' I say. I should try to make things better with Michael. We have a baby. We can't fall apart.

'I think you should. I'll call if I need you but I've got this.'

'Oh but Gavin's brother is coming in later to get the cake toppers. Apparently, he lives nearby so can whip in.'

'Boss, I think I can handle giving him the cake toppers. Honestly, take a day, I'll be fine,' Risky says. And I know she is capable.

'OK, thank you,' I say, packing up my computer and putting it in my bag. 'I'm very lucky to have you,' I tell her, because I am. She is a lovely assistant. A true romantic, and an actual nice person. Apart from the anal, which makes me wonder if she has a dark side. Or do sweet people do anal too? All I know is I'd take it up the nose if someone was offering it to me right now.

'I'm lucky to have you too,' she says. 'Now come on, go be a mum for an afternoon, you deserve it.'

Ruby

When I wake up my first thought is for my mother. It's very annoying to be programmed to care, when I would rather just forget about her entirely. I send her a message, just for my own peace of mind.

Good morning, Mum. Here is a picture of Bonnie from the park yesterday.

I attach a photo of Bonnie playing. My mother doesn't reply but the message shows as 'read'. She isn't dead. I can now get on with my day.

Surprisingly, Bonnie doesn't fight me as I get her into her buggy this morning. Getting dressed isn't awful, breakfast doesn't end up on the floor. She watches TV as I get ready and doesn't scream the house down when I turn it off. I give her some raisins to eat on the way to her new nursery, and she says thank you. Which almost blows my brain right out of my head.

'Where do you think the mouse is now?' she asks me on the way.

'Probably with his family,' I say, confidently, yet shivering at the thought of a bunch of mice breaking back into my house.

'Why are we going this way?' Bonnie asks me, realising our route has changed.

'You're going to a new nursery today, how exciting,' I say.

'Why?'

I don't give her an answer.

We arrive at the location, and a tatty door with an intercom. I ring the buzzer and the door clicks open. Almost immediately a strong smell hits me as we go inside.

'Pooh! What is that?' Bonnie shouts, pinching her nose in a cartoon fashion.

'I don't know,' I say, covering mine too.

The smell is terrible, but the dirt on the floor is worse. This place is not clean, it feels depressing and the few children, all much younger than Bonnie, look like zombies with streams of green snot hanging from their noses. A young woman comes over to us, her clothes covered in paint. Her hair is greasy. I want to ask her if she has ever even heard of dry shampoo. I did notice there was no Ofsted rating on their website but assumed it was because it was newly opened. Nothing here looks new.

'Hello, I'm Maria. Are you Ruby and Bonnie then?' she asks me.

'Yes . . . ' I reply. 'What is that smell?'

'Oh,' she says. 'We have a blocked toilet. Should have it fixed today, they kept cancelling. But they said they'd come out today so that's good.'

'How long has it smelt like this?' I ask.

'Only three days. Hello, you must be Bonnie?'

Bonnie turns her head to the side, suddenly very shy. Or nervous. Or repulsed.

'Say hello, Bonnie,' I say. She doesn't. I undo her straps and try to get her out but she goes stiff as a board.

'Come on now Bonnie,' I say gently. 'Do you want to play with the other children?'

After looking at the other children, she shakes her head. I ask her again. This time she screams no, and throws her arms around my neck, almost choking me. I can't pull them apart.

'Bonnie, come on now, this is your new nursery.'

The stench is horrific, but we are here and I need to work today. I can find somewhere else, but for now, this is it. They will get the smell fixed, and maybe the cleaner is ill. I'll suggest I pay week to week as it's mid-term.

'Bonnie, please, come on.' But she won't let go. She is crying painfully, and screaming. It's not her usual tantrum, it's more desperate than that. More genuinely upset than her just trying her luck.

'This happens a lot,' Maria says. 'Separation anxiety. It's normal when a child has been one-on-one with the mother until now. She'll settle – sometimes it takes a week or so but they always calm down.'

She thinks Bonnie and I have been one-on-one until now? I don't correct her.

I look around the room again. The children are playing with toys. There isn't much laughter, or much action happening yet. But it's only 8.30 a.m. And maybe the older children aren't here yet?

'Ahhh, you'll miss your mummy? I know. But Mummy has things to do. Here, come to Maria. I have Barbies, do you like Barbies?' Bonnie shakes her head. She has never had Barbies; I don't want dolls in the house.

'What about Lego?' I suggest.

'No.'

'Play dough?' Maria chimes in.

'No.'

'A book?'

'No.'

'Would you like to ride a bike?'

'No.'

'Have a snack?'

Maria is sounding a little desperate now.

'Maybe it's best you just go, I'll see you in two hours.'

I peel Bonnie off me, Maria pulls her away. She is crying so much her head has turned purple. She doesn't want to stay, she doesn't want me to leave. Would I want to stay in a dirty new place that stinks of drains? No. But it's a nursery, she is safe here. The toilet will get fixed, the floor will be swept, and I need to work.

I head for the door without looking back. The sound of Bonnie's screams follow me down the street. For the first time I think I understand what people mean by 'mother's guilt'. I never imagined I'd be the kind of person to feel it.

Lauren Pearce – Instagram post
@OfficialLP

The image is of Lauren in a bubble bath. There's a highly indulgent level of bubbles. It is the middle of the day. Candles are lit and the edge of the bath is visible and made of solid marble. There is a glass of champagne next to her. It isn't clear who took the photo.

The caption reads:
Self-care, guys. Who is with me? If we don't take time for ourselves then what do we expect? I feel blessed to be living the life I am living, but that doesn't change the voices in my head saying I don't deserve it. My anxiety is a daily battle. I wake up and have a green juice, I exercise, I do all the things you're told to do for a better life, but then BAM, when I don't expect it, fear creeps in and takes over my day. A voice tells me I don't deserve this. I am living someone else's life and any minute I will lose it all. I try to be strong. Every day I tell myself, 'You are alive, you have it all, you are loved', but my self-doubt tries to take all of these things away from me. The battle is real. Maybe all of these bubbles will get me through the day #AD #selflove #selfcare #VeuveClicquot #spon #bubbles

@TeddyFerrington12: I'll give you something to be anxious about love

@LaurensGirl: I wish I could hold you to make you feel better. I could, if you answer your DM's. I sent you my number. Call me. Wee culd be friends.

@Gapetour40: NOTICE ME

@uptowncreek: Bet Gav loves boning you. I would.

@policypipeline: Not being funny, but do you think it's appropriate to talk about solving anxiety with alcohol? Not really the right message to all of your young female followers, is it? Please be more responsible if you are going to present yourself as a role model.

@Adriannaspeaky: Thank you for talking out about anxiety, even if you don't really have it.

Beth

As I open the front door to my house, I am met by the sound of laughter. It is Michael and his mother, they are on the sofa. She is rubbing his feet. Tommy is in his bouncer on the floor.

'Hi,' I say, softly.

'Beth, you're home.' Michael jumps up to give me a kiss. He seems nervous to see me. Janet sits back, raises her hands up then lets them slap down onto her thighs, as if to say, 'Well that's the end of that then.'

'Yes I thought I'd call it a day at the office, I wanted to see you and Tommy. Janet, hello,' I say, politely, nodding in her direction.

'Beth,' she says, barely raising a smile. She can hardly look at me after Dildogate.

I walk over to Tommy and pick him up. He cries immediately.

'He's hungry,' Janet informs me.

'I know, it's time for a feed, which is why I rushed home.'

'We have a bottle heating up,' Janet says, getting up to get it. Michael goes all weird.

'It's OK, Mum. Beth can feed him herself if she's home.'

'But I was looking forward to giving my grandson a bottle. Oooooh,' she says, like I was walking towards her with an ice cream that I dropped just before it reached her mouth.

'Beth, is it OK if Mum gives Tommy a bottle?' Michael asks me. My boobs are so full, I'll have to pump. Which feels so stupid when I am in the room with my baby. But anything for an easy life when it comes to Janet.

She comes over to Tommy with the bottle, picks him up and starts to feed him. The milk in the bottle looks different.

'Wait, that milk is so white,' I say, knowing my breast milk is usually a little more yellow. I look over into the kitchen and see an open box of formula on the counter. 'Is that formula?' I ask, the ball dropping.

Michael says nothing.

'It's good for the big babies. They need it. I didn't breast feed Michael,' she says. I know this because she brings it up a lot. Every time we see her, in fact. It isn't normal for a mother of a forty-four-year-old man to repeatedly talk about not breast feeding him. I think she feels terrible about it and has spent Michael's entire life trying to make up for it by being extremely overpowering and offering regular foot massages.

'Michael, we didn't discuss this? I've been pumping like a mad woman to keep the supply up. There's still a load in the freezer, why are you giving him formula? NO, Janet, get that bottle out of his mouth. Is that the first one or has he been having it without me knowing?' I ask.

'First one,' Michael tells me, and I feel relief that I intercepted at exactly the right moment.

Tommy starts to cry. I made him jump and he is starving. Janet hyperventilates like I've attacked her. 'Michael,' she screeches. I didn't even touch her.

'We said we would keep going with breast feeding until

he was six months. I'm happy to keep pumping, why aren't you happy to keep giving it to him?' I ask Michael. He looks like a bullied kid, being forced into admitting to something by a strict teacher. 'My maternity leave is coming up. I want to breast feed my baby when I'm not working in a few weeks. Can we not just stick to the plan, it's all that's getting me through being away from Tommy this much?'

'I never breast fed any of my children and they are all perfectly fine,' Janet says, getting her breath back.

'Are they though?' I snap. Wanting to explain to her how monumentally fucked-up her son is, but managing to hold myself back. 'Well, this is not your baby,' I say, more gently, taking Tommy out of her arms. I sit on the sofa, undo my shirt and feed him. I'm trembling, I am so cross. Janet walks over to me and drapes a blanket over my shoulder.

'There you go,' she says. 'To protect your modesty.'

I rip it off immediately. She snarls at me but turns it into a passive-aggressive smile.

'I just didn't want you to feel exposed, I can see you're not back to your pre-baby self yet. Mind you, you've always been a little bit . . . ' Instead of words, she uses her hands to speak for her. And in the air draws the outline of a very curvaceous body.

'I'm quite proud of my curves, thank you,' I say, unsnapping the other bra strap, letting my other boob flop free. I sit feeding my baby right in front of both of them. Both of my breasts out and in plain sight. I am in my own home, this is my baby. If they want to have a problem with my body then they can go and sit outside.

There are a few moments of silence. Tommy's guzzling noises are all we can hear. But I'm not finished.

'You can't make decisions like that without me, Michael. It isn't fair,' I say.

'Isn't fair?' Janet says, ready to fight. 'Do you think it's fair to abandon your baby immediately after he's born?'

'I have not abandoned him, I'm working.'

'Poor Michael, having to do all of this on his own. That isn't fair,' she says, in a baby voice, laying her hand on his shoulder, like a supportive lover.

'Oh, but if it was me sacrificing my business, that would be fair?'

'You are his mother. It's your job.'

Janet is the antithesis of a feminist. Misogynistic women are worse than any man. Literally fighting against their own kind. It takes a whole other level of arsehole to pull that off.

'Some of us have lives beyond our children, Janet. In the long run it will mean they're better off.'

'What's that supposed to mean?' she says, aghast.

'Beth, come on. Mum just came round to see Tommy,' Michael says desperately. He cannot handle confrontation with his mother. He is terrified of her. I am not. If 'the worst' happened and we fall out and she never wanted to see me again, fine. That is not a situation I fear. In the meantime, to bridge the gap between that beautiful day and now, I will not be taking parenting advice from someone I consider to be a terrible example.

'I mean, she was just a mum. She never worked. She doesn't understand balancing a career and a child,' I say to Michael, deliberately going for the jugular. Michael looks like he might have a breakdown.

'Your style of parenting is very different to mine, Janet. I have a successful business. I am the main breadwinner in our family and that is something Michael and I are both very proud of. Right Michael?'

The two women in his life stare at him, both needing his approval. I always suspected he slagged me off to her; now I am certain. He's been whining about the childcare. How dare he? I am doing my absolute best.

'Just a mum? *Just* a mum?' Janet says, her crocodile tears appearing.

I feel guilty. Because this is what she does. She makes people feel guilty and fundamentally I am a nice person who hates confrontation.

'Look, I'll feed him then go back to work. But please, don't give him formula, OK? There's plenty of breast milk. If it makes you feel weird to give it to him then, Michael, can you just do it?'

He nods. I lift Tommy up and take him into the other room and feed him privately.

I feel so let down by Michael. Made to feel selfish and cruel. How dare he moan about all of this to his mother? It is such a betrayal.

Arriving back at the office, I feel upset that I was pretty much forced to leave my own house. I was excited to spend the time with Tommy, but the truth is, it's too confusing for everyone if I try to mould work and motherhood together right now. I just need to get this wedding out of the way, and then I'll be able to be with my baby. Alone. No Michael, no Janet. Head down, power on. I can do this.

As I walk up the stairs to the office I hear Risky groaning. There is a thumping sound. I run to the door. Is she being attacked, bludgeoned to death in the office? I burst in.

'What the hell?'

Risky is on my desk, her jeans on the floor and her crop top round her neck. She's having sex with Gavin's brother. It's so weird, I can't do anything but stare. It's like walking in on someone else's dream.

'Beth!' she screeches, pushing him away and gathering her clothes. Gavin's brother, Adam, zips himself up as Risky frantically gets dressed. Her face flushed, her little boobs staring at me like frightened children. Adam scrambles to dress himself, then picks up the cake toppers from the side. He turns back to Risky, and politely kisses her on the cheek before he leaves.

'Sorry. Not cool,' he says to me as he goes to leave. But not before turning back and winking at Risky one last time. Absolutely none of this makes any sense.

'Would you like a cup of tea?'

'No,' I snap.

Risky has been doing her best to be a good employee this afternoon, but I can't even look at her. I saw Gavin's brother's penis come out of her. I saw it glistening as he pulled up his trousers. Yesterday, she was my sweet, romantic, slightly ditsy assistant. Sure, with a penchant for anal but I never thought she was the type to shag a client's brother on my desk. What the hell was she thinking?

And yet, I get it.

'Beth, please let me explain,' she says, desperately. 'I really love this job and I . . . '

'Oh, I know you do,' I say, like a teacher. 'You love it so much you rubbed your vagina all over the contracts.' I pick up a piece of paper from my desk with two fingers, like it is laced with something dangerous.

I'm acting like I'm really annoyed. In a way, I am. She is in breach of contract, I could sack her. But mostly, I am jealous as hell. I want to ask her how it felt. It looked so good. Her face, lost in pleasure. His penis, lost in her. Both of them so beautiful, the sex so lustful. A part of me wishes I'd been quiet, just watched and captured a memory for myself like in the park. But this time with beautiful people, actually worth wanking over.

But I am her boss, it is my job to be annoyed.

Also, I cannot involve my assistant in my fantasies. That simply is not OK.

'Are you going to fire me?' she asks, fearfully. I wait a few beats to answer, to keep my authority established.

'It's lucky for you that this wedding is coming up. I can't do without you right now. Let's get the job done, and the job done well, and then I will have a look at how we move forward. OK?'

'OK.' She turns and walks back to her desk with her head slightly drooped. An email pops up a few seconds later.

I am really sorry, boss. It's just that I've been feeling so insecure about this guy I'm seeing, and how he just wants anal. My vagina needed some love too, you know?

Oh, I know very well what it feels like when your vagina needs love, but I can't tell her that. We sit in silence as she waits for a response. I leave it as long as I can.

'For God's sake, Risky. What do you think, you have to live up to your name?' I say, coming out from behind my desk and heading over to hers. 'Adam is our client's brother. He is Gavin's best man. He could tell Gavin about this, which really wouldn't be good for my business. It will sound like it's part of the service.'

'I know. But he came in here and was so sweet. He said Gavin had told him about me. I mean, Gavin Riley had talked about me? It made me feel so beautiful. I had the cake toppers in my hand and then next thing I knew we were kissing. He's so fit.'

'You cannot sleep with all the handsome best men that we work with, OK?'

'I know but he's Gavin Riley's brother. I was star-struck. He was begging me for sex and I . . . '

'He begged you?'

'OK, no, he didn't need to beg. I mean, he just looked at me and maybe I . . . '

'Maybe you what?'

'Maybe I kind of jumped him.'

'You jumped him?'

'Yes. I saw an opportunity and I just took it. I mean, who wouldn't?'

190

'Um, um . . . ' I say. 'Someone who takes their work seriously?'

Risky looks devastated. 'I'm sorry, boss. It won't happen again, OK? Please, I don't know what came over me.'

'I know exactly what was about to come all over you,' I say, heading back to my desk and trying to seem nonchalant. 'So . . . how do you *jump* someone then?' I ask, as I pick up some contracts and pretend to look through them.

'You just, launch yourself at them, I suppose. I mean, it's good to have an idea that they'd be up for it. But he was definitely up for it. So, I just threw myself at him and started kissing him.'

'And then what happened?'

That's it, I've blown it now. I've stepped down from boss to best friend and there is no going back. But I need to know.

'And then we just got down and dirty, I suppose. It's all about confidence, isn't it?'

'Is it?' I ask. Thinking about my body and wondering if, after being with the same man for ten years, and having had a baby, I could be confident enough to just 'jump someone'. Also, what am I thinking? I can't 'jump someone', I have a husband, a baby and milk spouting from my tits. But it's all I can think about. Sex with strangers. I know I won't be able to get the image of Risky and Adam out of my head. That's going to be in my dreams tonight, and there is nothing I can do to stop it.

'Well, please try not to jump anyone else while you're at work, OK?'

'I won't.'

We can't have been quiet for more than a minute before another email pops up.

Just to be clear . . . can I jump him while I'm not at work?

'No Risky. Please. Don't jump our clients full stop, OK?' I say, standing up.

'OK. Absolutely boss. No problem.'

'Good. Now, can you find me the contracts for the magicians please?' I need to double-check they know not to bring any doves. Mayra is scared of birds.'

'Sure boss.'

She does as I ask. I sit at my desk and wonder if I will ever experience the thrill of spontaneous rampancy ever again. I am pretty sure I won't with my husband.

But what if I could with someone else?

I do. Or she might overindulge in it, like my mother. Either way, these few years of prepubescent eating will be the best of her life, before vanity, weight management or health inevitably ruin her relationship with food forever.

Eating ice cream on the beach with my dad is one of my favourite memories. The luscious taste, abundant joy. I can take myself back there if I concentrate hard enough. The sound of the ocean, happy families on the beach. Me and my dad licking our ice creams, catching the drips that run down the cones with our tongues. Not missing a single morsel of the heavenly sensation of our sweet treats or the joy we found in each other. I can still taste the ice cream. For me it was always vanilla, for him chocolate. He'd say, 'Don't tell your mum I got you two scoops.' And I'd keep that secret like a love note stuffed into my pocket. My dad was fun. Somewhere inside of me, his influence still shines.

On the way home with the shopping, I walk past a little toy shop. I'm generally extremely conservative about the toys I have in the house for Bonnie. I can't bear it when you walk into homes and wonder if any adults live there at all because of the grotesque amount of child paraphernalia that litters their living space. Bonnie has all the essentials. Lego, books, a small art station, cuddly teddies and a neat kitchen that Liam put together for her at my request. He's good like that. Very handy. I was upset though, when Bonnie saw it. It was me who had paid for it and researched the perfect one that would suit her need for fun and my need for order. The assembly was going to take hours and so Liam offered to take on the task. When it was done, looking fantastic in the far corner of the living room, Bonnie was thrilled. She hugged her father and thanked him.

'It was Mummy's idea,' he said, realising Bonnie was excluding me from her overt display of gratitude. 'Go give Mummy a hug and say thank you.'

But she didn't and wouldn't, because at two years old she had no care for the importance of ideas or financial transactions. All she saw was her dad huffing and puffing and working to create a toy that she loved. As far as she was concerned, I had nothing to do with it.

Inside the toy shop, there is a large cuddly mouse. I don't like it. Even a toy rodent gives me the shivers. But rather than deny my child any more joy off the back of my illogical fears, I pick it up and pay for it. At home, I put it on the kitchen table. Then on the sofa. Then on the coffee table. Nowhere feels right, or exciting enough. Eventually, I put it in her bed. The cuddly mouse tucked under the duvet, its horrible head resting on the pillow. I decide that is the most fun place for Bonnie to discover him.

After a spinning session on my bike, I shower and pluck my face. The body hair is the worst it could be at the moment. I have a wax appointment booked at a new salon next week, and it can't come soon enough. I'm nervous about what the technician will be like, but I'm desperate. There is no way I am turning up to Lauren Pearce's wedding looking like this. I got very hot on my bike, and despite having a fan aiming directly at me, it was a struggle. I cut the forty-five-minute class by fifteen minutes and had a simple dinner of green vegetables and prawns to make up for it, before continuing my work on the images of Lauren.

I have her looking as perfect as she asked me to, and I must admit, I've quite enjoyed working on her. She has probably never even heard my name, but I play a vital role in her life. Her selfies on Instagram are so staged. The angle she chooses is the edit, really. Not like the shots for a magazine, or the professional pictures that will be taken at the wedding – she needs me for those. I am like her partner in crime, a silent investor keeping her business afloat. I am quite enjoying that power.

I wonder if she is excited for her wedding or dreading it the way that I was dreading mine. I didn't want all the attention, I didn't want such a big event. I knew something would go wrong, I knew it and felt so foolish when it did. I haven't been as foolish since. The only way to get really hurt is to let people get close to you. I won't make that mistake again.

I open the file on my computer called 'MENSTRUAL DIARY'. In the file, there are also some of my wedding photos; I printed out the only ones I remotely liked. The ones showing us exchanging vows are nice. I look happy, actually very happy. And I was. I thought I'd found the love of my life. Someone I could give as much of myself to as I would ever be willing to give. There are pictures of us holding hands at the drinks reception. I am smiling in most of them. The camera has caught multiple shots of Liam just staring at me. I do believe he loved me. Just not enough that he'd risk breaking our code of trust.

I open one of the images in Photoshop. It's of me, standing

next to Liam. We are looking into the middle distance. I don't remember if we were posing, or if there was actually something grabbing our attention. Liam looks so handsome in it. He's taller than me, which I liked. He has a slim frame, a nice face with a thick black beard and black hair all around an inch or so long. He has dimples that only a select few know are there, as he doesn't shave very often. We don't really look like a couple. Or maybe now I just can't imagine myself in the relationship we had.

Liam was a gentle person. Friendly, sociable. His friends never really took to me. I'm sure I took him away from a more fun life while we were together. He didn't seem to mind, I never stopped him going out when he wanted to. We used to have long dinners that involved hours and hours of conversation. I thought a relationship based on a genuine interest in each other was really wonderful.

We met when I worked in advertising. Generally, the people were abhorrent, but Liam was a freelance designer who would often be on email chains. Occasionally everyone was called in for physical meetings, and I met him in one of those. He followed me down the street afterwards and asked me for a drink. I obviously said no, but he was persistent. He had my email address and asked again later that day. It took a number of tries until I eventually gave in. I arranged the first date for after a wax and we surprisingly had a very nice time. I saw him again a few days later, then went quiet until after my next wax. I saw him every five weeks for around a year. He never lost interest. It all felt extremely out of body and not at all like my life. I only allowed him to have sex with me during the two weeks after a wax. The lights had to be off and I often kept a top on. I told him I had an issue with menstruation that made sex painful during other times in my cycle. He respectfully didn't question it. I hid my body from him, I played hard to get, and then I'd come on strong when my body was how I wanted it to be. It was the best I could do.

And then he told me that he loved me.

I backed off after that. Told him I didn't want to see him anymore. That the feelings were not mutual. If this turned into a real relationship, I kept thinking, I wouldn't be able to hide for weeks on end. I'd have to tell him or, worse still, show him my body.

He got upset one night and asked me if I didn't fancy him.

'I've tried so hard to get close to you,' he said. 'I don't know what more I can do. You don't seem to want me physically and I want to know what I can do to make it better.'

The fact that he presumed the problem lay with him devastated me. I knew I had to tell him, maybe even show him the truth about my body.

I took a deep breath.

'I have a condition called polycystic ovaries,' I said, looking at the ground. It felt like I was telling him I was ridden with a shameful disease that I had brought upon myself. 'It means I may have trouble conceiving. It means I am in constant battle with my hormones. It means . . . it means . . . '

He waited for me to finish. He was good like that, never speaking over me. Always giving me space to just be.

'It means I have thick hair all over my body. It's repulsive

198

and I understand if it turns you off me. I wax as often as I can.' I lifted the skirt of my dress and revealed my hairy legs to him.

He laughed and I felt stupid.

'Come here, Ruby,' he said to me, calling me over to the bed. 'I have hair all over my body too, do you think I'm repulsive?'

I told him I did not. He tried to make love to me, but I said I couldn't do that. That it would take time for me to be able to let myself go in that way, that I couldn't guarantee I ever would at certain times in the cycle. He respected that. He was relieved. He just wanted me to love him.

Then he asked me to marry him.

I look so thin in my wedding photos. Pale. Gaunt. My dress was lovely, I thought. I made it. It was inspired by a Victorian wedding dress that I found. I did my own hair and make-up, of course. But I didn't do it very well. In Photoshop, I warm the tone of my skin a little, plumping out my cheeks, filling out the gaps under my eyes. It's a subtle difference, but it makes me look better. The dress has ruffles all across the front. I chose that to distract from how flat my chest is. I enhance my breasts a bit, adding a cup size or two. It looks better.

Why stop there? It's for my eyes only.

I drag out my hips, giving me a much fuller figure than I would ever allow, but often dream of. A voluptuous shape, a bottom that men would admire. It looks good on me, I can't deny that. I smooth away the veins on my hands, shorten my fingers a little, plump them up. I put some extra shine onto my hair, make my feet smaller and take away the veins on my neck.

I look lovely. An image I would be quite delighted with. I suppose if my pictures were being seen my millions of people, I'd want this work to be done on them too. Maybe Lauren Pearce isn't as crazy as I thought. It's nice to look at photographs of yourself that boost your self-esteem. But of course, this isn't real.

I look at the photo for a while, wondering what a different life I could live if I could make those changes to myself for real. It would be better, I don't doubt that for a moment. I'd be happier. I'd probably still be married.

My phone rings. It's the nursery. They keep calling and I keep letting it go to answerphone. This time I feel bad and listen to the message.

'Hello Ruby, it's Maria again. Please could you let me know when you'll be able to collect Bonnie, she really isn't having a good day . . . '

I shut down my computer and get myself ready to leave. It's Friday tomorrow, Liam will come and take over at six. I'm looking forward to the weekend where I'll only need to take care of myself.

I take one last look at the retouched wedding photos and leave the house.

Beth

'What?' Risky says, picking up her phone.

It is very aggressive for her. I pretend not to notice and shift my gaze to my computer screen.

'Yeah, and I meant it.' She gets up and moves over to the window. 'I said it because it needed to be said.' She starts to pace up and down. Whoever is on the phone is really annoying her. I carry on pretending I haven't noticed.

'Why? What do you mean, *why*? Because it doesn't feel right, that's why.' She covers the end of her phone with her hand and lets out a frustrated sound, rolling her eyes at me. 'You can't just ignore it,' she continues. 'No, you have to at least acknowledge it. It's like it's not even there. Well of course it matters, it's my fucking vagina.'

Oh wow. She is talking about sex. I get up slowly. I'll sneak into the bathroom until she's finished. But she sees me get up and rushes over, putting her hand on my arm and squeezing it tightly as her frustration mounts.

'I don't hate it, I like it, but that isn't the point. It's not all I want. You're giving me a complex about my vagina. I don't need that in my life, OK? Is there something wrong with it? Why won't you have sex with it?'

I check to make sure she isn't drawing blood on my arm, it really hurts.

'Oh yeah? Well then it's over, OK? I can't do this anymore. That's all you want, and I want respect. Do you know what else wants respect?'

The guy on the phone and I hang tight for her answer.

'MY VAGINA.'

She hangs up on him, lets go of my arm and screams at her phone.

'Well that seemed to go well?' I ask.

'I love it up the bum, Beth. But my vagina needs it too,' she says, utterly forlorn. So much vagina chat for one afternoon.

'Shall we get on with some work?' I suggest. 'We're on a deadline here, Risky.'

She ambles back to her desk, her mind clearly still focused on sex. Sitting down, she picks up her phone and starts angry texting. Then she starts smiling, and her phone rings. This is fascinating.

'Hey,' she says, heading back to the window. 'Yeah, I did it. Yeah, I guess so . . . I mean, if you want us to be?' She is making her legs go all kooky and twirling her hair. 'Ha-ha, oh you do, do you?' She giggles. 'Oh yeah? I do too. What, now? Adam, I'm at work.'

'ADAM!' I say in a loud whisper. She shrugs as if she just can't help herself.

'No, not here,' she says. 'No . . . OK, OK, give me a second.'

Risky winks at me – any authority I had as a boss has all but evaporated – and takes her little pink dildo out of her bag and disappears into the toilet.

'OK, OK, I'm nearly there,' she tells him. 'They're black . . . and lacy . . . I'm not wearing one. I'm not!'

She shuts the door. I am left alone at my desk, in my office, while my assistant cracks one out in the bathroom, over the phone with my client's brother. How the actual hell is this happening?

The office door suddenly pops open.

'Michael, what are you doing here?'

'Tommy wanted to surprise Mummy at work,' Michael says, coming into the office holding my baby.

'Right, um, well how lovely,' I say.

'Where is Risky?' he asks me.

'Oh, she's in the toilet. She might be a while. Big lunch.' I wish I hadn't said that.

'Everything OK?' he asks me. I should be happier to see them.

'Yes, yes, fine.'

'Oh my goodness,' Risky says, coming out of the toilet. (That was quick.) 'You need to prepare me for this level of cuteness.'

She takes Tommy from Michael as he unclips the carrier. 'Hello gorgeous baby. Oh, he's got your eyes, Beth. And your nose, Michael. He is the perfect mash-up of both of you,' Risky coos. She makes funny faces at Tommy, he smiles.

'How lovely of you to drop by.' Why am I sounding so formal with my husband? 'I mean, you should have called ahead and we would have tidied up,' I say, giving Michael a kiss on the cheek.

'Oh God, you guys kill me!' says Risky. 'I'm always telling

Beth how you have my dream marriage. You're very special you know, Michael. Taking care of the baby like this while your wife works. Such a modern man.'

'Oh, thank you,' Michael says, blushing. 'It's just what you have to do, isn't it?'

'I suppose so, but not all dads are willing to do it.'

Risky's praise is nauseating. A dad fulfilling his potential as a parent doesn't mean he should be branded a hero.

'Have you fed him?' I ask.

'Nope, I thought you'd like to feed him?'

'Great. Risky, bring him here, would you?' She does as I ask. 'Come on little man, come to Mummy.' He latches onto my right boob and we both feel the release of it. I love him so much. Everyone told me I would feel a love I had never felt before, but I didn't realise it would feel so different from how I feel about everyone else in the world.

'How great does Beth look for someone who just had a baby?' Risky says to Michael. 'I keep telling her what a hot Mumma she is but she won't believe me.'

'Risky, please!' I say, hoping she shuts up. I don't want Michael to be forced into noticing me and then lying about how he feels about it.

'Yes, yes she's looking well,' Michael says. One hundred per cent less enthusiastic about my appearance than Risky.

'And what about those whoppers?' she says, pointing at my breasts. 'I bet it doesn't feel fair, for them to look so amazing but you're not allowed to touch them.'

She thinks she's hilarious. Risky prides herself on saying whatever she wants and being very open about sex. To be fair to her, she is talking to a married couple who shouldn't be finding this so excruciating.

'Yes, they are nice,' Michael says, not knowing where to look. He manages almost everywhere except at me.

'Oh look at you, getting all shy,' Risky says. 'Look Beth, he's blushing.' I pretend to tend to Tommy. I can't look at Michael. Someone even saying the word 'hot' around us has become unbearable.

'Sooooo, do you think you'll have another one?' she asks Michael. 'People always ask women that, but that isn't fair, so I always make sure I ask men too.'

'Um . . . I don't know about that, we'd have to . . . '

I wonder if Michael is going to say 'have sex'. But of course he doesn't.

'. . . Move, probably. We'd need another bedroom. And we don't really want to move, do we Beth?'

'No. We don't want to move.' I give Risky a firm eye, urging her to shut up but she doesn't get my point.

'Well, I suppose the joy of having one is that you get your marriage back nice and quick. You hear such terrible stories of relationships falling apart after babies. One of my mum's friend's husbands just left her after twenty years because she totally lost her sex drive after their third kid.'

'OK, Michael, I think Tommy is full,' I say, standing up. Poor Tommy doesn't know what is going on and starts to cry hysterically. 'I'm sorry love, we have a big meeting in about twenty minutes and I need to prepare for it. Can you take him home?'

Michael can't get Tommy in the carrier quick enough. He

is screaming and wants more milk. Risky is faffing, she can't cope with a baby crying. No one can, it's a horrible and traumatising sound. But nothing is worse to me right now than Michael staying here and Risky trying to spark a conversation about our sex life.

'Bye love, see you after work,' I yell down the stairs, over the sound of Tommy's screams. My nipples are spouting and soaking my top. I could cry at the thought of what our marriage has become.

'That was nice,' Risky says as I come back into the office.

'Yeah, lovely,' I reply as I sit back at my desk.

'Here,' she says, handing me some tissue for my leaking boobs. I pat the outside of my shirt, then shove a couple of nipple pads in my bra.

Risky gets another text message. She grins and replies enthusiastically. Looks like she's got the horn again.

I pretend not to notice.

Ruby

When I picked Bonnie up from nursery at five p.m. she was sitting in a corner alone, with bright red eyes and an exhausted face.

'She didn't settle all day,' Maria tells me. 'It would have been much better if you had picked her up when I called.'

I told her I was sorry, but that it had been impossible for me to leave work. Maria said that Monday must be different. 'Bonnie has separation anxiety and needs to be settled in slowly.' It's the worst she'd ever seen from a three-year-old, apparently. She asked for me all day long.

My little girl asking for me? I'd resigned myself to that never happening. Frustrating as it is for her not settling in, it's nice to know she needs me. This week hasn't been entirely terrible. Bonnie has watched a lot of TV in the time we've spent together, but we have had some nice moments too. More in a few days than we have had in months. Maybe Bonnie is responding to that, she wants to be with me more. But I try not to think about that too much, because what it also means is that I have been neglecting her for a long time, and that the moment I put more effort in to our relationship, her behaviour towards me has changed. This is quite a frustrating realisation.

Bonnie refused to get into her buggy. But only because she wanted me to carry her home. She wrapped herself around me and wouldn't let go. Her head lay gently on my shoulder. My back is sore from carrying her for nearly a mile, but I wouldn't have put her down even if she had asked me to. I don't remember the last time she held onto me like that. It gave us both a great deal of unexpected comfort.

'I have a little present for you at home,' I whisper into her ear to cheer her up. She cuddles me even tighter.

'What is it Mummy?' Bonnie asks excitedly.

'You'll have to wait and see.'

Her gorgeous blue eyes are sparkling at the thought of it; the excitement helping her to forget the agony of the day.

'It's up in your room,' I tell her as I open the front door.

Bonnie runs up the stairs as quickly as she can, I follow her up. In her room she scans the floor then looks in her toy box.

'Maybe try your bed?' I suggest, and she immediately finds the cuddly toy all tucked up.

'A mouse,' she says, pulling it out from under the duvet and hugging so hard she squashes it almost completely.

'Do you like him?' I ask.

'I love her.'

'Oh, it's a her?'

'Yes, and her name is Mummy.' She is delighted with her choice of name. I'd prefer not to have a mouse of all things named after me, but this isn't the time to express that.

'Good, well I'm glad you like it. Why don't you play with Mummy while I go and make your dinner?'

'I want to play with Mummy, Mummy,' she says, putting the mouse back on the bed.

'OK, well you do that and I'll call you when dinner is ready.'

'NO, I want to play with you.'

'With me? Why?' I ask. I never play with Bonnie. I have always been extremely proud of her ability to play alone. I am not one of those mothers who gets down on her hands and knees and builds Lego towers.

'Let's play shops,' she says, getting a case full of plastic food items and a little cash register.

'Bonnie, I really do need to get your dinner on . . . '

'You can't cook my dinner if you haven't been to the shops though, can you?'

'I guess not.'

I sit on the floor, resting my back against her bed while she arranges things into what she considers to be a good enough shop to satisfy her imagination.

'OK,' she says, looking at me like I know what to do next. It takes me a minute to get into character.

'Oh, right. I'd like a tomato and a cucumber, please?' I say.

'No, you want the pasta,' she says, forcefully.

'OK, please can I have the pasta and the tomato sauce?' I say, playing along.

'NO! You want the pasta and the cheese,' she says, snatching the fake tomato sauce out of my hand and forcing the plastic cheese into it instead.

'OK, Bonnie,' I say, calmly. 'I'll have the pasta and cheese please.' Determined to play nicely.

'But *I* want the cheese Mummy,' she insists, her arms crossing.

'Bonnie—'

'NOOOOOO, I WANT THE CHEESE,' she screams, unreasonably. Going straight to a level eight.

I keep my voice calm. I don't want to upset her, but I don't want her to talk to me that way either. She finds my response unbearable and exits the bedroom, thumping her way down the stairs. I sit on the floor, surrounded by plastic food, and I have a major revelation. Toddlers are crazy no matter what I do. It isn't my fault.

As Bonnie plays alone with her kitchen upstairs, I make her a dinner of sausages and mashed potato. She eats it in her chair with a big cushion on it, while I play *The Gruffalo* audiobook through my Amazon Alexa. I ask her if she would like more, but she turns her head to the side as if I have said the cruellest thing imaginable. It makes me laugh. I'm not sure I have ever laughed at this behaviour before, but parenting is slowly becoming clearer to me. It isn't easy, but that doesn't mean I shouldn't be doing it. All I have to do is think of Ross, and what he has been through. I bet he'd swap his agony for even just one more day with Verity, whether she was having a meltdown or not.

I let her watch the TV for a bit before we battle through a bath. She refuses to get in, then thrashes about so much that she slips and bangs her head on the side. No real damage is done, but the tantrum elevates to a solid nine. Getting her into pyjamas is like trying to dress an octopus. Eventually she is in bed, a story has been read, soft lighting fills the room and a vaporiser emits a gentle lavender scent. She falls asleep within minutes, holding onto Mummy the mouse like they have shared a lifetime of love.

I watch her from the door. Maybe the trick to parenting isn't trying to manage her reactions, but rather, it's trying to manage my own. And above all else, at least my daughter is alive. Maybe I am lucky after all.

Lauren Pearce – Instagram post
@OfficialLP

The picture is of Lauren in workout gear, sitting in the classic Dandasana yoga pose. She has taken the photo herself, using a mirror's reflection. She is smiling. Fully made-up. There is a green juice on the mat next to her.

The caption reads:
I'm doing better. Much better today. Silly me getting myself in a state and sharing that with you all. As if you don't have your own problems to worry about. The thing about anxiety is that we all have it on various levels. We all have to manage it. And I can, and I will. Less than two weeks until I say 'I DO' to the man I love. Feeling thankful for him, and for the people I have around me. And I am grateful for the large and the little things in my life that bring me joy. Everything from my smoothie, to my dog, to the clothes on my back. Am grateful to be alive. We all should be. #loveyourself #selfcare #womensupportingwomen #greenjuice #yoga #vegan

@quincybones: That's it girl, get those pelvic floors nice and snappy and cheer the f*ck up.

@delorously: I like it when you share about your anxiety. If someone like you has it, then it makes me feel like less of a mess.

@reason675: oh my fucking god when will you actually shut the fuck up you vain vacuous asshole.

@eagerbeaveronly: So much respect for you. QUEEN. You are beautiful inside and out.

@lovelollyed: literally never loved another human as much as I love you.

Ruby

With Bonnie upstairs sleeping like an angel, I sit on the sofa looking at the pictures of Lauren. I keep flicking between the originals and the ones that I have worked on. Of course I have made her more beautiful. In fact, I have made her perfect. But she really wasn't so bad to begin with. There are plenty of untouched photos of her and Gavin leaving various parties and on red carpets. Her dresses are always skin-tight. Either her boobs or legs are shown off, sometimes both. She is every bit the stereotype of the trophy wife. A bit of an airhead, laden with designer clothes, if she is wearing anything at all. The Internet is full of quotes that her PR has made on her behalf. Banging on about empowerment and anxiety like she has a clue about it. She needs to spend a week with my mother, then tell me she understands mental health.

She is a fraud. But she is also my source of income at the moment, and all of this will buy me an exceptional new handbag and very possibly a new painting for my living room. What is the expression? *One man's trash is another man's treasure?* Maybe in my case, it's more 'One woman's insecurity is another woman's art budget.' I shouldn't joke. Mental illness is nothing to take lightly. Which is why Lauren Pearce using it to gain career traction is so offensive to me.

I text my mother.

Mum, how are the cats today?

'Delivered' turns to 'read' immediately on iMessage. Luckily she has never realised she can turn that function off, as it's very useful to know she has seen the message, and that she isn't dead. I get back to the images of Lauren.

My job is to make something that isn't real, not look fake. That takes a lot of skill. When I used to work for an advertising company, which was awful, there was never the concern that something looked fake, all we had to do was create a picture that lied about how life-changing the product was. I was forever making some anorexic model with limp hair look like she had the locks of a Grecian goddess, just to sell some shampoo that didn't even work (I know this, because I tried all of the products myself), but all anyone cared about was that the hair looked incredible. A level of incredible that is literally unachievable by anything other than a wig. So full, so shiny, not a split end in sight. I'd create the impossible hair to promote the impossible product. And the people who were behind it were vile. They spoke about women like they were idiotic pieces of meat, stupid enough to believe they could look like a digitally created picture. It made me very uncomfortable. Rebecca used to work for them a lot too, but she moved more into celebrity photo shoots with magazines and took me with her. That was never a moral decision for her – I'm not sure Rebecca has morals about what she does – but then I'm part of the machine so what good are my morals really?

Rebecca used to send me some really horrific emails back

then. The agency would book models that were so thin, so ill-looking. I can spot a girl with an eating disorder a mile off. One time, the photos of this poor girl were so upsetting to look at. The ad was for a denim brand. They claimed these jeans gave you the perfect bottom. This woman had no bottom. She was gaunt and pale and her legs looked hardly able to hold her up. Whoever cast her should have been fired, but apparently she was a well-known model and quite a catch for the campaign. Rebecca sent me the images with the simple instruction: 'Make her look like she isn't dying.' It broke my heart. I felt for her as I warmed her skin tone, took away the dark shadows under her eyes, fleshed out her thighs, and gave her the bottom that the jeans promised to give every woman. What I did to her would make her problem worse. She looked fantastic by the end, meaning she would get booked for more work. Her credibility as a model would continue to rise, and she would continue to starve herself. I always wondered what it must feel like for a model like her to know that she'll be 'fixed in post'. Was it a relief to know it didn't really matter how she looked, because someone like me would alter it anyway? Or did it destroy her, to see that her real image was never good enough, and that it needed to be reworked on a computer to make it printable? Either way, the entire experience of advertising was excruciating. These days I mostly work off the demands of the women in the photo, although Rebecca requests changes too and the subject of the photo never contests them. I have no reason to feel bad about it. Even though I do.

Unable to stop snooping on Lauren Pearce, I find an interview that she did with the *Daily Mail* a few years ago. They ask her when she plans to have children. A stupid question to ask a twenty-five-year-old (as she was at the time) who isn't even married yet. Her answer is breathtaking.

The lemon-haired beauty wants her daughters to know the value of their bodies.

'If I am lucky enough to have daughters, I'm sure it will be very hard. I want them to love their bodies, like I love mine. But it's hard, especially with Instagram and Snapchat and other social media apps where filters can make anyone look perfect. It's a fake world, but my job as their mum would be to keep it real.'

I have no sympathy for this woman or her hypothetical daughters. She is a liar and a hypocrite. Living in her perfect bubble of money, fame and potential motherhood. Trying to make a dime out of her fashionable issues with mental health, and the fake body she flaunts as real. It really shouldn't be allowed.

'Come on, please, Bonnie, Daddy will be here soon,' I say, holding her shoes and coat. It is finally Friday evening, Liam is due at six and he is rarely late. I am waiting for him in the hallway.

'What will you do when I'm with Daddy?' she asks me, as I tie her laces. It is the first time she has ever asked such a question.

'Tonight, I have a dinner with friends, and the rest of the weekend, I will work,' I tell her. Because that is what I do at the weekends, along with taking long walks, sometimes buying a new handbag, occasionally making a dress. I spare the detail that I will spend most of tomorrow in a salon, having hair ripped out of my body by someone I don't know, who may or may not send a message on WhatsApp to a group of her friends later in the day, telling them they won't believe the woman that came in that day. Before describing me as disgusting.

'What is work?'

'It is what grown-ups do so that they can earn money to buy food and clothes, and other essential items.'

'Do I work?'

'Do you earn money?' I ask her.

'No.'

'No, you are a child. You don't work, you play. When you are a grown-up you will work, and you will have to choose what it is you do.'

'What work did you choose?'

I pause. Did I choose what I do? Not exactly. I have landed in a place I never expected to land.

'I make pictures look pretty,' I tell her.

'Pictures of what?'

'Of people.'

'What people?'

'Women.'

'How do you make them pretty?'

'I . . . I colour them in, I suppose.'

'Can you colour me in, to make me pretty?'

'Don't be silly.'

She lets out a moan. A moan way more in keeping with

the version of her I am used to. She wants me to answer the question.

'So why are the women in the pictures not pretty?'

'Because they don't think they are.'

'Why don't they think they are?'

'Because they think there is something wrong with them.'

'What's wrong with them?'

'Nothing.'

'Then why do you need to change them?'

I stare at my daughter. She stares back at me. She wants an answer to a simple question but I have no idea what to say. When explaining my job to an innocent child, it feels completely ridiculous.

'Why can't you make me pretty, Mummy?'

'Because, because . . . '

The doorbell rings and I feel, quite literally, saved by it.

'Daddy!' yells Bonnie, exercising an immediate mood change, and running to the door and knocking me over. I've always been cast aside by Bonnie's love for her dad. It's something I came to accept from around five minutes after she was born. Bonnie opens the door before I have the chance to get up. Liam sees me on my bottom in the hall and rushes in to my aid.

'Ruby, Christ, are you OK, did you fall?'

I brush off his hands and shoo him away. He knows I don't like to be touched.

'No, I was just putting on her shoes and she knocked me over.'

'Oh, OK, good. Hey Bon Bon!'

Bonnie jumps up into his arms. That used to be my favourite place too.

'How was your trip?' I ask him, knowing it's important that we manage polite conversation in front of our daughter.

'Oh, it was OK. You know, work. How was your week in the end?'

'Hard, actually. I have a lot of work on at the moment.'

'Mummy makes women look pretty for her work but she won't make me pretty,' Bonnie says, jutting out her bottom lip.

'That's because you're already as pretty as you could possibly be,' he says, reminding me of the answer I should have given her.

'Anyway, she's started at her new nursery now so that's good.'

'And how was it, do you like it?' he asks Bonnie, to which she shakes her head violently and then rests it on his shoulder.

'It's smelly,' she answers.

'She's being silly, it was great. It will just take a bit of time for her to settle in,' I add, not looking him in the eye.

'Right, well I'm glad that's sorted. And it probably didn't do any harm for you guys to spend a bit more time together anyway,' he says, putting on the brakes and stopping the world from turning.

'Excuse me?' I ask him, slowly. Possibly with some steam coming out of my ears.

'Well, you know, you two spending some quality time together would be nice, no?'

'Are you kidding me? All I do is work, and parent, work

and parent. Is that not enough for you?' I am saying this through a fake smile, as if Bonnie doesn't understand English.

'All I mean is you drop her off at eight every morning, and pick her up after five. She comes to me every weekend. So maybe spending a few weekdays together isn't such a bad thing. Did you like spending time with Mummy, Bonnie?'

She nods her head furiously. 'We caught a mouse,' she tells him. He raises his eyebrows with surprise; he is well aware of my phobia. 'We set it free in the park.'

'You did?' he asks me. But I have frozen, both physically and emotionally. I can't think of a damn thing to say.

'OK, well we better get going if we want to get a movie in before bedtime,' Liam says, snapping me back into the hallway.

'Her bedtime is at seven, please don't keep her up late.'

'I know, don't worry,' he says, offering Bonnie a cheeky smile that she delivers right back to him. He's the fun one. I'm the boring one who never spends any time with my child, apparently.

I give him the bag I packed for her. It's a nice bag, a Kate Spade tote, I tell him not to lose it. I shut the door behind them as they walk off down the street making silly faces and laughing.

It isn't my fault I am not as much fun as him.

Beth

All of my feelings about Michael not touching me are turning to rage. I am so angry I could burst. I have the right to a sex life. What if I have married a man who never works this out, and I have to either break my family in half to satisfy my own needs, or just commit to a life of no sex? Could I do that? Live a sexless life? Maybe I could. I mean, do we even need sex?

I do. I need sex. That doesn't make me crazy.

All that has happened so far is accidental voyeurism, and continuous erotic fantasies both when I am awake and asleep. If I don't get laid soon, I'm worried I might jump Risky.

I came home early from work today, in time to feed Tommy before bed. And early enough that Michael can't possibly tell me he is too tired to speak to his wife.

'We need to talk about the other night,' I say to him, as I tuck into a jacket potato with tuna that I brought home with me. He was offended that I didn't want his shepherd's pie with a parsnip topping. But the second best thing to sex are carbohydrates, so it's happening. He can't deny me them both.

'Oh, Mum will be OK, she just loves Tommy, that's all,' he says, choosing a subject he can handle rather than the one he knows I am referring to.

'I don't mean what happened with your mother, I mean what happened with us, in bed. Michael, can you look at me, please?' He does as I ask but looks terrified, then cross. I refuse to allow our sex life to be a forbidden subject. I have been fantasising about watching strangers fuck in forests, this simply can't go on. I am not enjoying feeling like a pervert. 'Michael, I love you so much, but we have a problem, you know that, don't you?'

He sits down next to me. 'I know,' he says, pitifully. This feels like progress.

'Michael, do you fancy me?' I ask, bracing myself for an answer that I am not emotionally prepared for.

'Of course I do,' he says, tenderly.

'Then what? What is the problem?'

'There isn't a problem, Beth. Why are you always making me feel guilty?'

OK, here we go . . .

'I'm not trying to make you feel guilty. I just need to know. Is your lack of interest in me my fault, or is it something else?'

I want to avoid suggesting that there is anything wrong with him, even if it means aiming the blame at myself, because I am trying to create a safe space for him to tell me why this is happening. I think I am doing quite well.

'Yes, it is your fault,' he says.

I immediately want to cry.

'My fault, how?' I ask, telling myself to stay strong. I am not the one in the wrong. I am a good wife, I am a good person, I am not the one with the problem.

'There's nothing sensual about you anymore, nothing subtle. You make me feel like all that matters is sex. If I don't want it, there's something wrong with me. Well, have you ever thought that there might be something wrong with you?'

'Yes, Michael. All the time. I wonder if there's something wrong with me every single day.'

'And?'

'And what?'

'And have you worked out what it is?' he asks.

Is this really the man I married?

'No,' I say, knowing he is about to tell me, and knowing it will hurt.

He takes his time, as if really working out how he will say it. And then he does.

'You aren't very good in bed.'

'Pardon?'

'You make love like you're alone. It isn't very sexy. It's not what I like. Take the other night as an example, I was clearly not in the mood but you forced yourself on top of me and writhed around like you were possessed. It wouldn't have mattered if I was there or not.'

'It wouldn't have mattered if you were there or not? We were making love! You kissed me. You had an erection?' I say, feeling like I can't stand up, or raise my voice, or do anything else that might emphasise the fact that he clearly thinks I am a sexual monster. I take a deep breath and force myself to speak calmly. 'You could have asked me to stop, Michael.'

'Could I? You weren't taking any notice of me.'

I don't know what to say.

'It's not how women should behave.'

'Excuse me? '

'From the moment you got pregnant it was all about you. How you were feeling, how birth would be for you. How I would take care of Tommy, so you could work. Being a mother has made you selfish. Sex-crazed.'

'OK, Michael, I think you're really upset. I didn't mean this conversation to turn nasty. I just wanted to talk about our sex life.'

'No, you wanted to tell me it's my fault.'

'No, I . . . for God's sake, people are out there hurting each other. Cheating on each other. And I don't want that to happen to us.'

'Are you cheating on me?' he asks, his eyes squinting.

'No, that isn't what I said. I said people are, and I don't want us to . . . '

'To what? To cheat on each other? Are you threatening me with infidelity?'

'No, I wouldn't do that. I'm just saying that—'

'You're just saying that if I don't have sex with you, you'll cheat on me? Great, I feel really horny now.'

'You've just twisted everything I've said.'

'Well, that'll go well with your twisted brain, won't it?' he says, like a petulant teenager who I will never be able to reason with.

'Michael, stop it. You're being ridiculous.'

'Am I? Well maybe this marriage is ridiculous.'

Wow.

'Look, I'm sorry if that's how that sounded, but it isn't

what I meant. I am not cheating on you, and I have no plans to.'

Maybe that was a lie.

'Good,' he says, heading to the living room door. 'Because with all the childcare that I'm doing, I know which parent would get the judge's vote for custody.'

'What did you just say?' I ask him slowly, every hair on my body standing up, my spine breaking through my skin and the Mumma Bear in me preparing for attack.

'You heard me,' he says, standing firm.

'You're not doing childcare, Michael, you're being a parent. Can we at least get that straight?'

'Don't test me. If you cheat on me, I'll not make it easy for you. And I'll take Tommy, you can bet on that.'

He leaves the room. I am left dumbstruck.

I came home to try to and work things out. Now, to be quite honest, he can go fuck himself.

Ruby

WhatsApp chat
Group name – Falmouth Forever

Yvonne: Feel fat, hate my clothes. What are you all wearing?

Jess: Urgh, me too. Kids ruined me. Jeans, grey top with puffy sleeves, boring.

Sarah: You are NOT FAT. Me, on the other hand. I was doing so well but I'm too busy to go to Pilates. I'll probably wear what I wear every time I go out . . . a black smock.

Ruby: I was thinking about wearing some velvet, maybe? ;)

Yvonne: LOL. Can't wait to see you in velvet Rubes, can't imagine it ;)

Every time I meet my friends for dinner they send a flurry of text messages explaining why they will look terrible. Very often the complaint is dress-size related. As if they will walk in, and one of us will scream in horror at their weight gain.

I went to university with Yvonne, Jess and Sarah. We were

at Falmouth, all doing degrees in Fine Art. I very much enjoyed the course, but living by the coast in a place that had a rampant surf scene was more challenging than I'd envisaged – when I first applied, I hadn't realised my condition would get worse.

But I managed to make good friends, and twenty years later we're still in touch. We are all busy but manage to meet two to three times a year for dinner. I generally arrive kicking and screaming but quite enjoy it by the end. It's always a little surprising when I get invited as, since they witnessed Liam's outburst at the wedding, I have been even more cagey than usual. But they seem pretty determined to keep me in the group, all reminding me regularly of the times that I apparently 'saved them' from total despair.

I'm not capable of giving myself that much credit. But I suppose what they are saying is true. I have, at different times, rescued them all from something. Jess' experience is the one I remember most clearly. We all shared a house, which I hated because women seem to want to walk around wearing just towels or underwear. They never saw me in anything less than full-body velvet. It was at university that I truly made it my 'thing'. Dressing gowns, trousers, tops, coats, dresses that I made, vintage discoveries. Looking back, I realise I looked like a sofa, but it got me through university. Like a punk who pierces her face, or a biker covered in tattoos, I claimed velvet as my look. I couldn't afford full-body waxing back then, and the hair growth was still quite recent. I didn't have a grip of it at all, and one stupid night I decided to shave. I had shaved my legs and armpits before, of course. But this night, I shaved everything. My legs, my arms, my stomach, my nipples. I even reached around to my back and shaved that. I felt like I had won the greatest prize on earth. I came out of the bathroom with just a towel around me. There was no one else home to see it, but the walk from the bathroom to my bedroom, with my shoulders exposed, felt like the most joyous victory lap imaginable. My friends were in a pub and I hadn't wanted to go because my need for solitude was starting to develop. But that night, I felt free.

I joined them in the pub. I even drank alcohol. Three drinks in total, my first in ages because I'd developed another fear of losing control. The drinks went to my head pretty quickly. I found myself flirting with a guy at the bar. He seemed to find me attractive, and I'd not flirted or been flirted with for a long time because I hadn't allowed it to happen. I told myself to enjoy that night, the skin underneath my only sleeveless velvet dress loving the sensation of the air on it. I felt like I could fly.

Jess was getting off with one of my guy's housemates. At around eleven p.m. they suggested we went back to theirs to continue the party. We said yes. Jess and her guy went into the living room, me and my guy went into the kitchen. He made me a disgusting cocktail, which I drank because I was already feeling loose and had managed to convince myself that I was someone else. After a while we began kissing. It got quite heated so – most out of character but obviously fulfilling an unconscious desire – I asked him to take me to his room. I was a young woman, I had my needs. He did as I asked.

He took off all of his clothes and got into bed. I stood looking at him, my velvet armour clinging to me as if it knew what was about to happen. He asked me what I was waiting for. I told him nothing. I took off my dress and my tights. I got into bed. He kissed me, and laid his hand on my stomach, then leaped out of bed, shaking his fingers like there was something sticky on them that he wanted to get off. He yelled, 'What the fuck was that?' And pointed to my belly.

I ran my hand over it. Stubble so sharp it made a sound when I rubbed it the wrong way.

The guy, Jonny, was now switching between laughter and obvious repulsion. 'Did you shave your gut?' My presence in his bedroom was impossible to understand. What was I even doing there? Why did I think this could be me?

I got out of bed and got dressed. I didn't say a word. He laughed at me as I left.

I felt I couldn't go without letting Jess know, so I quietly peeked into the living room, very aware that I could walk in on my friend having sex, which was not something I wanted to do. What I saw was Jess fast asleep on the sofa, and the guy she was with lying naked next to her. One hand in her underwear, the other hand wrapped around his penis – he was about to have sex with her.

I immediately ran to the couch, pulled his hand off her and shook her as hard as I could.

'Jess, wake up,' I yelled, repeatedly. Shaking more and more violently until she came around.

'What the fuck are you doing, you crazy bitch?' the guy said, still naked. Still with his hand on his penis.

'She was asleep, you animal,' I said, wanting to spit on him.

'She was gagging for it,' he groaned. No care for the damage he could have inflicted.

I did the button up on Jess' jeans, and put her arm over my shoulder, managing to get her out. We staggered with great difficulty for the fifteen-minute walk home. My back was killing me, but it wasn't worse than what we had escaped.

The next morning I told Jess exactly what I had seen and what had happened to her. She found the whole thing very hard to cope with, but was back at the pub and getting off with guys again within a few weeks.

I didn't get intimate with another man until I met Liam. And I never drank again.

We are all mothers now.

I have to do a little mental preparation before I meet Yvonne, Jess and Sarah. It isn't that I don't like them, I do. But the more time you spend alone, the harder it is to be sociable. These women see each other a lot so they're quite relaxed with each other. Because I see them less they ask me a lot of questions and I find it quite overbearing.

There is an awful lot of pressure to be a 'woman's woman'. Everyone's talking about 'women supporting women', and 'the power of female friendship'. It's enough to make me stop reading the papers. Female relationships being written about like a bond men could never understand. How we are 'stronger together', how 'magical things happen when women unite'. How girls run the world, according to Beyoncé. I don't know if I'm particularly on board with any of that. I'm not sure I particularly like women, just because they are women.

My relationship with the fairer sex has always been extremely complex. For most of my life they have fought against me. It started with my mother, then the girls at school, picking on me in the changing rooms and making monkey sounds at the very sight of my flesh.

These women, my friends, are not cruel to me, despite me being quite unpleasant a lot of the time. After Liam said those awful things at our wedding I was so embarrassed that I barely saw them until Bonnie was born. They turned up unannounced at my house, like they were hosting some ridiculous intervention. Luckily, I was wearing my dressing gown. I allowed them in. They gathered around Bonnie like mad aunties. I didn't admit it to them, but I enjoyed their visit. I told them I would resurface on the proviso we never talked about the wedding, that they never asked me any questions relating to what happened, and that they never showed up at my house unannounced again. They agreed to all of the above. Each stating again how much I had helped them at various times, and how they all owe me their support.

Maybe they are right, because as well as helping Jess to escape rape, I once punched one of Sarah's ex-boyfriends in the face because I saw him kissing another girl outside the college library. I went home and told her right away. She cried and accused me of lying, then went to his house where he opened the door with a black eye and a half-naked girl standing behind him. Sarah apologised to me and said that I could rely on her friendship forever. She's kept this promise.

I am wearing a black velvet version of the usual dress this evening with extensive costume jewellery and a fantastic Saint Laurent shoulder bag. When I am this hairy I go full throttle on my accessories. They're the ultimate distraction. I was supposed to be freshly waxed for this dinner. I wanted to cancel, but they always give me hell if I try to do that.

'Ruby, you look so skinny,' says Yvonne, as I walk into the tapas bar in Soho. My instinct is to snap at her. What a hideous way to greet a woman. 'So skinny' is a loaded 'hello'. 'So skinny' is not a compliment. It's oozing with, 'What is the matter? Are you depressed? Do you eat? Are you ill?'

Women go on and on about wanting to be valued for more than their looks, but they do this to each other. They greet each other with compliments, often fake. I don't want to look like a praying mantis. But if I gave in to food I'd swell up like a pregnant rhinoceros. Staying thin is a consistently agonising task. All women know that. Yvonne is projecting her own delusions about her size and possibly hoping I greet her with the same false positive. I don't. She's put on weight and it's not worth denying.

I am the last to arrive and they all stand awkwardly for me. They've all been told to get off me when they have touched my body. They've all been snapped at, told to shut up. Warned not to mention things enough times to be wary of how to be around me. I don't feel good about being so demanding, but there is no doubt my time with them is easier since I set such boundaries.

Their children are older than mine because it didn't take them as long to find husbands. They all live in Queen's Park.

All living the dreamy London mum life, which centres around their kids' social activities and dinner parties.

'So how is Bonnie?' asks Jess. She had her babies at home and runs a charity for pregnant women who live on the streets. The charity ensures they get the best chance possible for a safe delivery. She likes to tell stories about how homeless women, who have everything against them, still have wonderful experiences of birth. I have asked her many times not to relay them around me. She gets upset – once she even said I was selfish, which I suppose is true. But I explained about Bonnie hammering down onto my birth canal for hours, before being cut out of me, and how I now have a high chance of prolapse if I stand still for too long. That put an end to the happy birth stories.

'Bonnie is alright. She was ill this week though, and we had a terrible time with her nursery so I was forced to find somewhere new.'

'Oh no,' Yvonne says. And I immediately wish I had lied, because then she does that thing that people do when they are very happy with something in their life, and start recommending it to you over and over again despite you telling them it isn't right. 'I can speak to the ladies at the nursery Florence used to go to, they're so lovely. Oh God, I miss them. I can ask them on Monday.'

'No, don't do that,' I say. 'I've found a new place and I live in Kentish Town anyway, I couldn't take her down there every day.'

'Oh, but it's so good. Seriously, worth the commute,' she says, not listening to me.

'I can't take her to nursery in Queen's Park, I don't live there. I found a new place. She just needs to settle in.' I'm trying to stay calm and rational.

We all stop to order some drinks as the waiter has been hovering over us. The others order a bottle of wine and I order an Arnold Palmer as a special treat.

'Oh, you know who I could ask,' says Sarah to Jess. 'I could ask Mary, the one who runs the place Sammy used to go to, she's got an extension I think, so she has more room.' Jess nods cheerily, as if it's a great idea.

'Where is it?' I ask.

'Oh, just off the park,' Jess says.

'Which park?' I ask, preparing my eyes for an enormous roll.

'Queen's Park,' she and Sarah say in unison.

'I don't live in Queen's Park,' I say. Again.

'Yes, but this place is sooooo good, you could just . . .'

'No. No, I can't just. I don't live there, I don't want to go there. You can stop making suggestions now, I'll work it out.' I don't like being mothered, it makes me uncomfortable. It is a side-effect of never having been mothered. It makes me feel like someone is putting a hot, heavy blanket over my head. Being cared for is very claustrophobic for me.

There is an awkward silence. There are always awkward silences. I actually don't find them that awkward because the thing that I want to stop, has indeed stopped.

'Are you OK, Ruby?' Sarah asks. 'You seem even more tense than usual.'

They all find this funny. I tell them there is nothing wrong, but they insist I share whatever's on my mind.

'Liam said something,' I say, causing them all to take sharp intakes of breath. They have been warned countless times not to talk about Liam. They obviously tried to investigate further after the nightmare of the wedding, but I shut it all down. I shut them down, then I had Bonnie, and I shut the marriage down.

'It's OK. In this particular capacity I'm happy to discuss him, you can all breathe out now,' I say, reassuringly, and they all do. Jess' eyes light up; for some weird reason she reminds me of the mouse.

'He made a comment that has upset me,' I say.

'Uh-oh,' Jess says, darting her eyes at Yvonne who makes a 'yikes' face. 'This is never a good start.'

'What did he say, my love?' Yvonne says gently. She definitely owes me a sympathetic ear.

The time I 'saved' Yvonne was possibly the most remarkable. I walked in on her making herself sick in our third year. She had lost a dramatic amount of weight and insisted it was just the stress and pressure of the final exams. When I walked into the bathroom and caught her, fingers wedged firmly down her throat, she looked at me with a look that maybe a murderer would have given me, had I have walked in on them mid-stab. She was scared, threatened, but also determined to carry on.

She ran to the door and slammed it shut, almost trapping my fingers. I hammered for her to let me in, but she wouldn't. So I sat on the floor in the hallway and talked to her until she calmed down. I told her I could hear everything she was doing, and that if she was sick I would know. Her problem was a secret and she couldn't bear for me to hear her do it,

DAWN O'PORTER

so she slumped on one side of the door, and I sat on the other. We stayed like this for hours not saying anything, while she cried and cried. I never left, not even once. Eventually I coaxed her out. She held me and cried some more, admitting to having done this for years with no one knowing, that she hated herself for it, that she wanted to stop. I sat with her and held her hand while she called her mum and told her. Something that very much came from her. I can't imagine calling my mum when upset, it would be like burning my toe and then jumping into a fire. I forget other people receive comfort and support from their mothers in times of need. I then drove Yvonne to Bristol to her family home, where she stayed for six weeks until she felt like she could return. To my knowledge, vomit-free.

Essentially, she hated her body. Which is why I think I connect with her the most.

'He said something about me never spending any time with Bonnie, and it's really struck a nerve,' I continue.

'Oh,' Sarah says, in an indecipherable way.

'Oh?' I push, noticing Jess throw her a look. Sarah feels confident to carry on.

'I mean, the weekend thing is odd.'

'Odd?' I ask, trying not to snap. I invited this judgement, I know that.

'Yes, Liam has her every weekend. We invite you to things with the kids but you never come because you don't have Bonnie, ever. It's just odd, that's all. For Liam to have her every weekend.'

'But he wants her at the weekends. I have her all week.'

238

'You don't though, do you? She's at nursery,' Sarah continues, like she's been wanting to say this for ages.

'I'm working.'

'I know, we all work. But we see our kids at the weekends, that's the whole point.'

'I work too much, and I'm feeling like shit about it,' Yvonne says. I am grateful for the attention to be on someone else. She is a lawyer. She quickly realised having an art degree was utterly pointless and retrained after Falmouth. I've always been quite impressed by that. It sounds boring as hell but the level of study is extraordinary, and I think it's brilliant that anyone should achieve such a qualification without giving up. She's a clever woman, and maybe my favourite out of the three. Jess works for a women's health charity, while Sarah does something in the arts that is never clear to me no matter how much she explains it. She doesn't make art or sell it, but by the time she's explained that far I've usually switched off.

'I'm actually thinking about going freelance; getting out of the grind, taking on less clients, spending more time with the kids,' Yvonne says, as Sarah and Jess nod. I join in for show. 'They'll have grown up before we know it,' Yvonne continues. 'And I'll look back on these years knowing I missed most of it because I worked so much. I don't want to feel that way.'

'You have to follow your heart,' Sarah says, offering nothing but a cliché.

'I think it's good to be a busy working mum,' I say. 'Sets a good example.'

'I agree,' Yvonne says. 'But I feel distant from the kids. It makes me . . . ' She sets her glass down and puts her hand to her face. She is crying. The other women lay hands on her body, Jess leans in to hug her. I remain still.

'You're a fantastic mum,' Jess says. 'And Ruby's right, it's good that your kids see you as a working woman. Providing for your family.'

'I know, I know. Sorry Ruby, I know this was supposed to be about you—' blubs Yvonne, nodding and crying. 'It's just that when they run to Daddy, and don't come to me with their problems, or when they hurt themselves . . . I'll always blame it on the fact I don't see them from Monday to Friday, you know? Rob picks them up every day. By the time I get home they are in bed. It's not what I want anymore. I feel like I'm serving myself and failing my children.'

'Then you must do what makes you happy. If you think you can do it freelance, then do it,' says Sarah.

I'm quite surprised. I've not seen this side of Yvonne before. She always seems to have it so together these days. I've always been a little jealous, to be honest. We actually share the same feelings, in a way. Liam's relationship with Bonnie is very upsetting for me. I never considered that my issues could apply to other women too.

'Here's to being a shit mum,' I say, raising my Arnold Palmer. They all clink glasses with me, raising their bare arms into the air as our glasses touch. I think we are all happy to move on from that conversation. It has no real resolution. If you are a mother and you work, you will always probably feel like you're letting your kids down in some way. We just need to live with that. I brush my feelings back under the table.

'So Jess, how is all with you?' I ask.

'Oh, you know, my life is just one constant negotiation. Do I choose my husband's happiness or my own needs?'

'Explain?' Yvonne urges.

'Sex,' Jess says. 'Sex and marriage do not go hand in hand.'

'Oh my goodness, a married woman is going to talk about her sex life? Controversial,' Sarah says. And she is right, we have discussed this before. These women used to talk about their sex lives in detail, until they got married and that kind of talk just stopped. A mysterious consequence of getting wed. A sudden respect for the sanctity of a sex life. Jess is obviously keen to smash that code.

'He's so moody. He grumps around the house all annoyed, and I know it's because we don't have enough sex. But why would I want to do it with someone who's being so grumpy? But what always happens, every single time, is I give in and have sex with him just to snap him out of his strop. Afterwards I feel like I let myself down, but he is practically cartwheeling around the house. Such is a woman's plight. Sex with moody husbands. Who signed me up for this shit?'

We all laugh. One thing I really do like about my friends, is how much they make me happy to be single. But also, how because of them, I am not entirely on my own.

Lauren Pearce – Instagram post
@OfficialLP

The image is of Lauren's lower abdomen and thighs, she is wearing a very sexy black body suit. Across her lap we see white silk. A wedding dress? In the other hand she has a glass of champagne.

The caption reads:
Not long now until I get to wear this and say 'I do' to my best friend. Talking of 'I do's, shall we all say it to ourselves today? 'I do' accept myself, and I AM good enough. #Ido #love #selflove #happiness #mentalhealth #Happiness #AD #VeuveClicquot

@kellyclarkvillee: I accept you as my hero!

@helloprettiestone: SHOW US THE DRESS. Oh my God I cannot wait . . .

@selmaslemaslema: Is it true about Gavin? My friend says she knows one of the women. Bless you if it is. I hope you have good people around you.

@elasticbrain: You and Gavin and GOALZ. I wake up every day wishing I was you. How did you get that man? What is the secret?

@harrietgallently: I tried that granola you were promoting. Tasted like my gran's armpit.

9

Beth

It's like when you're hungry and you find yourself standing at the fridge with a mouthful of cake, but don't remember getting there. I'm behind the tree again.

It is lunch time, prime time, and it isn't dark. This is a 'dogging hotspot', I know that now, I read it online.

A car passes but doesn't stop. I see a little movement behind a bush on the other side of the clearing and I tell myself I am safe, even though maybe I am not. Is that part of the thrill? I'm still trying to work that out. People would hear me if I screamed.

The rustle moves a little closer. Maybe it's the couple?

Another car drives past. It doesn't stop. Then a man appears from behind a tree opposite me. He is wearing a mask. It should be terrifying, but the mask only covers half of his face and it is a kid's mask, some kind of animal. Maybe a fox? Yes, a fox. If I wasn't so horny I'd think he was stupid. But I read that a lot of people wear masks. It's an anonymity thing, and

I think that is fair enough. I try not to pay it too much attention.

The man stands in the clearing and holds his hand out, as if asking me to join him. I shake my head. I'm not here for that. I see there are other people behind the trees. He puts his hand out again. This time I wonder if I should. I was led here by my sexual desire, I am craving something new. I deserve to have my libido acknowledged and appreciated. It weirdly feels like a safer space than my own bedroom. I don't want the complexities of emotion; I want the satisfaction of sex. I come out from behind the tree and walk over to the man.

He takes my hand and leads me to a tree stump. There are definitely people watching us. He smiles at me. I wish I could see his eyes. He is tall, slim. He could be very handsome, I wish I could see. But then he could be very ugly. So maybe it is best that I can't.

I now can't imagine him any other way than ugly.

He begins to undo his jeans. Another rustle behind a tree. Tommy appears in my mind. My baby. Michael too. Still my husband. Reality strikes.

'I can't, I'm sorry,' I say. The man is getting closer to me with his hard penis in his hand. He stays still, and puts up no resistance, but he continues to masturbate himself, as if that will change my mind.

'I'm sorry,' I repeat, shaking my head. 'This isn't who I am.' I walk away slowly, wondering if he will jump on me and make me go through with it. But he doesn't. I pick up the pace and I run as fast as I can towards Lauren's house. It's the only destination I know, but obviously I can't just pop in so I go into a local pub and order myself a drink.

'Gin and tonic, please.' Just the one is OK, I'm craving it. Tommy's next feed will be a bottle anyway. And I need a moment. I have things I need to think about. These feelings are not right. Do I have post-natal depression? Is that why I suddenly hate my husband and want to have sex with strangers?

But I don't feel sad. I just feel out of control of myself. Part of the responsibility of being a parent is keeping yourself safe. To think what could have happened. How horrible would it be for Tommy to live his life knowing that his mother was bludgeoned to death in a park whilst being raped by a tall man with a fox mask on. I can't go back there. That is not the answer.

I can't believe this is me. I was always a sexual woman. Some might say, too sexual. I lost my virginity at fifteen; not too early, not too late. Boys were never scary to me. They liked me, I liked them. I was a good flirt, a good shag. I didn't expect relationships from sex and was happy to have the fun. My parents loved me, my influences were good, my friends were not wild. It was all good fun until I got to university and had a boyfriend with a strange quirk. He used to leave money on my bedside table after sex. I'd tell him I didn't want it. I'd insist he took it back. But he made sure that one way or another I took it. By either hiding it in my bag or throwing it at me then running away.

'You're my little whore,' he would say, as if the whole notion of paying for sex really turned him on. We spent most of our time high and in bed, so there wasn't much outside of that to judge him by. The sex was good, not too rough. He occasionally said things like, 'You are so worth the money,' or, 'You could charge double.' But he wasn't mean to me and he didn't force me into anything emotional or physical that I didn't want to do. He just insisted on paying me, that was his fantasy. And I was a broke student, so in the end just gave up fighting it and took the cash. I even held off on dumping him before Christmas because I had to pay to get home for the holiday.

It wasn't until I was about twenty-six that I realised that made me a prostitute.

I battled with the repercussions of that for some time. Feeling dirty and ashamed. Like I should have just broken up with him, like I should never have spent the money, and posted it through his letter box instead. I always said to myself that if I ever had the money I would give it all back to him. It was such a small amount, really. About £300 in total, I only went out with him for a couple of months. But at that age, it felt like a lifetime and £300 to a skint student was a lot. I could pay him back tomorrow if I wanted to. But I have no idea where he lives, and I certainly don't want to ask people if they know and draw attention to it all. Also, I was so high for most of that time that I actually have no recollection of his surname. Sometimes I wonder if I ever even knew it.

I can't change the past. It's always quite surprising to me how things feel terrible in retrospect, but at the time they really don't. A nice guy, fun, non-violent, a weird sex thing, money was exchanged that paid for my family's Christmas presents. It didn't feel wrong. But often, when you are living an experience, and things seem OK, you really don't worry about what is wrong with it. Especially at that age. I didn't think about my future when I was twenty-one. I didn't think, 'If I take that twenty pounds from the side of the bed, it will haunt me for years.' It didn't haunt me at the time, surely that is all that matters? So, I always try to put myself back there, when that dark and heavy thump of anxiety and regret tries to keep me awake at night, I tell myself it is OK to have been questionable. I also remind myself that people are out there doing actually terrible things. Rape, murder, fraud, betrayal. My experience was nothing like that, but still, it challenges my self-respect. And that is very annoying.

I've always thought my marriage was quite normal, until recently. Maybe I'll look back on it one day, and not believe I was in it. It's feeling less and less like where I should be every single day.

I realise I have finished my drink. Whoops. I order another one.

When I met Michael, a safe, sexually unambitious man who didn't demand anything weird in the bedroom, I felt like maybe he redeemed me. He was vanilla, I was absolved. Most women have had some kind of relationship they are not proud of. A one-night stand, a guy who you stayed with who got you to do kinky stuff you weren't even into. An affair. The list goes on. Well mine was inoffensive really. No one got hurt. But it left me with shame. Michael took it away. I had my own business, I didn't rely on him for anything. And he was

249

gentle and I felt relieved that my deviant days were over. The past is the past. Everyone is allowed to have dubious stories that make no sense to anyone like they made sense to you at the time. That's called living. I was adventurous at that age, I was wild. I have spent most of my adult life trying to justify my actions.

I ended up seeing a therapist for a few years in my late twenties because I felt so disgusted by myself. I never knew if it was a comedown from all the drugs I took at uni, or a reaction to how that relationship made me feel. Either way, therapy helped. My therapist told me it was OK to have done those things. That all I have to do is give myself permission to have acted in that way, give myself permission to have been young and unbothered by the consequences. She said all I was doing was role play, the transaction was not important. I was neutral back then; if it wasn't hurtful at the time, then why should it be hurtful now? She was right. At the time it was OK. Marrying a man contaminated by innocence also helped. I have to beg the question, would Michael have been the man I chose, if I wasn't trying to mask my shame?

I don't know the answer to that. As women, we are raised to believe all men want to screw us. When one doesn't, especially when it's the man you love, it's incredibly confusing. It feels like the problem must be me.

Until now. Michael isn't making me happy. He isn't who I thought he was. But then look at me; a middle-aged woman regretting my past and present over a gin and tonic while I avoid work and my child. As if that is going to make anything better. I finish my second drink.

A man heads over and sits next to me at the bar. He orders a beer. He didn't need to sit in that chair, there are plenty of others to choose from.

'Waiting for someone?' he asks me.

'No,' I reply. Wishing I'd said yes. I really want some time on my own.

'Drinking alone in the afternoon? That's usually a sign of one thing.'

'That I'm a single woman out gagging for sex and should therefore be approached by men I don't know and hassled until I give it up?' I say, accusing him, when actually it's kind of true. I am gagging for it.

He is around fifty, annoyingly handsome, well dressed in quality casual clothes and he blatantly wasn't hitting on me. I realise that immediately.

'I wasn't going to say that, actually. I was going to say that drinking alone in the afternoon usually means you have something you should be talking about. But sure, I'm a man, so presume the worst.' He picks up his drink and walks away to a table in the corner. I feel like an idiot.

'Hey,' I say, calling him back. He stays where he is, so I go over. 'I'm sorry, that wasn't fair.' He looks up at me.

'I have a daughter. You just did what I've always told her she should do. So I guess I should just sit over here and shut up.'

'You don't need to shut up. Again, I'm sorry. I'm not having the best day.'

'So maybe you do have something you need to talk about?' He pushes a chair out with his foot. And gestures to the barman to get me another drink. I don't turn it down. 'Or we can sit here for a few hours, play backgammon and pretend our real lives aren't happening?'

'That sounds like a really nice idea.'

I guess I'll have to pump and dump.

Coming out of a pub drunk when it's still light is like walking down a tunnel towards a fleet of trucks, all with their head-lights shining right into your face. I'd maybe fall to the ground if the man wasn't holding me up. I never caught his name. It's not like you can ask again after an hour of sitting with someone in a pub, is it?

He remembers mine.

'Beth, I'll hail you a cab,' he says. I shout the word 'Booooooring' like a thirteen-year-old girl who has just been told to button her top up to cover her cleavage.

'No?' he asks me. 'Then what do you want to do?'

I manage to straighten my legs and hold them still enough to put my face opposite his. My head is like a balloon tied to a stick, it keeps flopping down towards the ground. I haven't been drunk in over a year. I just chugged four gin and tonics in one hour. That's a lot for me right now.

'I want to kiss you,' I say. 'I want to kiss you on your mouth.' I manage to keep my head steady enough to make my first attempt. He pulls away, looks up the street and seems a bit cross.

'What are you doing?' he says, like I just tried to hit him.

'Sorry, I thought we . . . ' My shame taps me on the shoulder. Another man who thinks I'm a giant sexual oaf.

'It's OK. But what about this?'

He holds up my left hand, he's referring to my wedding ring.

'Oh that,' I say, looking at my ring like it's a scumbag ex-boyfriend. 'This is what I think to that.' I take it off and throw it into my bag. 'Does that bother you, because it doesn't bother me?'

'No. I understand that feeling,' he says.

'Take me to your house,' I demand.

He looks both ways and puts his arm under mine to help me. We're at his front door within a few minutes.

'Wow, you're really rich,' I say, as we walk in. Which is rude. I'm drunk and behaving like a student. It's a house in Highgate. The entrance is beautiful, ivy growing up the front of the building. The living room he leads me into doesn't feel like a bachelor pad. 'You have great taste for a man.'

'My ex-wife did most of this. She didn't want the house when we split. She wanted all my money though.'

'What a bitch,' I say, smiling. It's a joke, and thankfully he gets it. This is OK.

He is at a little bar pouring us some drinks. He hands one to me and I drink it quickly before reality dares to remind me who I really am.

'Look at us, two strangers alone in a house together. I've had enough booze to pretend to be someone else for a bit, have you?' I say, wiggling around flirtatiously.

'I don't know if I need to pretend to be someone else, but I'm certainly happy you're here,' he says, with all the assurance of a man in his fifties who doesn't have personal or intimacy issues. I put my drink down and sit on the sofa. He does the same. I channel Risky and throw myself at him.

His hands are stroking me and squeezing me. Touching me more passionately than my husband ever has. It feels unreal, like it's someone else's body, but it isn't, it's mine. This is what I want and need. It's what I deserve. It feels good. I feel good.

I take off my jeans and lie on the sofa. He goes down on me. Michael hasn't gone down on me since before we were married. The last time he did it, he stopped before I came and said he just couldn't stand the taste. Why am I just realising how cruel that was? I have a gorgeous vagina. This man is reminding me of that. It's like I'm a bowl of warm chocolate and he's eating his way out of me. He's so good at it. I have my hands on his head. I want this to be filthy. I come very quickly. I'm not done.

I bring his head back up to my face and lick and kiss his lips. He starts to undo his jeans. I don't want a quick fuck on a sofa in the missionary position. If he comes quickly and that's all that happens, it will have been for nothing. I need more from this. I pull away from him and reach for my bag. I almost fall off the sofa but he catches me. He must think I am getting a condom, but I'm not. I have a little pot of Vaseline lip balm. I tell him to take off his jeans, and I smother his penis with the Vaseline. He tells me I'm 'so hot, so sexy'. I look him in the eye and ask him if he's feeling naughty. He tells me he is.

I am a sexual woman and he is so lucky to have me on his sofa. But I am getting what I want out of this. And I'm going to enjoy every minute of it.

I turn myself around, and when he tries to enter me I guide

him upwards. I think of Risky. I want to be more Risky. 'I want you in my arse,' I tell him over my shoulder. He hesitates, but not for long. He undoes my bra. It's a nursing bra and it falls to the sofa. My breasts full of milk, my baby at home, Michael. I get those thoughts out of my head. I deserve this. He gently pushes his penis into my bottom at my request. I've never had anal sex before, I don't know what brought me to it in this moment. The need to feel dirty? In control? Desired? Or just that my vagina belongs to someone else? If I do it this way, maybe it isn't so bad? Or maybe I just need to reclaim my slutty side.

The man is gentle but passionate. He pulls my hair and scratches his nails down my back. As he starts to ramp up, and I know this will end soon, I tell him to go harder. 'Harder, harder,' I say, and he slams into me. Air popping from my anus, making fart sounds that I don't allow to bother me. It doesn't matter. It doesn't hurt. I thought it might. He is so turned on, and that makes me feel so good. This is as much for my head as my body, I need to be ravished. He pulls out and comes all over my bottom. He falls back onto the sofa and pulls his shirt over his penis. Why did he do that, was there poo on it? I look down on the sofa, there are huge wet patches underneath me from where my breasts have leaked. I'm trying to stay in the moment and keep reality at bay, but it's hitting me now. What am I doing? This is not OK.

'Oh God,' I say, getting to my feet. 'I'm so sorry, I don't know what that was about.'

'What that was about? You being so sexy?'

'Yes, that. Me asking you to do that, that isn't who I am.'

'It's OK.'

'It's not OK. Oh God.' I realise the milk is pouring from my nipples down my tummy.

'Wait, are you lactating?' he says, throwing his t-shirt at me to catch the drips. 'How old did you say your kid was again?'

I don't remember what I told him.

'Oh God. Please, I need to go, I don't know what I was thinking.'

Another small but audible air pocket pops out of my bum. They are not actual farts, but still. This is not ideal.

'Here,' the man says, passing me my soaking wet, heavy nursing bra.

'Thank you,' I say, as I turn around and put it on. I get dressed. He politely doesn't watch me. I suddenly don't feel sexy. I feel flabby, pale, and like I want to hide.

'Are you going to be OK?' he asks me, kindly. 'I wouldn't have done that if you hadn't asked.'

'Will I be OK? I don't know. I just need to go home. I'm sorry for all of this. I have a baby and a husband, and I don't know what I'm doing.'

He stands up. He puts his hands on my arms. 'It's OK. OK? Everyone has the right to act out of character sometimes. Don't beat yourself up about it. You're OK, and this is between us. It doesn't have to collapse your world.'

He's a really nice person.

'My husband and I are having problems,' I tell him. 'I have a baby. He is four months old. I work full time. I'm not sure I'm coping with everything as well as I thought I was.'

'Being a parent is hard. Don't beat yourself up, OK? We can only do the best we can.'

'I'm not sure this is me doing my best, do you?' I look down at my boobs and laugh. He does too.

Thank God this happened with him.

'Maybe not. But rather than give yourself a hard time for what you did, try and fix the reason you did it.'

'Your daughter is a lucky girl,' I say.

'Yeah, maybe. Maybe not. Here.' He hands me my trousers and starts straightening the cushions on the couch. I wonder what happened with him and his wife. I know people can't be judged on one encounter, but right now I feel like if I was married to someone like him, I'd never let him go.

'Thank you for not making this worse,' I say, sincerely.

'Thank you allowing me to fulfil a fantasy I never thought I would.'

'Really?'

'Yup, never gone there before. Big box ticked here so please leave feeling charitable.' He smiles again. 'Can I get you a car?'

'No, I'll be OK. Thank you.' I kiss him on the cheek and leave.

I've done it now. I've cheated on my husband. I am that wife.

Lauren Pearce – Instagram post
@OfficialLP

The image is of Lauren's left hand, a diamond glistening in the light. It is laid over a man's hand, presumably Gavin's.

The caption reads:
Days to go. I love this man. Feeling so so lucky. Commitment, together . . . bring on forever!! I dedicated my life to you, my love. Is it Saturday yet??? #LOVE

@genedder: You deserve happiness, you bring nothing but light.

@happyguuuuuu: You help me get through my day. You bring such joy. Keep being you!

@nailedforeveryours: The DREAM

@yellagain: More pictures of Gavin please!!!! Can't wait to see your dress

@unitednotabit: Excuse me while I vomit into my shoe.

Beth

'What happened to you, you look like you've been dragged through a bush backwards,' Michael says to me as I walk into the house. The word 'backwards' rebounds in my head. All I hear is 'anal, anal, anal'. It's like he knows.

I feel like I just murdered someone and buried their body. This secret will kill me. I cheated. I never thought I would actually do it, but I did. I am that person.

'Lauren wouldn't stop talking so I couldn't pump. Look, I'm leaking everywhere. I have to go and shower,' I say, calmly.

Michael looks at my soaking chest when I open my jacket and looks suitably horrified by the mess of it.

'You're drenched.'

'I know. I missed Tommy so much today, I think it sent my milk supply into turbo speed and I had no time to pump.'

'OK, well go and have a shower and I'll bring the pump to the bedroom and leave it out for you, OK?'

He is being nice. Which is confusing. I need him to remain horrible now, because of what I just did. I rebelled against a husband who was mean. I need him to stay mean.

In the shower, I let the warm water wash away the milk on my body and the sperm from my back. I have an uncomfortable sensation in my bum. It's a little sore.

I keep trying to think of the man's name. Robert? Peter? I wish I could remember.

'The pump is ready for you, I screwed the bottles on,' says Michael, opening the door a little but not coming in. He feels like a stranger.

'Thank you,' I say, turning the shower off. I could have stayed in it for days, washing away what I did. It's a shame you can't shower away your feelings.

In the bedroom, Michael has plugged in the pump and left it all ready for me, along with a glass of water and a biscuit on the bedside table. I tie the towel around my waist and hold the funnels in place. Sitting on the bed, in front of a full-length mirror, I watch the bottles fill with milk. It feels so good to get it out. My boobs decrease in size. I put the full bottles on the bedside table and then lie back, putting my hands over my face as I start to sob.

'Beth, are you OK?' Michael says, coming in to check on me. He takes a towel off the back of the bedroom door and lays it over my chest. I'm too tired to rip it off and tell him I have the right to bare my breasts in my own house.

'I'm just tired. It's been a big few weeks,' I say, wanting him to go away. I need to be alone. Why am I never alone?

'I'm sure you are. Well, the wedding is at the weekend, and then you can take some time off, and be with Tommy. You're doing great, OK? I'm proud of you.'

What is happening? He was supposed to be cruel to make this easier.

'You're proud of me?' I say, looking at him through my fingers.

'Yes, I'm proud of you. It takes a lot to have a baby and then get right back to work. But you've done it, and Tommy and I are proud of you. And I'm sorry, OK? I'm sorry for what I said, I know how painful that must have been.'

He smiles and lays his hand across my belly. He kisses me on the face. I'm so confused.

'Kiss me,' I ask him. I get a peck on the lips. 'No, kiss me,' I say again, pulling his face towards mine. He is trying to get away, but I am holding his head so hard he can't. I keep kissing him, regardless of him not wanting to. Eventually he breaks away from me and stands up.

'What is wrong with you?' he says, a look of disgust on his face. 'I just said sorry. I hoped we could talk and you turned it into that again. It's like you're a sex addict, it's all you think about. And have you been drinking? I can smell it on you.'

There isn't much point in saying anything. I just lie still, allowing his words to thump down onto me, like I'm a pavement in the rain. I'm a cheating ex-whore, married to a man who finds me repulsive. Craving sex from strangers and demanding sodomy in nice houses. All the while selling the concept of love and matrimony to a woman who, if rumour has it right, is being cheated on. I am the worst.

'Yes, I've been drinking,' I tell him, rolling my head to the side. He can pour his judgement all over me. I don't care anymore.

'It seems like such a waste, but I'll throw this down the sink,' says Michael, holding the bottles of breast milk, looking very cross. 'Drink your water, eat your biscuit and get some sleep.'

He leaves. When the door closes, I throw the glass of water at it and scream.

10

Ruby

I stop by the park on my way to my wax appointment. Ross is sitting solemnly on the bench. It isn't clean. He has his top off and is sweating. He looks sadder than usual.

'Are you alright?' I ask him as I sit down.

'I forgot the wipes. I'm so stupid,' he says, looking at the bench with disgust, like the pigeons made their mess to spite him. I check my bag, but I don't have any either.

'Bloody pigeons, they have no respect,' I say, smiling at him. He manages a little one back. 'You look like you have more on your mind than usual?'

'Yeah, I have a big weekend coming up. Family stuff, I always get anxious. But I'll be alright. Where's Bonnie today?'

'Oh, she's at nursery this morning. I was actually hoping that I would see you. I wanted to thank you.'

'Thank me? What on earth for?'

'For saying all the right things.'

He laughs to himself. 'Well that would be a first.'

'I needed to meet someone like you. You've given me a perspective that I think I needed.'

'All problems are relative. You can't compare everything to the death of a child.'

'True, but it certainly made me assess what is important. Like I said, I needed it, so thank you.'

'You're welcome. I guess it's good that something positive can come from all this,' he says, dropping his head again. He is so heavy today. Of course he has days like this. I'm not sure I would ever get out of bed. 'My wife doesn't know about this bench,' he tells me, as if that bothers him.

'Really, why?' I ask, quite shocked by that. The bench should be for everyone who misses Verity, surely?

'She brushed her death under the carpet. She didn't want to talk about it. All I wanted to do was talk about it, I couldn't stop. I've seen a therapist twice a week since it happened, just so I can go on and on. I don't understand how she couldn't. She didn't want a bench. She thought it would be a place to wallow, rather than a place to feel connected to Verity. This bench feels like my lifeline some days.'

'It's a lovely thing to have,' I say, feeling a need to reassure him that she was wrong.

'I used to bring the girls to the park. You see it a lot, don't you? Dads on Saturdays with their kids. That was me. This was our favourite spot. I went ahead and organised the bench without telling my wife. It's my special place where I can be with my daughter. I find it so peaceful here.'

'It is.'

We sit for a moment looking out. I notice the time and realise I better get going.

'I have to get to an appointment,' I say, standing up. 'Thanks. Again. I hope your weekend is OK and not too stressful. Families are hard.'

'They are. Bye Ruby.'

'Bye.'

Something tells me he'll be there a while today.

I have a wax appointment at ten a.m. I travel across London on the underground at rush hour to get there, I am now very hot. I underestimated the weather and wore velvet instead of cotton. The waiting room is packed, everyone is young and, to my self-deprecating eye, extremely beautiful. I walk purposefully to the receptionist. She is young, too.

'Yes, I have an appointment at ten,' I say, feeling like an old hag.

'Great, and your name?'

'Ruby.'

'Ruby . . . yup, there you are. OK, you're in for a full body today?'

I can't believe she just did that. Any number of these people could have heard. I can't speak. I just stand still, like a pillock.

'Is that right, Ruby? A full-body wax?'

Oh my God, she did it again. Is this woman thick?

She needs an answer from me. There are two women in the queue behind me, why is this place so busy?

I am so desperate for this wax. I have to be brave. I nod.

'OK great, you'll be with Pete today, he'll be right out.'

'Pardon?' I ask, I must have misheard her.

'Pete, he will be your technician today.'

'Pete? Is that short for Petra?'

'No, Peter. He does our full-body waxes. You'll love him, he's very quick.'

'He's a bloody man!'

'Oh, God yeah, sorry. Don't worry, he's gay.'

She looks at me as if she just solved all my problems.

'I can't do that, is there a woman available?' I ask. I have done an enormous amount of mental preparation to come here today and I have found peace with using a new technician, but not Pete.

'No, sorry,' she says, getting impatient. 'Will you take a seat?'

I sit on the sofa next to a young woman in a short skirt. I look at her legs – not a single hair in sight. Why is she even here? If she knew what was going on underneath my dress, she would be sick. I might be sick.

'Ruby,' says a man who I presume is Pete. He is about five foot six, blond, also not hairy. I can't put myself through this.

'Sorry, I've changed my mind,' I say, getting up. 'I don't need it after all.'

'Are you sure?' Pete asks, confused. I tell him I am very sure. Instead, he calls for a Hannah. Hannah jumps up and says 'Yay' and they kiss on each cheek and disappear into the back. To wax her perfect fanny, no doubt.

This is not the salon for me.

I've been waxing like clockwork for more than twenty years

and have never missed a cycle, but it's like the universe is conspiring against me.

Due to the failed wax attempt, I pick Bonnie up at nursery after two hours, just as Maria insisted. It gives me a little spring in my step, to do something that suggests I am actually a reasonable parent. Maria said she didn't cry as much this time, but she refused to play with the other kids, saying they were babies and that she wanted more three-year-olds. Maria said there are other three-year-olds who come to the school, but they are all on holiday.

'All of them, in the middle of a term?' I asked, in my most accusatorial voice. She nodded and told me I could only bring her for two hours a day until she was settled. It's too hard on the other kids when Bonnie loses it the way that she does, apparently.

Bonnie clung onto me when I came to pick her up. I'm trying not to get used to it, because she will no doubt hate me again soon. The second we were out of the building I covered her hands with anti-bacterial gel. That nursery is a Petri dish. The toilet still isn't fixed. It's a real dump of a place, I need to find somewhere else.

I bring Bonnie to the park. It's either this or more TV at home.

I look over at the bench with the plaque on it. Ross was so upset today, I wish I'd sat with him for longer. If I'd have known what a disaster my appointment was going to be, I would have. I really enjoy seeing him. A homeless man is sitting on it eating half a sandwich that he found in the bin.

He eats quickly, dropping crumbs on the floor that pigeons gather round his feet to eat. He smiles at the pigeons, like they are his friends, then breaks up the final bite of the bread and throws it down for them. By the look on his face, he got as much pleasure from that as he did the food in his belly. The homeless man realises I am looking at him and he smiles at me. I smile back, and even offer him a little wave. He does the same. Poor man, I wonder where he will sleep tonight. I think Ross would be happy to know that this man has found a moment's peace on Verity's bench.

Bonnie is in the shrubbery looking for the mouse. If she finds it, I will scream and we will leave.

The homeless man gets up and moves on. The bench is now empty, other than the pigeons that are walking across it, picking up the last few crumbs that he dropped. I walk over and shoo them away. They have pooed all over it. Ross won't be very happy about that. Using the wet wipes that I picked up on the way here, I clean all of the bird mess off the bench.

Bonnie is now on her hands and knees underneath a hydrangea bush shouting, 'Mousey, come on mousey. Mousey, mousey.' It would be cute, if she weren't trying to draw the attention of a rodent. I throw a smile in her direction, she doesn't catch it. I spend so much of my time regretting having a child, and fantasising about how much easier my life would be if my only responsibility was hair removal. But the idea of anything happening to her is so unimaginable. Ross has given me a perspective that should have been obvious all along. I know how it feels to have someone I love taken away from me, so why wasn't losing my dad lesson enough? The

Lauren Pearce – Instagram post
@OfficialLP

The picture is of Lauren sitting in a gazebo in a garden. She is surrounded by Bianca roses. She is wearing white lacy underwear, her hair is perfectly tonged.

The caption reads:
Today I woke up and smelt the flowers. Feeling like the luckiest girl alive. When life gives you lemons, surround yourself in roses. That's the expression, right? #TWO MORE SLEEPS

@wellyturnips: your life . . . it's perfect. Lucky, lucky girl!

@MikeyinDisguise: Show us your mum again. I love a MILF.

@harriethartly: Looks, love and millions. You nailed it.

@bettyblack: SHOW US THE DRESS!!!!!!!!!!!!

@iamtheonebutyouarethetwo: Gavin could have had any woman in the country but he chose you. I find this FASCINATING. Not being mean, you're nice and everything, but Cheryl Cole is single again . . . just saying!

@garindagale: So bored of the me me me posts. Disappointing lack of #realness. UNFOLLOW.

Ruby

Even though I have made versions of the same dress over and over again in the past twenty years, I like the ritual of starting from scratch each time. Step one is always measuring myself, just to be sure. I start with my bust: thirty-five centimetres. My waist: twenty-seven and a half centimetres. My hips: thirty-eight centimetres. Just as I was at university. I knew I hadn't changed, but it's nice to see the numbers. A satisfying visual after all the hard work.

I measure as a size six, but because of my height I generally have to buy size eight clothes. Which is why making my own works much better for me. Also, finding dresses with the level of coverage I like usually involves me looking like a frump, or having some random key-hole detail somewhere pivotal, like on the back above the zip. A pointless and very annoying detail when you have a hairy back and shoulders.

On top of this, I have quite long arms. I need a thirty-three-centimetre sleeve, which most brands do not accommodate. My dress pattern is unique to my body and satisfies both my need to be protected and my desire to be stylish.

A while ago I purchased a large roll of slightly stretchy crimson velvet. It's a vibrant colour. I have been saving it for a special occasion. Maybe Lauren Pearce's wedding is that occasion? I realise I won't be at the main event, that I will be in a back room working – and I'm relieved that I won't have to socialise – but that doesn't mean I can't step up with my dress, does it? The best thing about my design is that the velvet is very soft and comfortable. I could sleep in it. Not that I would. But working for an entire day in it is not a problem. The only issue is the heat. I'll find a way to deal with that on the day.

I cut a pattern following the outline of the black one that I made in high school and cut the fabric to size with my traditional shears. I do this every time, I really enjoy the process. I stitch it all together on my Singer sewing machine, putting a light lining in, to avoid any friction. I add a slightly larger puff on each shoulder, for some extra drama. The sleeves are a little longer with tighter elastic so they don't ride up at all. I will be fully hirsute at this wedding, and whether I am alone in a room or not, I cannot take the risk of exposing myself.

All in all, the dress takes me four and a half hours to make. It's an evening of my life well spent, to produce an outfit that will have me living confidently outside of my house. I put it on and look at myself in the full-length mirror in my bedroom. The colour is exciting and the fit is perfect. I'll wear this one a lot, I am sure.

I stand staring at myself in the mirror. It's never an easy thing to do. Although if I force myself to be honest, I am not an unattractive woman. I'm too thin, I'm too pale. I wear my attitude like a coat of armour, it warns people away. But my hair is long, the curls are thick. From my advertising days I know that it is desirable. I have deep brown eyes and the bone structure of someone who means business. In a dress like this, I pass as good looking. With my own style. In my own way. Which, when I really break it down, I think maybe I actually quite like.

Beth

'Boss, what is wrong with you?'

Risky's voice is there in the background somewhere. My stare stays fixed to the window.

'Beth? Beth? Seriously what's going on with you today?'

She is right next to my desk now. She is looking at me like I am a child who just did an emotionally charged pee on the floor. Annoyed, but with sympathy and concern for what made me do it.

'Sorry,' I say, snapping out of my daze. 'Sorry, just a lot on my mind.'

'I know. A four-month-old and a major celebrity wedding in two days. Yeah, you've got a lot on. What do you need? Can I order you food? Download a podcast? Massage your feet?'

I look at her like she is joking. She isn't.

'Oh, nothing. I just need to get through it. OK, I'm back in the room. What did I miss?'

Risky is thinking. She likes to fix things. She is wondering how to help me survive the next few days. I am wondering the same thing.

'I've got it,' she says, clapping her hands. 'I know what to do. Get your things, I'm taking you to the spa.'

'The spa? No Risky, that's a massive waste of time. We have so much to do.'

'Yes, we do, but we can work there. There's a warm floor you lie on, and Wifi. Come on, I am insisting.'

'Who's the boss here?' I ask, not moving.

'You are, and that is the problem. You're not taking care of yourself. Come on, if we get there before lunch it will be quieter. Chop chop.'

She is standing over by the door now. I clearly have no choice. And maybe a foot rub from a professional would be nice.

'What is this place?' I ask as we arrive. It's not like the spas I have been to before, where people walk around in towelling robes and uncomfortable slippers, sipping cucumber water and eating almonds and dried fruit while panpipe music fills the room as people wait to be called in for their overpriced treatments.

'It's a Korean spa,' Risky says, confidently. 'Heaven.'

We pay at a reception desk. It's very cheap. I have to fill in a form – Risky has been before so doesn't need to. It asks if I am breast feeding or pregnant and Risky urges me to lie.

'It's just a hygiene thing,' she says. 'Just get out if you start lactating in the hot tub.'

'Oh, I probably won't go in it anyway, I don't have my swimsuit,' I tell her.

'Swimsuit? Boss, this is a Korean spa, you have to be naked. That's the point.'

'What?' I ask as she hands my form back into reception. 'Naked? Are there men in there?'

'No, just women. Come on, you'll love it.'

I stand still. I don't want to get naked with other women. I don't want to get naked with Risky. I don't want to. I just don't.

'Boss, come on. You need this,' she says, making a scene. The two Korean ladies behind reception are looking at me like I am pathetic. Now I do want to emotionally pee on the floor.

'Can I wear a towel?' I ask Risky, following her reluctantly.

'Not in the water!'

In the changing rooms, I am first struck by the absolute lack of luxury, relaxing vibes or glamour. In each locker there is a thin cotton robe and some rubber slippers. The lighting is stark. Risky strips immediately like she is running down a beach towards the sea and can't pause or she'll chicken out. She throws her clothes into the locker and, just like that, my assistant is naked in front of me. Her young, tight body, unharmed by slow metabolism or childbirth. Small breasts sitting perfectly on her chest, nipples so dark they look like raisins. A vagina like a Jackson 5 hairdo. Up the sides of her body, stretch marks run like snail trails across her hips. She isn't perfect, but she is utterly beautiful.

'OK, your turn,' she says, hands on hips, her legs slightly apart. 'Boss, you have to stop staring at my vagina or I'll have to file a sexual misconduct case against you.'

'God, I'm so sorry,' I say, shaking my face and pulling myself together as I begin to undress. First my maternity jeans, then

my shirt. I fold them neatly, putting them into my locker. My
heart is thumping at the thought of removing my underwear.

'Boss, seriously. We have a wedding in two days. As much
as I want you to relax we can't be here all day.'

I reach around and undo my bra. It's OK, Risky sees my
boobs every day when I pump. I fold it up and put it under
my clothes in the locker. I then slowly pull down my knickers,
and pop them in too. And so here I am, naked in a changing
room. A tall skinny woman with a nice tan storms in. I grab
the robe and put it on.

'OK, you ready?' Risky asks.

'My body has changed a lot. I could have done with some
mental preparation before I got naked in front of people,
that's all.'

'You look amazing,' Risky tells me. 'I love this place. Women
of all shapes and sizes walking around like the fashion industry
never even happened. I love it. My mum and I come here all
the time.'

I look around and see that she is right. A large black lady
is sitting on the edge of a small pool. Her extra-long breasts
dangling over the rolls of her belly. She is chatting and laughing
with her friend who is immersed in water. On the other side
of the room, standing in line for a shower, is a very thin lady,
maybe in her seventies. She has short white hair, her breasts
are mere flaps of skin with nipples. Her knees have hoods,
her neck wobbles when she moves. Her pubic hair is straight
and grey. To her right, there's a short woman, maybe in her
forties. Her red hair is the exact colour of her pubes, and goes
down nearly as far as her knees.

All of these women are so different, yet they are all the same. I take off my robe and hang it on a hook.

'OK, I love this one. It's really hot and the minerals in the water are purifying and make your skin feel so soft,' Risky says, stepping down into a small pool with steam rising from it. She respectfully looks away as I lower my naked body into the water.

'This is very nice,' I say, settling in.

'I told you so!' she says, proudly.

After a few moments, the large black lady comes to get in. I'm not so down with the etiquette and as I smile at her, it is impossible for me to ignore the pinkness of her labia as it gets closer to my face. It sinks under the water and her breasts float up like life rafts in front of her.

'I could never drown with these attached to me,' she says, smiling.

Risky kicks me under the water because she finds it funny.

'Aren't women amazing?' she says, leaning over to me.

'Yes,' I say, feeling perfect in my skin for the first time in a very long time. 'Yes, we absolutely are.'

Ruby

Liam is here as he's agreed to take Bonnie for the afternoon. Maria is insisting on just two hours a day at the nursery, just until she starts to settle, and I simply cannot keep her home any longer to watch TV while I work. I might not be the one getting married on Saturday, but it is a huge event and I can't bear the idea of being surrounded by beautiful people whilst feeling so grotesque myself. I have made yet another wax appointment. Who knows how it will go this time!

I told Liam the nursery is insisting on a long induction process. He has no reason to question me further and isn't suspicious as to why we can't do full days. I have never lied about our child's welfare before, so he fully trusts me. I have warned him that Bonnie misses her friends, which is why she keeps complaining. I realise I need to find somewhere else, and I am also working on that. I can't do any of the things I need to do with Bonnie home, hence him taking some time off work to help. He's very generous like that. Never complaining about being with Bonnie. I've only recently realised the amount of effort it must be for him to have her every weekend. That doesn't leave much time for him to have for himself. Or to find a new relationship. He's never mentioned anyone else, and neither has Bonnie. I can only hope and presume that there isn't anyone. Which is good. I'm not ready for that.

'So what are your plans?' I ask him, as I finish putting Bonnie's shoes on and zip up her jacket. I'm still quite upset about what he said the other day, but I am trying not to show it because what is making me most upset is that I think he is right and I'm not sure what to do about it.

'We'll go get some food. Then head to the park. Or we could go to Pret and get a picnic. Shall we go feed the ducks, Bon Bon?'

'Yeeeaaaaah,' she says, sounding so joyful and cute that both of us smile.

'OK, well be good. Home for six please, and no sweets. I don't want to be dealing with a sugar rush tonight, I'll work after I've put her down so I need bedtime to go well.'

I don't know why I say this, because actually I have finished all the work that Rebecca sent through. I got it all done early, so I could go for this wax.

'So you're very busy then?' he asks me, lingering a little longer than usual.

'Yes. I have some pictures to do, but mostly gearing up to a big job next weekend. I'm going to a wedding. Lauren Pearce, you know the . . . I mean, I don't know what she is, model I guess? She's getting married.'

'Yeah, she's marrying Gavin Riley. You're going to the wedding? That's crazy, how come?'

'I'll be retouching the photos on the day, so she can post them. It's ridiculous, and not the kind of thing I would choose to do.'

'Are you kidding? Gavin Riley, he's seriously impressive. Wow, that's really cool,' Liam says, notably impressed.

'Sure, maybe it is "cool". I'm being paid well and that's why I am going. And is he impressive or was he just born into the right family? It's not like he set up the business, is it? Also, I've heard he is a relentless cheat. Which makes him awful.'

'Harsh,' Liam says, raising his eyebrows.

'But true,' I say, raising mine.

'Maybe,' he says, hovering by the door for a while. 'If you're working at the weekend, why don't you take this afternoon off and come with us? We could grab food, go feed the ducks?'

'No, I have too much to do. You two go, you'll have more fun that way.'

'More fun than us all being together? Oh come on Rubes.' He always used to call me Rubes. I found it embarrassing at first, then grew to love it. It feels nice to hear it again. 'You don't hate me enough that we can't spend one afternoon together as a family, do you?' Liam says quietly, so that Bonnie, who is climbing into her buggy, doesn't hear him. It doesn't please me to think that the father of my child thinks I hate him. Hating someone and being angry with them are very different.

'Come on Mummy, pleeeease,' says Bonnie looking up at me. Her beautiful eyes begging.

I am dressed well for this weather, I suppose, with good coverage. I could just put some tights on under my green velvet dress. Liam knows not to touch me. I am desperate for this appointment, but my daughter's happiness is somehow succeeding my need for personal comfort. It's a new and complex emotion, but one I am surprisingly happy to pursue.

'I could join you, I suppose,' I say. This will, of course, mean I am hairy for the wedding. But I have made a great dress that offers full coverage.

'Just give me a minute.' I go upstairs. Tights, blusher, a red lip. I remove a few hairs from my chin and dab a little witch hazel on to reduce any redness. I put on extra deodorant as it's a warm day. Back downstairs, both Bonnie and Liam look very excited.

'You're coming, Mummy?' Bonnie asks.

'I am,' I tell her.

'Let's not bother with the buggy, she can walk, can't you Bon Bon?' Liam says.

'Yes, I'm a big girl.'

Liam and I take one hand each.

One of my earliest memories is of a family picnic. I was around five, we sat on a red tartan rug and the fluff kept sticking to my food. My mother had made sandwiches and had various salads and dips in Tupperware boxes. I'm sure she did this a lot, but I only remember it the once. My recollections of my early years are hazy, but I do have some happy memories to refer back to.

My father was very proud of his wicker picnic hamper and kept mentioning the joys of drinking wine out of an actual wine glass in the middle of a beach. I remember Mum telling him to stop going on about it, but laughing at him at the same time. He leaned over and kissed her. She told him to get off. This was a common dynamic for them. Believe it or not, it was a sign of affection. They were flirtatious back then. I remember hints of it.

My dad had brought a skipping rope with us that day, and while they both took an end each, I jumped over it.

'Faster, faster,' I would shout, and they would oblige, speeding up until my little legs couldn't take it. I'd crash to the sand laughing and exhausted, and they would laugh too.

Funny to think of me being a happy little girl. I had no idea what cards life had decided to deal me at that point. I was innocent. My relationship with my parents was all that mattered, really.

'Can I have chocolate?' Bonnie asks in Pret a Manger, as Liam gathers far too much food for us to eat in the park. He winks at Bonnie and puts a Rocky Road bar into his basket.

'Rubes, anything particular you would like?' he asks me. I shake my head, then pick up an apple and pop it in the basket.

'That is far too much food, you two will never eat it all. Waste of money,' I tell him, as he loads it onto the counter so the cashier can ring it up.

'Oh, I bet we will, right Bon Bon?'

Bonnie nods enthusiastically.

'There wasn't much point in us calling her Bonnie if you insist on only calling her Bon Bon, was there?' I say, taking my apple and putting it into my bag. Liam mimics what I said in a silly voice and makes Bonnie laugh. I huff off and wait outside.

'If she eats all that she will feel sick,' I say, when he comes out. He stands in front of me and looks me directly in the eye.

'Ruby, will you please get off your high horse and drop your standards for an hour or so while Bonnie and I try to enjoy your company at the park?' He picks Bonnie up, and whispers, 'Stare at her until she gives up' into her ear, loud enough for me to hear it. They both, trying not to laugh, squint their eyes, as if waiting for me to say something. I hold as long as I can, insisting that they are being ridiculous.

'OK, OK, but you will not eat that entire bar of chocolate all by yourself, OK?' I say, warning my daughter with my scowl and starting to walk away.

'There she is, I knew she was still in there somewhere,' Liam says, referring to my softer side. 'And of course she won't, half of it is mine. Right Bon Bon?' he says, making her scream, 'NO WAY.' They both laugh so hard you would think someone just cracked an incredible joke.

'Are you coming or not?' I ask firmly, a small smile trying to break out from underneath my stern expression. Liam passes me the two paper bags bulging with food and helps Bonnie up to his shoulders.

'Do you have to . . . ' I start to say, before Liam stops me with a defiant look and a cheeky wink. He storms past me, Bonnie screaming with delight way above his head.

'Well wait for me,' I say, catching them up. 'Bonnie, hold on please.'

'Chase us, Mummy,' she says, as if she has never been happier.

'So tell me more about this mouse,' Liam asks, as he lays copious amount of food out on top of the paper bag that he has fashioned into a base for our picnic.

'Mummy caught it,' Bonnie says, proudly.

'Oh, she did? With her hands?' Liam asks her, winking at me.

'No! In a bucket,' Bonnie says, correcting him. 'She caught it in a bucket and we took it to the park and let it go back to its family.'

'Wow, it sounds like you two are a super hero duo.'

'We are,' Bonnie says, raising her hand as if to punch me. I close my eyes expecting impact, but Liam explains.

'It's a fist bump,' he tells me.

'A what?'

'She is giving you a fist bump, look.'

He punches Bonnie's hand, and they both look very pleased. Bonnie holds her clenched fist up to me again. I punch it and feel a million years old and totally out of the loop.

'Daddy, did you know that Mummy is hairy like a mouse?' Bonnie says. The piece of apple I just ate jamming in my throat, causing me to cough like I just smoked a Marlboro Red in one drag.

'I did, yes,' Liam says. I still can't talk, so I wave my hand frantically as if telling him to shut up. 'I kind of like it, don't you?' he continues, realising I can't tell him to shut up, and taking full advantage of it.

'It's funny,' Bonnie says, and I finally get the apple up.

'OK, Bonnie. Let's play hide and seek. You go hide, now, go on.' She drops all of her snacks and immediately runs behind the nearest tree.

'ONE, TWO,' I yell, hoping Liam has moved on.

'You still can't talk about it, huh?' he asks me.

'THREE, FOUR. No, Liam. I don't like to talk about it. Not in the park, not at home, not at my wedding.'

'Oh here we go, really? I know. I fucked up. But Jesus, Rubes, how many times do I have to say that I'm sorry?'

'No amount of sorry will change the look of joy on my mother's face when you humiliated me. So no amount of sorry will make it better, OK?'

Liam exhales loudly. I've made him feel so guilty about this for so long, and I know he regrets it. Of course he does. But I just can't bring myself to let it go.

'Mummy, what number are you on?' Bonnie yells loudly, from her secret hiding place that's right I front of us.

'TEN.' I shout, running towards the tree.

'I still love you.' Liam shouts after me. I keep running.

11

Ruby

It's the day of the big wedding. As I get dressed, I picture myself in the hours before mine. I allowed a system to take control. A system of tradition that I wasn't comfortable with but accepted as part of the process. I wore white underwear, I made a cream dress out of a thick, silky fabric. It had a high neck, ruffles across the front, I added splits in the sleeves. I, of course, had my customary wax. I wore more than the usual make-up, I had my hair blow-dried by a professional. I sat in a chair, looking at myself in the mirror for much longer than I normally would. I stared at my face, reminding myself that my husband-to-be made this decision all by himself. I never applied any pressure to get married. He wanted to. Love and joy was inside of me somewhere, and for that morning I allowed it to flourish. I was a bride. A wife-to-be. I think maybe I thought life was about to change forever. Acceptance of myself on the outside and the inside, all because someone else was willing to do the same.

But Liam blew it. He squeezed out my recklessness and smashed it on the floor. I immediately crawled back into my shell, with even less inclination to come out. Now, every day when I get dressed, my aim is to cover as much of my body as I can without looking like I am dressed like a nun. I am sure Lauren Pearce's wedding will be full of young women exposing flesh like they are produce in a butcher's fridge. Not me, I will be in my usual velvet armour. Albeit in a fabulous colour.

I consider shaving my entire body, but it's never worth it. Within hours the hair would start to grow back and that is very uncomfortable. I pluck my chin and I pack my tweezers. Twelve hours is a long time, and who knows what will sprout from where by the end of the day. I put on the crimson version of the dress but it's too hot for tights. It's a warm day and I've packed a portable fan to keep me cool. I presume this 'back room' will at least have a window?

Rebecca has told me to bring a sandwich. She said she was sure there would be something available for us, but that I shouldn't rely on it. I don't eat sandwiches, so I make a neat packed lunch of some rice cakes and crudités with a generous amount of hummus in a Tupperware box. I also pack deodorant and a pair of tights in case I do get cold. You never know if there will be air conditioners or not. I have my computer, of course, my charger, and an Internet dongle in case there is no Wifi. All of this requires one of my larger totes. A cheeky Anya Hindmarch with a pair of googly eyes on it. It's quite ambitious on the fun factor, considering who owns it. But I quite enjoy the irony of that.

A car is waiting for me outside my house. It's a Mercedes – apparently they're providing a fleet of cars for the event. Every guest has been sent one as the wedding party don't want random taxis showing up. I was asked by Rebecca to #Mercedes with a selfie of myself on the way. I told her I would do no such thing. I am going to this event to work, I am being paid. I have no obligation to enter into the brand support just so that Lauren Pearce and her famous husband can get loads of things for free.

The driver isn't chatty, so it's a fine journey as we travel about forty-five minutes west of London. I spend most of it thinking about Bonnie, and what a mess I have made of her nursery situation. After a wax, it is top of my things to have sorted by the end of next week.

A text comes in from my mother.

Not answering my calls? I hope you are a better mother than you are a daughter.

I don't reply, despite the barrage of attack I would like to throw in her direction. It's never worth it.

'What is happening? Some kind of festival?' I ask the driver. There's tape and barricades and wardens in high-visibility vests as we enter a small village.

He looks in his rear-view mirror and raises his eyebrows as if I am joking. I find it irritating.

'It's for the wedding?' he says.

'Ohhhhh.'

'Apparently there are five hundred guests,' he tells me, proud of his knowledge. 'That's why all the roads are closed. And to stop the press getting too close.'

I had no idea it would be an event of this magnitude.

I have been told to call Rebecca as soon as I am out of the car, and that she will come to meet me at the entrance. As we pull up, I text her. I really don't like talking on the phone.

Hello Rebecca, I'm arriving now.

K, dwn in 5

There is no need for that level of abbreviation. Rebecca is one of those women who goes on about being busy all of the time. So many emails end with something about her not having much time. It's just a subtle way of telling people not to try to get any more out of her than she is offering. If she knew who she was conversing with, she wouldn't bother.

I get out of the car and wait on the step. There are literally hundreds of people rushing around. Florists wheeling in huge arrangements, caterers with trays of glasses and food. Trucks pulling up, being unloaded with God knows what. I even see two people carefully carrying an enormously tall white box, which must be the cake. I don't know what it is about me that wants to go and push the box over. But all of this wedding joy is triggering my own wedding trauma. I remember choosing all of those things. The cakes, the flowers. It all felt so out of character for me, but I went along with it all because I was in love. It was important to Liam to be traditional and he was important to me. I became a bride. I chose cake toppers. I selected food I thought my guests would enjoy. I played the part. And then he ruined it with a 'joke'. My self-awareness is too feisty a beast to take humour on the chin.

And here I am at Lauren Pearce's dream day. How does a

model who uses fake mental health issues to sell products get to have this level of joy in her life and not me?

'Ruby,' calls Rebecca, coming up behind me. She is wearing red trousers and a cream blouse. Her brown curly hair is tied up untidily, and she has accessorised with large, fashionable earrings. She has a simple lick of mascara on, rosy cheeks and a solid red lip. She knows how to make casual look good. Well you would, when you spend your life surrounded by magazine people and photographing models. The trousers are a little controversial for a wedding, but I suppose they offer her a little more flexibility as she will be moving around a lot, squeezing into small spaces, and doing what she can to get the perfect photo. She's not a small woman. Tall, with solid thighs. I haven't seen her for a number of years and there is definitely a little more weight around her middle. The mole on her face is as prevalent as it ever was and the first thing you notice, even when you know it is there.

Her unpleasant aura is still as powerful. We don't bother with pleasantries that go beyond a simple 'hello'. As always she gets out of conversation by implying how busy she is with various comments and gestures. She does, however, look me up and down without complimenting my dress, which obviously means she hates it.

'OK, follow me and I'll show you your room,' she says, leading the way. She looks around, seeming a bit on edge.

'Are you looking for someone?' I ask her.

'Nope. Just checking out locations for possible photos.'

She's like a sniffer dog, always on the job.

'Thanks for coming early. Lauren wants a lot of getting-ready photos. Everything from her bath, to putting her underwear on. She wants to approve each shot and that will mean giving her a few options so we will have to work quickly if we're going to make these posts feel live. You OK with that?'

'Well I don't have anything else to do today, so I'm sure it won't be a problem.'

'OK, Lauren is in there.' She points at a door off a long corridor. I am curious to see Lauren in real life. Whatever real life is, to someone like her. I've erased her flaws in picture form, I now want to see them in the flesh. I've built quite the dislike for this woman, and she's done that all by herself with her Photoshop requests and ludicrous Instagram feed, yet still I am met with a small thrill at the thought of seeing a major celebrity move and breathe. This day is actually quite exciting. I am pleased I took the time to make a good dress.

'She has her mother with her. I just took loads of pictures of them but need to get more. She has two bridesmaids but they're in their own rooms with their own PRs, which is so weird I don't even know what to say about it. Gavin is in a room on the other side of the house. I'm about to go and get some shots of the cake, then I'll get some of Gavin and his groomsmen, so then you can get working on those while I go and photograph the bride. She's being quite intense.'

'Intense?'

'Snappy. She wants photos but doesn't want photos. Fucking brides, I swore I'd never do weddings.'

'Why did you then?'

'The money. I'm being paid like a footballer to shoot this wedding. So we better get to it. The contract stated they want one shot of the champagne fountain and some bottles around it, followed by Gavin and then the reveal of Lauren and photos of the day as it progresses. Oh look, here comes Lauren's mum.

'Hey Mayra, this place is a maze, isn't it,' Rebecca says, conversationally, waving Mayra over.

'A maze? I don't know why you all have to abbreviate everything,' she says, which seems unfriendly.

'Pardon?' Rebecca asks.

'Did you not have time to say "amazing"?' Lauren's mum says. Her tone is quite spiky and I dislike her immediately. Neither of them think to involve me.

'I said this place is a *maze*. As in, there are loads of corridors and it's quite hard to find your way around,' Rebecca says. Two not very nice ladies having an awkward chat. I don't try to make it three.

Mayra laughs, but doesn't apologise. 'Oh, I'm so used to Lauren doing that. It's so confusing to me. Anyway, have you photographed Gavin and his groomsmen yet?'

'Nope, I'll get there in about fifteen minutes, I reckon.'

Lauren's mum looks at her watch. 'OK, I'll go and let him know.'

She walks quickly away from us.

'She's a real piece of work,' Rebecca informs me. 'No wonder Lauren is a mess. Anyway, this is your room.'

'Wow,' I say, walking in. It really is stunning. The way she was talking, I'd been imagining myself stuffed into a broom cupboard. But this is really magnificent. Beautiful, opulent fabrics surrounding the windows and furniture. A four-poster bed with multiple fluffy cushions and a bathroom of pure marble with an enormous bath.

'Goodness me, this is wonderful,' I say, almost wanting to do a twirl when I walk in. I'm delighted to spend the day in such a gorgeous and unexpected place.

'Lovely, isn't it. OK, the Wifi code is on that pad over there. Here's the first card with photos of the venue and Lauren and her mum. If you could find one of the champagne that would be great, just make sure the colours pop. And can we just do a few test shots? My flash has been playing up and I need to just check the exposure.'

'Um, OK,' I say. 'Snap away and I'll have a look at them on my computer.'

'OK, thanks. If you stand by the window that would be good. The back light is what's worrying me.'

I walk over to the window slowly, unsure why it matters where I stand. She raises the camera to her eye and points it at me, I quickly dart to the other side of the bed.

'No, no, sorry. I don't want to be in any photos if that's alright.'

'No one will see them, it's just so I can check stuff.'

'No. Sorry, I really don't want to be in any pictures.'

Rebecca looks annoyed. Tough shit. Nowhere in my contract does it state I have to be in any photographs. I don't want to do it, she'll have to find someone else.

'OK. Then can you take the photo? I like to test with people in the shot. Would you at least do that?' she asks, sarcastically. As if I have just personally offended her. I tell her I will of course take some photos. She goes to the window and poses awkwardly. I take a few pictures. She checks them on the camera, then asks me to take some more. She leans against a chair, sits on the bed. It is a very strange five minutes as we barely say a word; she really isn't very easy to get along with. She takes her camera, checks the photos, makes a few adjustments and finally seems happy.

'Are we done?' I ask, wanting her to get out so I can enjoy my room.

'If you need anything, there will be staff catering happening in about five minutes in a staff tent downstairs. Maybe you could grab something and bring it back up? The guests arrive at two so Lauren will be right in the throes of getting ready then, and I want to get the images to her quickly.'

'OK, thank you,' I say, wondering if she will leave now.

'Great, well, you have my number if you need me. I'll keep popping back with the cards, and I guess we just get on with it?'

'Great,' I say, opening the door to encourage her exit. I want to swan around this room and pretend it's in my house. She hovers by the door. 'Was there something else?'

'I'd really appreciate you getting going, please don't treat today like a spa break.'

'Oh, yes. Of course,' I say, getting my computer out of my bag and setting it up on a little desk near the window. It's such a strange feeling to have someone talk to me that way. I really have no authority in my life and I respond to it quite negatively when faced with it. 'I'll get on much quicker if you leave me to it,' I say, regaining some control. I don't like being spoken to like someone's employee. Finally, she leaves.

I immediately lie down on the bed and stretch out my arms and legs. It's gloriously comfortable. I love hotels, and occasionally splash out on one on a Saturday night while Liam has Bonnie. It's been a while, I am due a mini-break.

I get up and look out over the grounds from the window. It's a stunning location and a gorgeous summer's day. On the lawn there is an aisle created between two sections of about three hundred chairs. At the end is a flower arch, there are explosive arrangements everywhere. The flowers alone must have cost tens of thousands. Even with my cold heart, I have to admit it looks very pretty. This place is the dream location for a day such as today. It's what you get, I suppose, when you sell your body for hundreds of thousands of pounds and marry one of the most successful businessmen in the country. Oh to be the future Lauren Riley.

Realising Rebecca's work might take some time, considering the effort needed for uploading all of the pictures of Lauren and her mother, I wonder if maybe I will take a walk down to the staff tent. I could fill up my water bottle, maybe get some extra crudités. I'm intrigued by this fantastic location, I want to know more about how much it will cost for me to come and spend a weekend here. I'd never leave the room. I'd sit by the window and read Brontë novels all day long.

I walk through the kitchens and out into the gardens to the staff tent. Multiple waiting staff are lining up to receive their free lunches. I see a side table with some fruit and coffee. I take an apple, a satsuma and a black coffee. I know the pace of work is about to ramp up, but even these few minutes are a bonus I didn't anticipate.

Just as I'm walking up the beautiful staircase back to my room, Lauren Pearce appears at the top. It startles me . . . she is a real person. Of course I knew that, but here she is, skin and bones, right in front of me. It's harder to dislike someone when you see them in the flesh. The reality of everything you created about them in your head now challenged as their eyes move, and their skin breathes, and they become actual people, instead of objects I have worked on. She has a nervous demeanour. She is delicate and pretty. She is wearing a white tracksuit, her hair tonged to perfection. I won't have to do much to it today. I had always imagined her to be more bolshy, or loud, or overconfident, but she is gentle and timid. Her smile spreads across her face as she sees someone behind me. She runs quickly past.

'Dad, you're here,' she says, as she throws her arms around him.

I can't believe what I am seeing as the man approaches, the coincidence hitting me like a cosmic message I know must mean something. I hurry back to my room. I don't want him to see me.

Beth

'Double-check that the favours are to the left of the forks please. And that the leaves with the names are in the middle of the napkin. Oh, and then do the chairs. Five inches from the table, no less, no more. It's what she wants.'

I have everything in order, I think. I am waiting for the last-minute drama, there always is one.

'Hey boss, so Tom the magician is ill, but he's sending a replacement. I've forwarded the NDAs and I'm waiting for them to be emailed back to me. I made it clear no one is allowed on site until they have sent one through. Just letting you know,' says Risky, reeking of efficiency. I'm very glad for it.

'OK, that's OK. If he's weird or crap at magic, we just send him home. Simple. Shame about Tom, he's good. Anything else?'

'The florist just gave me the buttonholes for the groomsmen . . . ' She is holding a tray with them laid out. She stands looking at me as if waiting for approval. 'Shall I go and give them to them, or do you want to?'

Ah, she is asking me if she is allowed to go and see Gavin and his brother. 'Give them to me, I'll . . . ' There is a massive crash in the marquee. It sounds like glass. A lot of glass. 'Shit!' I say, running over to see what happened. 'OK, go and give them to him. And then leave!'

'Yes boss.' I see a cheeky smirk on Risky's face that she immediately tries to hide.

In the marquee, one of the waiting staff has knocked over a perfectly compiled pyramid of coupé champagne glasses. She is sobbing in a chair with around three other members of staff trying to calm her down.

'It's OK,' I tell her. 'Why don't you go to the staff area and have a cup of tea? I'll have someone deal with this.'

'I'm sorry,' she says. 'I'm having a terrible time at the moment, I'm not quite myself.'

'Go to the staff tent and get yourself together, I need everyone to forget their problems today, and just get through it. You're not in trouble, OK?'

She nods and hurries away. All feelings must be cast aside today. The only emotion I want to see is pure joy from the wedding party. Everyone else, me included, needs to just deal.

Every time I think about Michael I want to throw up in a flower arrangement. I keep trying not to think about Tommy, because when I do I become riddled with a guilt that makes it impossible for me to even pretend to want to celebrate the concept of love today. I just have to get through this wedding, then I can work on the state of my own marriage.

I'm walking towards the groom's quarters to find Risky, when she suddenly appears in front of me, running and crying. My first thought is that she has been attacked.

'Risky, Risky, what happened?' I ask, running towards her. 'Are you OK? Did someone hurt you?'

She can barely catch a breath.

'Risky, pull yourself together. What happened? Was it Adam? Did he upset you?'

'No. No. No . . . It's Gavin, he's . . . '

'He's what? What is Gavin doing?'

'I can't. Boss, no. I need to unsee it. This can't be happening, I just can't take it.' She is hysterical. I put a hand on each shoulder and tell her to breathe.

'Risky, calm, calm, calm. OK, what did you see?'

'Gavin.'

'Yes, I gathered that. What is Gavin doing?'

'I can't say it. I can't. That room down the corridor, the third on the right. Go look.' I start to make my way down there, terrified of what I might see, Risky following close behind. I'm thinking the absolute worst. 'Quietly boss, be really, really quiet.'

I approach the door nervously and push it open. 'Holy shit!' I say, shutting the door quickly but quietly. 'Oh my GOD.' There is always a last-minute drama, but this takes it to a whole new level.

'Did you see?' Risky says, catching a breath at last.

'Yes. Yes I did.' I am now becoming hysterical myself.

I take some long slow breaths.

'Is that really happening?' I say, not really asking. I saw it with my own eyes. It was absolutely happening. No doubt, not a single bit. Gavin is in that room a hundred per cent having sex with . . . oh my God!

My nipples start to leak.

'Quick, Risky, I need to pump. Where is it?'

'Follow me,' she says, as we race down the corridor.

*

'So what are we going to do?' Risky asks me, a blanket over her shoulders like she has just been rescued from a sinking ship. She is sipping water, holding the bottle with both hands. Shivering, despite it being quite warm. I am sitting opposite her in a small room, my breast pump on. We are working out our next move while the bottles fill up.

'We have to tell Lauren,' Risky says, every bit the woman's woman she preaches to be.

'What? No Risky, we can't do that. We can't do anything.'

'He's cheating on her. It's so bad, and with *her*? It's horrible. The worst. Lauren needs to know. All of those rumours, there are so many. They're all true. If he can do that, he can do anything. She has no real friends. It's down to us to save her.'

Oh God, the crusade. Women supporting women can be really limiting when you need a wedding to happen.

'Listen, Risky, no marriage is perfect. OK? Do we really believe Lauren has no idea who she's marrying? She's made her decision, this is what she wants. It isn't up to us to crush her dreams.'

'But he just . . . on their wedding day . . . with . . . '

'I know, I saw. But seriously. It's not down to us to fix this. We're here to do a job, and I think we just have to do it.'

'Beth, in the nicest possible way, you have the perfect marriage. Maybe you just can't accept that love isn't always a Disney movie.'

I can't handle this anymore.

'For God's sake Risky, no marriage is a Disney movie. I got shagged up the arse by a stranger the other day because my husband refuses to touch me. When are you going to understand that relationships are just shit?'

Silence. To be fair, I just gave her a lot to process.

'Michael refuses to touch you?' she asks. I am glad she chose to focus on that part of my sentence.

'Yes. It's been really terrible for a long time. He has some weird sex phobia and it's made me do something terrible and now I'm in such a mess and I don't know what to do about it.'

'Beth,' she says gently, coming close to me. 'Why didn't you say?'

'Because I am your boss and we have a wedding to get through. I don't like to bring my personal life to work.'

'You sit there with your tits out half the day. I watch your nipples being stretched like rubber bands, milk squirting out the end of them. You can tell me anything, OK?'

She hugs me and it feels very strange to consider this very young girl my friend. But I do.

'But wait, you got done up the arse by a stranger? Beth, that's pretty full on.'

'Inspired by you, Risky. Quit with the judgemental face.'

'Hey, I'm not judging. I'm actually impressed – I thought you were a prude.'

'I think I am a prude. Can we stop talking about it? It's making me feel weird.'

'OK, yes. For now we can. Also, we need to get back to Lauren and Gavin. Lauren needs to know what we saw. God, I hate rich white men.'

'You're right,' I say, 'but it isn't our job to sort that out.'

'But what about the sistership?'

Bloody hell, she is so annoying. 'What about the sistership, Risky?'

'What's the point of feminism if we don't help women? How can we just watch her marry a cheat? Cheating is the worst thing you can do in a marriage. People who cheat should be punished.'

'OK, OK Risky, remember what I just told you?' I say, my guilt not needing a hammering.

'Yes, but you had good reason.'

'Maybe Gavin has good reason?'

'To shag someone else on his wedding day? And her own—'

'I know, I know.'

'Look Beth, we could let this go, or we could exercise the power afforded to us by recent feminist movements and actually save a sister from a life of mental abuse at the hand of her cheating husband and her cruel, cruel . . . Oh God, I'm going to tell her.'

She runs out of the room. I realise that entire exchange took place with my left boob hanging out. I reclip my nursing bra, do up my shirt and hurry after her. I catch her up as she is knocking on Lauren's door.

'Risky, please. Can we at least discuss how we do this, we can't just barge in, this will be devastating for so many—'

The door opens and a whole new nightmare stares me in the face.

'Anal man!' I screech clear as a bell, when I see my recent sexual conquest standing in front of me. His face doesn't jog any memory of his real name.

'Wow,' he says, alarmed by such a graphic hello.

'What? This guy?' Risky asks.

'No, another man,' I say, trying to cover my tracks. 'Look, it's another man.'

'Is Lauren in here?' Risky asks him, moving on. She will deal with me later.

'Yes, who shall I say it is . . . '

But Risky bursts past him before I have a chance to answer.

'Come in,' Anal Man says sarcastically. We stand for a second staring at each other. 'Well this is strange,' he says.

'It is. I, er . . . '

He leans in and whispers, 'You just called me Anal Man, is that my new name?'

'No. Look, oh God sorry, can we catch up later, I really need to . . . ' I push past him too.

'Sure, why not. Anyone else wanna come in?' he jokingly shouts down the corridor, before shutting the door. When he turns around, Risky and Lauren are standing opposite each other. I am in a corner begging the ground to swallow me up. What is he doing here?

'Are you OK, love?' he asks Lauren protectively.

'Yeah, I'm OK Dad. This is Risky and Beth, they're my wedding planners.'

Dad? Anal Man is Lauren's dad? For fuck's sake!

'Lauren's dad? Wow,' says Risky. 'The plot thickens . . . '

'What's wrong, Risky? Did the cake not show up or something?' Lauren asks.

'The cake showed up,' Risky says, mentally preparing herself.

'OK, well what is it then? Something is wrong, isn't it? Oh God, is it the ice sculpture? Did it smash?' Lauren is doing her best to guess while Risky prepares to blow up her life into a billion pieces.

'The ice sculpture is fine. I . . . I . . . Oh I can't do it, Beth, tell her.'

'What? Why me?'

'Because you're the boss?' Risky says, as if that makes any sense. Lauren turns to look at me. She is worried now, maybe starting to panic a little. Why would we burst in like this if it wasn't serious? I have to tell her, but how?

'What is it, Beth?' Anal Man asks.

The room is suddenly deathly still. I have no choice.

'Lauren, Risky and I just saw something we wish we hadn't seen.'

'What?' she asks nervously. 'What did you see?'

I take a deep breath and hang my head. I can't look at her while I say this.

'We saw Gavin having . . . he was having . . . '

'Having what?' Lauren asks, a little tear appearing.

'Having sex with your—'

Right on cue, in storms Mayra. 'Right, let's get this dress on, shall we darling?' she says. 'Oh Ross, you're here!'

'Ross!' I yelp. 'Ross, that's it!' Everyone looks at me strangely.

'Having sex with who?' Lauren says. And I realise she hasn't moved an inch, or taken her eyes off me. Waiting for me to finish my sentence with her entire life depending on it.

'With her,' I say, pointing at Mayra. 'Risky and I just saw Gavin having sex with your mother.'

Lauren and Mayra lock eyes. Risky smiles at me, and mouths, 'Well done.' I feel like the worst person alive.

'Mum?' Lauren says, with so much pain in her voice that it hurts just to hear it. 'Is that true?'

'What? Of course it's not true. These women are trying to get publicity for their business. It's very obvious, darling. Now please, everyone out. It's time for the bride to get dressed.'

I start to leave. A part of me just wants this to pass over. I said it, it's up to them now.

'Come on Risky,' I say, urging her to come with me, but she doesn't move. She just stares at Lauren like she is a puppy in a shop window and needs to be saved.

'I saw it though,' she says, breathlessly. 'You're her mother, how could you?'

'Oh, take your lies somewhere else you vicious little girl. Making up tales to sell to the press to make money for yourself. Disgusting,' Mayra says. The venom in her voice is a bit startling. I step back and stand by Risky. I can't have her spoken to like that.

'Mayra, if you choose to lie to your daughter then so be it, but please don't make accusations like that to me or my staff.'

'Oh, I can't make accusations, but you can, is that it?'

'Is it an accusation though?' Ross says, chiming in. Lauren has not moved.

'Excuse me?' Mayra says, looking at him like lasers might come out of her eyes and kill him.

'It's not like you have no history of cheating on people you love, is it?'

'Ross, this is not the time.'

'Oh, I think this is exactly the right time,' he says, like he too has been waiting for this moment.

'For God's sake, what has got into you all? As if I would sleep with Gavin on the day of your wedding,' Mayra says, blushing now. Some sweat appearing on her brow.

'Well you slept with my brother on the day of ours,' Ross says.

'What?' Lauren says. 'Is that why you don't speak to Uncle Stewart?'

'Yes, the affair went on for years. I found out about it when Verity died. Turns out she needed him for comfort at the funeral, not me. I walked in on them in the bathroom.'

'Oh my God,' Lauren says, as if years of drama now make perfect sense.

We all just stare at Mayra, willing her to crack. Of course, she finally does.

'I deserve happiness too,' she says, pitifully. It's an obvious confession.

'No,' Lauren says, white as a sheet, despite the fake tan. 'No, this isn't happening.'

'I don't know how to stop it,' Mayra says, falling back into a chair. 'It's so hard to find anything that takes the pain away. Gavin does. I can't help it.'

Lauren starts to shake quite violently. It's unclear what will come out of her, tears or flying fists. She bends right down to Mayra, pushing her face as close to hers as she can before it touches.

'It will be all your fault. This time I will not fail.' And then she runs out of the room. Mayra looks at Risky and me and lets out an ear-splitting scream.

'Quick,' I say. 'We better follow her.'

Leaving Mayra to wallow in a stinking heap of her own destruction, Ross, Risky and I find ourselves in the corridor.

'You go that way, I'll go this way,' he says, desperately.

I run off with Risky to find Lauren.

Ruby

Staring into the bathroom mirror, I wonder why life does this sometimes. Why worlds collide in this way, why people jump into your life in such a way that it startles you to the point of reassessing everything, including yourself. You're being led down a path that you think is maybe going one way, but suddenly there is a fork in the road and you find yourself going in a direction you never imagined. For me, this means a road of sympathy instead of frustration. Understanding rather than judgement. Openness to acknowledge, rather than a knee-jerk reaction to shut something down. The man from the bench is Lauren Pearce's father. Everything I assumed about her has now been turned on its head.

I hear the door slam. I walk back into the bedroom expecting to see Rebecca, but instead I am faced with Lauren. This synchronisation of the cosmos leading me further into the unknown. She is looking out of the window. I must be in an alternate universe. One that is forcing me to stop and take stock. To realise that I have done the exact thing I fear people do to me to someone else: I have judged her completely by what she looks like and the tiny version of herself that she chooses to share with the world. I thought I had collated a detailed picture of the woman standing in front of me, but maybe I got her entirely wrong. I've failed to consider the layers that make up a person who is ridden with such self-loathing. I haven't considered that grief may have been part of her experience, nor that the bubble of the perfect life I wanted to see was formed off the back of something so painful and sinister, rendering her flaws irreparable and her pain more real than any Instagram post could ever convey. I want to tell her I am sorry. Instead I stay quiet, peering from behind the door.

She is still in her white tracksuit, her hair perfect. She is looking out of the window and crying. What could have happened now – last-minute nerves? Longing for the sister who should be by her side? She has something in her hand that she keeps looking at.

I'll give her the time she needs, she doesn't have to know that I am here. As I step back from the bathroom door, I hear the little white bottle she has in her hand rattle. It's a bottle of pills.

I'm sure she must just have a headache. Getting married is stressful. She is crying. A migraine? Oh dear. She pours the entire contents of the bottle onto a little table, sits down, and stares at the pills whilst crying harder and harder.

Is she planning on taking them all?

She pours a glass of water from the jug that is on the table and pops two pills into her mouth and swallows them. Phew. But then she takes another two, and then picks up some more. She takes them and picks up a few more. I don't have time to question myself.

'Wait,' I say, bursting out of the bathroom. 'Wait, Lauren. Don't do that.'

She looks at me briefly, but soon gets back to her pills. She picks up yet more.

'Please leave,' she says bluntly, putting them in her mouth. It's only another two, I see them on her tongue. That's about eight so far. Hopefully not enough to do any damage, but she really cannot take any more.

'Please, stop. Don't do that,' I say gently. My heart is beating so fast and I've started shaking myself.

'Seriously, just go. Whoever you are you shouldn't be here for this.'

I always thought that if someone wanted to commit suicide they should be allowed to do it. If that urge to die is so strong, and life has spiralled to a point that they don't feel they can own it anymore, let them at least have control of their own fate. But when it's in front of you, you realise that letting it happen is impossible.

'I can't leave, Lauren. I'm sorry. You must not do this.'

'Why? Who would care?'

'A lot of people would care. Gavin?'

She stares at the pills.

'Please leave me alone.'

'I can't do that, Lauren. I can't leave this room. Whatever has happened can be fixed.'

'You really have no idea so please, just go,' she says. I see that she is shaking. She looks so upset.

'Maybe I don't, but I know you.'

I move a little closer to her.

'You don't know me,' she says painfully. 'You, like everyone else, knows a version of me and that isn't even real.'

313

'Actually, I know you better than that. I know you hate your thighs the most, and wish they were thinner. I know that you have a mole on your right arm that you wish wasn't there. I know that you quite like your eyes, and that your left incisor slightly shades the tooth in front. I know that you like your bottom. I know that you have a tattoo of a V on your hip that you don't want the world to see.'

She looks up at me. I've confused her, obviously. Possibly even scared her a little. I keep going.

'I know that V stands for Verity,' I say, calmly.

'Who are you?' she asks nervously, like I have been watching her through a secret hole in her shower wall for the past five years. She stands up cautiously, some pills still in her hand.

'I'm Ruby. I'm the person who retouches your pictures.'

She looks a little relieved.

'And I know your dad. I've chatted with him. We met in the park. He's helped me realise a lot about myself. He told me all about Verity. It must be so painful, especially on a day like today. Is that what this is all about?'

'It's painful every day. But no, this is about me and my mother. You wouldn't understand. Please, just go, OK?'

'Have you and your mother had a falling-out?'

'You could say that.'

'Your dad told me she has struggled too since Verity died. Trying to present herself as happy when really her happiness is impossible. That must be hard. My mother and I don't get along either. I've barely spoken to her in twenty years.'

She sits back down, rolling the pills back onto the table. She puts her head into her hands and starts to cry.

314

'What happened today, Lauren?' I ask gently.

'She slept with Gavin.'

'She?' I ask, as if I must have missed something.

'Yes, she, my mother. The wedding planner and her assistant just walked in on her and Gavin. Downstairs, just now. On my wedding day. Did your mother do that to you?'

'Oh my goodness. No, my mother didn't do that. I see why you are so upset.' For a moment I wonder if maybe my mother isn't so bad after all. I quickly get that thought out of my head. She is as awful, just in different ways.

My words remind Lauren how upset she is and shift her focus back to the pills.

'I hate myself,' she says, picking a few up again. 'Today was the day I was supposed to gain something, not lose everything. Please, just go. I'm doing this whether you're here or not.' She puts more water into the glass.

'Lauren listen, you've got a whole life ahead of you. You've got your looks, you're so beautiful . . . ' I am annoying myself with all the clichés, and it gets on her nerves too.

'Oh, what would you know? All tall and skinny. Not in the public eye. You don't know what it's like to be defined by the way you look. I'm a body, a face. Feeling like a heap of shit every day because I know I've done it to myself. I'm in a cage. I have no one. No one who really cares.' She looks at the open bathroom door.

'Lauren, come on, seriously, there are other ways to cope. You don't need to have your mother in your life. You can just detach from her, not let her hurt you anymore. You don't have to do this to yourself.'

She realises I am not leaving and wipes her hand across the table, guiding the pills back into the bottle. She heads towards the bathroom; if she shuts and locks that door there will be nothing I can do.

'Wait,' I call, but she is walking towards her death and I'm not sure what to say to stop her. 'Wait,' I say again, scrambling to find my zip and yanking it down. As I run to the bathroom door and block it, my dress falls to the ground. My body is exposed, just my underwear is left. Other than my heavy breath creating a ripple down my body, everything is still.

'You're . . . ' she can't find the words. 'You're . . . '

'I'm disgusting.'

'No, you're . . . ' She still doesn't know what to say.

'It's OK, you don't need to say anything,' I say, not looking at her. Just letting her take me in, until I know she understands. 'We can all find a reason to hate ourselves, OK? We can't just pop some pills to deal with it.'

The bedroom door bursts open. Lauren drops the pills, the contents of the bottle spilling all over the floor.

'What the fuck!' screams Rebecca when she sees me. I try to cover myself but it's pointless. I reach down for my dress but my trembling hands can hardly cope. I get all caught up in it. I can't do it. Where is the zip? I need Rebecca to get out.

Two more women burst in. I try to escape into the bathroom but I trip over my dress and fall. Naked on the floor, I feel like a wild animal trapped in someone's house.

'Please, shut the door,' I plead, trying to pull my dress over me to cover my hideous body.

'What the actual hell is happening?' Rebecca asks, with her usual lack of grace. The other two women seem relieved to have found Lauren. The youngest woman goes straight over to her and hugs her, politely ignoring me.

'Thank God we found you,' she says before noticing the pills on the floor. 'Wait, were you . . .?' she begins, but clearly unable to find the words to ask if Lauren was about to kill herself. While the focus isn't on me, I get to my feet and pull my dress up.

'Seriously, what is going on?' continues Rebecca, so confused. 'Why are you in here, Lauren? Ruby, why were you standing in front of her naked? I'm sorry Lauren, I take full responsibility for Ruby's behaviour and will send her home immedi—'

'No,' Lauren says. 'No.' She comes over to me, lays her soft hands on me and helps with my dress. 'Please don't be embarrassed,' she says as her hand slides up my back, pulling up my zip. I allow her to help me.

'Thank you,' I say, feeling like maybe we understand each other.

'I just wanted to show her that she isn't the only one who feels defined by her body,' I say, keeping my head down. 'That we all label ourselves. We all decide what people see. That's all.'

I head sheepishly over to the window where I sit on one of the chairs. I am quite winded by all this. Quite damaged. Quite unable to be tough. We are all wondering what happens next.

After a painfully long silence, Rebecca says, 'Girls at school used to Sellotape raisins to their faces and take the piss out

317

of me. I've been terrified of women ever since.' Her harshness evaporates from her like steam from a kettle.

Another short pause.

'My belly looks like a dartboard after giving birth and I've put on so much weight my husband finds me physically repulsive and refuses to look at me, let alone touch me,' says a nice-looking but quite plump lady. 'Hi, I'm Beth, by the way,' she adds, smiling at me and Rebecca.

We all look to the young pretty one, wondering if she has any defects she would like to confess to. It takes her a minute, but eventually she thinks of something.

'I've got terrible haemorrhoids from too much anal.'

'Risky!' Beth yelps, horrified by her words. But the haemorrhoids did just the trick. We all, somehow, manage to laugh.

Suddenly Ross, my friend from the bench, comes in. He is hot and bothered. I've seen him look that way before. I turn my face away so he doesn't recognise me, but carefully spread the skirt of my dress over the pills on the floor, so he doesn't have to see what Lauren was about to do. I know how much that would upset him.

'There you are!' he says, hugging Lauren like the loving father he is. He reminds me of my own dad.

I am glad he still has a daughter to hold. It makes me think of Bonnie.

'Come on, let's find a way to sneak you out of here and I'll get you home, OK?' Ross says.

'Ruby?' I hear her say. But I have ducked into the bathroom and shut the door, I don't want her father to see me. When I am sure he and Lauren have gone, I come back out.

'What you did was very brave,' Beth says to me, seeming to understand my sacrifice.

'I did what needed to be done.'

'Yes, well, you did a great thing. Now I guess I better go and make an announcement,' she says. 'There are around five hundred people downstairs expecting to see a wedding. Including the groom. He has no idea any of us know what happened yet.'

'Good luck with that,' I say, not envying her task.

'I'll come with you,' says the one with the haemorrhoids. 'I'll find Adam, he can tell Gavin. You focus on the crowds.'

Before they leave, she turns back. 'This is the sistership right here,' she says. 'When women come together, the world gets better. We don't know our own power sometimes.'

Maybe she is right.

Rebecca and I pack up our things, then share a Mercedes home. She's much easier to get on with since she admitted to being picked on because of the mole on her face. It's like she set the elephant in the room free. I feel a little of the same thing.

From my sofa, in my dressing gown, I watch the drama unfold online. The press and social media are already speculating all sorts of theories as to why the wedding didn't go ahead. I just feel pleased it's not a far more sinister news story, and that Ross didn't lose another daughter today. Who'd have thought that, one day, this body would save a life?

I did good. And I feel OK.

12

Beth

Risky keeps starting sentences then giving up before the first word comes out. Eventually she manages to say what's on her mind.

'So this is what I don't understand: Michael just refuses to have sex with you?'

'Pretty much. I mean, he usually runs away from me before he gets the chance to refuse, but yes, he does not want sex with me.'

'Why?'

'If I knew that I'd probably be able to save my marriage.'

'Have you asked him?'

'Yes.'

'What does he say?'

'He tries to make out that it's my fault. He's suggested it's my weight. He's suggested I have an overactive sex drive. He's suggested I'm a bit mad.'

'That's cruel.'

'Yes it is.'

She hangs her head as if the love of her life has walked away from her. 'I thought he was perfect.'

'No one's perfect.'

While Risky stares into middle distance, like a child who just found out Santa isn't real, I concentrate on wrapping up the wedding details. The bill was paid in full within three days of the event. Or non-event, as it came to pass. The money came from Ross' account, as opposed to Gavin's, like the previous deposits had. This week has been busy for us, the contractors are all upset they haven't had any mentions on Instagram feeds, and of course I am the contact for all of them. I've been filtering things through to Jenny, as I really don't know what the answer is. Apparently, Lauren is willing to pay as opposed to post, so we need to work out what discounts were given and ask everyone to be patient. Risky is being quite useless. Following every mention of the saga in the press. Getting more and more upset about how Lauren is being portrayed in the thousands of tabloid articles that have come out about them.

'Listen to this one,' she says to me, standing up and coming over to my desk. '"Gavin was always unsure," says a source close to the couple. "But Lauren's drinking became too much in the end. In the final hour, he just couldn't go through with it." That isn't what happened at all, she wasn't drunk. That bitch Jenny, she's out there making this stuff up when we all know what Gavin did and why the wedding didn't happen.'

She's right. Jenny is still the PR, but only for Gavin. We

were sent a very aggressive email about how she's representing only Gavin now, and how any queries about him should be sent directly to her and not mentioned to anyone. She sent more NDAs. No mention of Lauren anywhere. It's like she's been blacklisted from brand 'Gavin'. Lauren hasn't done a single Instagram post or answered her phone since the wedding day. The press has been making her out to have alcohol problems, drug addictions, eating disorders, the works. The public support is all for Gavin. There is no mention of his infidelity. Maybe Jenny is good at her job after all.

'Why was he with her in the first place?' Risky asks, making a fair point. 'If he was just going to cheat on her then walk away without a fight?'

'I think some men just like to have a woman at home. A security against their loneliness. Someone they can rely on to make house and make babies. It's like money in the bank, they know they will always have it.'

'Yeah, unless two badass wedding planners foil their plan, right boss?'

'Right, Risky.' The only thing getting her through the heartache of her two favourite relationships being crushed is knowing that she exercised her feminism goals and rescued Lauren from an absolute rotter.

'I can talk to Michael for you, if you want?' she says. 'I will. I'll tell him he's been unkind.'

'Thank you. But really, I have to sort this out myself.'

'How are you going to do that?'

'I'm not sure yet, Risky. Can we just get this wedding tied up so I can work that out?'

'Sure boss, whatever you need.'

Tommy gurgles next to me. It's time for a feed. Risky takes him out of his bouncer and gives him to me. I unclip my bra and feed him.

'I love him being here,' Risky says. And I agree.

I couldn't take another week of not being with my baby, or another week of feeling like Michael was doing me a favour by looking after him. Or another week of anything that is happening in my house. So I insisted Michael went back to work and, as there are no longer any meetings, there is no reason why Tommy can't be with me in the office while Risky and I get this job completed.

'I'm worried about Lauren,' Risky says. And I agree because her radio Instagram silence is strange.

'I'm sure she's just recuperating. Heartbreak is terrible for anyone, let alone when the world's making you out to be crazy,' I say, stroking Tommy's head.

'I saw a pap shot of Gavin leaving their house this morning. He's still living there. I wonder where she is.'

'With her dad I'm sure. Hopefully nowhere near her mother.'

'I hope not. She's better off ditching that bitch. What an absolute horror of a woman she is.'

I'd hate to be a woman on the wrong side of Risky.

I never met any of Lauren's friends. Maybe she doesn't have any. A cliché of being rich and famous is that you are lonely, and I actually think that Lauren is exactly that stereotype. To think anyone presumed she had the perfect life. And then to be betrayed by her mother.

I'm ready to exit this world of celebrity drama now. My

maternity leave is beginning. Just me and my baby, and my terrible marriage that I still have no idea if I can fix.

Or if I even want to.

'We need to try and find her,' Risky says, radiating a new enthusiasm that I don't have the energy for right now. I'm tired, really, really tired.

'Risky, they're all grown-ups and they'll all work this out. Lauren doesn't need us.'

'Of course she needs us, we saved her.'

Risky keeps saying that. I might get her a cape for Christmas so she can feel and look like the superhero she thinks she is. Whistleblowing on Gavin has put her firmly in place as a woman who will, at some point, save the world.

'You could contact her dad?' she asks me. Causing me to almost drop Tommy and turn a neon shade of red. I hoped I had gotten away with that, but I suppose me yelling 'Anal Man' gave it away.

'I mean, I wouldn't say I know him,' I say, spluttering.

'OK, well you—'

'I met him yes,' I blurt, before she says it.

'Sure . . . you, er, "met" him,' she says, rolling her eyes and doing inverted commas with her fingers. 'Well can you contact him and ask him how she is?'

'Risky, it isn't our problem.'

She comes to my desk and sits on it, bending over to get her face as close to mine as possible. Tommy blinks at her proximity.

'Boss, there is a woman out there with no one to turn to. She tried to kill herself at her own wedding. She could be thinking about doing something stupid again. We have a responsibility to make sure she is OK.'

'Risky, please. I just want to get this job wrapped up and get back to my maternity leave.'

'OK, well if anything happens to Lauren and you knew a way to reach out to her, then that will be with you forever.'

'Woah. That's not fair!' I say, swapping Tommy onto my other boob.

'I'm just saying, if you know of a way to help someone you should do it. Her dad might be beside himself about it all. He might need help too.'

I think about Ross, and how kind he was to me that day when I acted like a drunk hussy and demanded anal in the middle of the afternoon. He didn't make me feel worse. He's a good person. Maybe he does need help. Lauren will be a mess and it can't be easy on him either, knowing his ex-wife had an affair with his future son-in-law.

'OK, I'll go and see him. I'll check in on Lauren. I'll make sure she's OK. Then can I get back to my life, or whatever is left of it . . . '

'Yes. Yes you can,' Risky says, heading back to her desk to read a text message. She looks very excited as she reads it.

'Who is it?' I ask, fascinated.

'Oh, um . . . it's Adam.'

'Risky, please, if this thing gets out it could be really damaging for my business.'

'Beth, there's so much gossip surrounding this wedding, do you honestly think anyone would care about me and Adam getting together?'

She raises a good point.

'Anyway, weren't you going somewhere?' she asks, suggestively.

'OK, OK, I'll go.' I get my bag and put Tommy in his sling. 'I'll go because I just want to put this whole thing behind me.'

Bad choice of words.

'I bet you do, you saucy minx,' Risky says, winking at me. She is relentless.

Ruby

I step out of the shower and begin my usual routine. I fully dry myself in the bathroom, then put on my dressing gown and button it up all the way. I peek into the living room to make sure Bonnie is safe in front of the TV, then go to my room, lock the door and get dressed. I've done this every morning for as long as I can remember.

But today, I push myself into something new. It's time.

I unlock my door. And I take off my dressing gown. I am wearing just my knickers and bra. Even when I am alone, I hate being unclothed. Just standing outside my bedroom this way is making my heart race. I go downstairs. The fear of the front door bursting open, people on the street seeing me. My stick-thin body, the fur. I keep going.

I get to the living room door. I see the top of Bonnie's head; she is still engrossed in *Peppa Pig*. I remind myself that she is my daughter. She has already seen it. She deserves to know the truth about her own mother. The more I hide myself, the more I will teach her to hide herself. I know the dangers of that.

Deep breath. Be brave.

With as much confidence as I can muster, I walk across the living room, in front of the sofa. Bonnie barely looks up, so I do it again. I am parading in front of her in my underwear, my body hair is at its maximum. By this afternoon, it will be gone, I finally made an appointment. But it will grow back, and I can't hide anymore.

I stand directly in front of the TV.

'Mummy, you're in my way,' she says, not even looking at me. She leans to the left to see the TV around me. It makes me laugh. I do a silly dance. Still, she doesn't look. I put my hands in the air and wiggle them around, I make silly faces, pulling the sides of my mouth wide open and sticking my tongue out. I turn around, stick out my hairy bottom, wiggle it from side to side.

Eventually Bonnie looks at me. 'Mummy, why are you doing that?'

I tell her I don't know, just because. But of course, my reasons are epic. I am doing this because I can't be afraid of myself anymore. Because I am ready to be liberated from the jail I have been in since school. Because I want my daughter to know that to fear yourself is a form of torture, and that to walk confidently in just your underwear, in the confines of your own house, without wanting to cry, is an experience that all women should be able to take for granted.

I have proved my point, and I am proud of myself. Enough for one day.

'OK Bonnie, five minutes, OK? Then we have to go.'

'OK,' she says.

As we reach the nursery door, I remind myself that everyone has the right to act badly. It's how we recover that matters.

'Bonnie, you're back!' says Miss Tabitha. She is clearly delighted to see my daughter, as are the other children, who swarm around Bonnie and start playing with her immediately. 'Hello Ruby, how are you?'

'I'm good, thank you. Thank you for allowing us to come back,' I say, graciously.

'You're welcome. We're just so happy to see you guys. This place isn't the same without Bonnie.'

'That's really kind, thank you. And I'm sorry. The way I behaved that day was unacceptable.'

'Really, it's fine. We all have bad days.'

'Thank you,' I say, turning to leave.

'Mummy, wait,' calls Bonnie, running over to me. She throws herself against me, wrapping her arms around my legs, squeezing me as hard as she can. She has never, ever done this before. I kneel down to her.

'Have a great day, OK?' I say, kissing her cheek. 'I love you.'

She runs off happily to see her friends. People would pay millions for a shot of the endorphins that just ran through my body. I clench my fists and shut my eyes, not wanting them to escape.

'You can stay if you like,' Miss Tabitha says. 'We have a music class?'

'Oh, that's sweet but no, I have an appointment I can't miss. Thank you though.'

'You're welcome.'

I wave goodbye to Bonnie, who is back playing with her friends. This is better. She is where she should be.

'Oh, Miss Tabitha?' I say, turning back before I leave. 'Bonnie will only be coming Monday to Thursday now, we're going to spend Fridays together. Do something fun.'

'Lovely,' she says, almost relieved. 'I'll make a note of it.'

It's now time for my next slice of humble pie.

Approaching the salon, I remind myself of what Miss Tabitha said. *We all have bad days*. Of course we do, I am not alone in my struggles. Parenting and polycystic ovaries are a terrible combination. I need to cut myself some slack on how hard I find it sometimes.

'I have a ten a.m. with Maron,' I say to the receptionist. I am prepared for her not to remember my name, and I have prepared myself not to be annoyed about it.

'Ruby, hi. Yes, she'll be right with you.'

'Oh, OK.' I take a seat.

'Ruby!' says Maron. 'No Bonnie this time?'

'No, I thought maybe best I come alone, don't you?' I smile, offering an olive branch.

'I think that is almost definitely going to be better for everyone,' she says, taking it. 'Shall we get you sorted then?'

I follow her into the treatment room.

'Here, get undressed and I'll be right back,' she says, handing me a big enough towel to cover myself when I have taken my clothes off.

'Thank you,' I say, waiting until she has shut the door.

I've learned a lot about myself over the past weeks. I know I need to stop pinning my existence on my condition. That I have to break free of its shackles and realise that, beyond it, there is a life I could be living if I allow myself the opportunity to embrace it. Better relationships with my daughter, my friends, myself. I have a long way to go, but right now, I can't wait to get this fucking hair off my body.

'Ready?' Maron says, tapping on the door.

'Oh yes,' I reply. 'I'm ready.'

Beth

I find myself at Ross' front door, seriously considering not knocking on it. He might presume I am crazy and turning up for more weird sex. But Risky will kill me if I don't report back with at least having spoken to him. So, I do three gentle knocks. Tommy is asleep in the carrier on my chest.

Ross opens the door. He looks at Tommy.

'Oh God, it's not mine, is it?'

'No, I . . . he . . . ' I realise he is joking. We both know there are multiple reasons why that cannot be the case. The timing, obviously. Not to mention the entry point.

'Hi,' I say, nervously. 'Sorry, I know this is weird, but I just wanted to check on Lauren. I haven't heard from her since the wedding, she's not posted anything on Instagram. I just wanted to make sure everything was OK and presumed you'd know?'

'That's very sweet, thank you. Come in.' We head into the living room. He tells me to take a seat. I choose not to sit on the sofa, but I do notice a little smudge on it that looks like someone has tried to clean a few times. It was almost definitely caused by my breast milk.

'Can I get you anything?' he asks me, making himself a drink from the bar in the corner. Like a lawyer in his office in an Eighties TV show.

'No thanks, better not.'

'He's cute, what's his name?' he asks.

'Tommy. He's a nice baby. I'm definitely going to keep him.'

Usually that makes people laugh. Not this time.

'Well, cherish every moment,' he says, looking down. I move on.

'So, about Lauren, is she OK? Do you know where she is?'

'Yup, she's upstairs. She hasn't come down since Sunday. It's normal when bad things happen – she takes a lot of solace from her childhood room. She shared it with Verity.'

Verity. Why do I know that name?

'My other daughter. She died when she was a little girl.'

Verity is the person who died. I remember now, he mentioned her at the wedding. That was his daughter? 'Oh my God, I'm so sorry.' I find myself wrapping my arms a little tighter around Tommy.

'Yeah, Lauren was only five when it happened.'

'It?' I'm winded. I don't know if I should be asking questions, but I find myself devastated for him. The puzzle of Lauren and Mayra's troubled relationship is starting to piece together.

'Verity drowned in the pool outside. She'd just learned to swim, so we were all being very relaxed about watching her. Lauren started screaming when she saw her at the bottom of the pool. I dived in to save her, but it was too late. The worst day of my life. I hope.'

'I didn't know any of this,' I say, wiping away a tear. 'I'm so sorry.'

'No, it's not something we really talk about. Especially Lauren. She has paid people to keep it out of the press. It hurts her too much.'

'I don't know what to say.'

It's odd, I knew there was something sad about him, and Lauren too. I presume losing her sister was the void Lauren told me about? And as for Mayra, she must be in agony. It's no excuse for what she's done, but it does explain a lot.

'It must be so hard, even still. Especially as it happened here.'

'I had the swimming pool filled in and I beat myself up a little bit every single day. I can't sell this house. The idea of someone else living here and not understanding what happened is too painful. So here we are. A messed-up family, trying to get through life. The world sees us as rich with a famous daughter. Apparently, that makes us lucky. Sorry, I shouldn't be telling you this. You're supposed to be in that new baby bubble with your husband.'

'Oh sure, yeah, the lovely bubble. That's how I ended up on that couch with you,' I say, and he laughs this time. 'I really am sorry, this must be so hard for her. For all of you.'

'It is. But you know what else is hard? Marriage. So maybe she's better off knowing about Gavin now rather than when she's got a few kids and is tied to him forever,' he says. 'Finding out you're married to a cheat when you've invested half of your life in them is no joke.'

'No, I can imagine,' I say, my own guilt tapping me on the shoulder. Like a little gremlin threatening to multiply and cause hell. 'Mayra seems like a real piece of work.'

'She is, but ultimately she's just as unhappy as I am. Verity's death hit her hard, she let Lauren down and she knows it. She's struggling with it all too.'

'You're so together,' I say, amazed by him. It's so strange being around a man with grown-up emotions and pragmatic approaches to big problems. There is no blaming, no name-calling, no bullying. It makes me realise what a mess Michael really is.

'I've learned the hard way. And have had a lot of therapy. Anyway, Lauren is OK. Or at least she will be. She's here with me and I'll get her through it. Thank you for caring.'

'Is there anything I can do?' I ask. He shakes his head. Then I realise that Lauren is standing at the door of the living room. She looks thin and tired. She has a pink velvet tracksuit on, and no make-up.

'Hi Beth,' she says.

'Hi Lauren. I just wanted to check in on you, Risky and I have been worried and wondered if there was anything we could do.' She walks into the room and sits down on the sofa, right on top of my breast milk.

'You must think I'm so stupid, all that planning for nothing,' she says, sweetly. Her dad puts his arm around her, and for the first time I realise she is just someone's little girl. A million miles from the major celebrity who the world is talking about.

'Actually, no I don't. I think you believed in someone and they let you down. I'm glad you two have each other.'

'Me too,' Lauren says, as Ross holds her tighter.

'We might be a mess, but we're our mess. Right Lolly?'

Lauren pats his hand and smiles.

'OK, well I better go,' I say. 'Tommy will wake up soon and he'll want feeding.'

'Can I get you a car?' he asks, as he did last time I was leaving his house. I say yes this time. And while we wait the three minutes for my Uber to arrive we say our goodbyes.

'Will you be OK?' he asks me, Lauren out of earshot, unaware of my random and rampant shag with her father.

'Yes, I don't live far.'

'No, I mean with your marriage. Will you be alright?' he asks, kindly.

'Oh, that. You know what, I don't know what will happen with my husband. But whichever way it goes, I have this guy. So I'll be alright, yes.'

'He's very cute.'

'I'm so sorry for what happened to you and your family,' I say. 'I don't know you very well, but you seem so kind and it must feel very unfair. You make me want to deal with my problems better.'

'Well, what I've learned is that saying the words that feel impossible to say is the best way to get through anything.'

'It's that simple, huh?'

'Yup, that simple.'

'Bye Ross,' I say, proud to know his name.

'Bye Beth. Bye Tommy,' he says, waving at my baby, whose sweet eyes have opened, taking it all in.

'See you around.'

He shuts the front door.

13

Ruby

As a rule, I would never answer my phone to an unknown number, but after the fifth or sixth call I picked it up. I wondered if my mother had finally done it.

To my surprise, it was Lauren Pearce. She got my number from Rebecca. She asked if she could come to see me. I said yes, of course, albeit slightly nervously. I'm not really looking to be anyone's support system right now, not when I am hoping to improve so many aspects of my own life. Nonetheless, I said that she could 'pop round'. I have vacuumed the floors and boiled the kettle. She arrives exactly on time at eleven a.m.

'Hello,' I say, as I open the door. She looks pale, and gaunt. She is wearing a big cardigan and her arms are wrapped around herself as if she is cold, despite it being quite warm outside. I let her in immediately.

'I don't think anyone followed me,' she says, like she is on the run. 'I snuck out the back of my dad's house and called an Uber from down the street. There are paps everywhere, but no one saw me.'

'I'm sure that can't be easy. Can I make you a drink, the kettle's just boiled?'

'Just water, please.'

The house feels very silent when I go into the kitchen to get the drinks. It's quite bizarre having a celebrity in the living room. Especially when the world outside is looking for her.

'Please, take a seat,' I say, coming back in.

'Thanks. Your place is lovely. You've got great style,' she says, looking around at the many things I have gathered over the years, to make my cave a place where I am happy to stay.

'Thanks, I am very proud of my home.' I don't have many guests. It's quite nice to have my good taste acknowledged.

'I wanted to say thank you. For what you did for me that day. For talking to me, and . . . and for exposing yourself to me the way you did. I'm sure that wasn't easy.'

'No, it wasn't,' I say, fighting my learned behaviour of shutting down a conversation that makes me feel self-conscious. She saw my body. There is no need to push her away now. I saved her life. At least in this situation I should allow my accomplishment to eclipse my humiliation.

'Well, you can add saving someone's life to the list of things you do well. I mean it, thank you. I was a mess that day. I wasn't thinking clearly.'

'Or maybe you were,' I say, controversially.

'What?'

'I mean, surely in the moment you decide to kill yourself you are thinking most clearly of all. You know something is

338

destroying you, you know you can't cope. The direction of your thought process is entirely focused. I think it's OK to admit that you knew what you wanted to do in that moment.'

'I did. But what I've realised since is that I wasn't doing it to get me away from anything, it was just to hurt other people as much as I could. I wanted Gavin and my mother to have to live with it forever. Which is not the right reason. Not that there are any right reasons. Anyway, you made me realise that finding a way to cope with everything is better than not coping, so thank you.'

'It's OK. Really, I'm just glad it ended the way it did. I mean, I'm glad you're OK, I realise things didn't go exactly to plan for your special day.'

'No, they didn't. God, every time I think about them together my skin crawls.'

'Yes, it's really difficult to comprehend, I'm sure. That's not the role you think your mother will play on your wedding day. I can relate to that.'

'You're married?'

'I was. It ended very soon after the wedding, unfortunately.'

'What happened?' she asks, sipping her water. I wouldn't normally offer this information, but I suppose Lauren Pearce and I have terrible wedding days in common. I don't have many other friends who appreciate how it feels.

'In his speech, my husband made numerous jokes about my body hair, and I felt very let down by it.'

'Oh. Why was he so cruel?' she asks, a look in her eye suggesting she knows all about cruel men. I don't like it – Liam is nothing like Gavin.

'No, he wasn't being cruel. He thought he was being funny. It was very ill-judged.'

'OK, so why did you leave him?' she asks, a little confused.

'Because of the jokes,' I clarify. 'You should have heard him. He said he was happy to be marrying me because he loved cats but was allergic to them. Oh, and another one was, he said that my particular breed of woman is almost extinct because most women remove their body hair. He made some wisecracks about how spotting one like me in the wild, catching it and domesticating it was no easy task, but that when you get one they're actually easy to tame. He basically compared me to an animal in front of all of my friends and his entire family. And my mother, which was maybe the most painful thing of all.'

'Why?'

'Because my mother is also not a good person. She's been cruel to me my entire life, she mocks my condition, calls me names. I didn't need the love of my life giving her more ammunition.'

Lauren looks confused.

'He compared you to a cat, but said he loved cats? Don't you think that, just in a very odd way, he was letting you know how much he loved you?'

'He made fun of me, Lauren. He outed my condition. I wasn't ready for that.'

'Well, what did he say afterwards?'

'He said he just wanted everyone to know that he accepted me.' I roll my eyes. Playing along with what I have always told myself, that Liam is terrible for what he did. But saying it out loud to someone whose husband was caught bonking her mother on her wedding day, suddenly I am questioning the level of the crime.

'Look, I'm sure you had all sorts of reasons to break up with your husband. But are you sure this isn't really about you and your mother?'

'Excuse me?'

'Well, you said he made you cross because he gave her more ammunition? It sounds like the real problem you have is with her.'

I allow silence to fall while my mind reassesses itself and I question nearly everything I have told myself to believe about my wedding day. Lauren must sense that she has said something I am struggling with.

'I bet you looked beautiful on your wedding day,' she says, trying to snap me out of my thoughts. 'Can I see pictures?'

'No, I'm not the kind of person to share pictures of myself.'

'Oh come on, I bet your dress was amazing. I love your style. It's so dramatic, I could never pull anything off like what you wear.'

I imagine Lauren in one of my dresses. She's right, it wouldn't work on most people. I am proud of my unique style.

'Wait here,' I tell her. A few moments later, I am back with my laptop. I open the file, 'MENSTRUAL DIARY', then show her the screen.

'So this is us moments after we said "I do" before the speeches. A little moment in time when I felt truly happy.'

'Ahhh, I can see it on your face. You look glowing.'

I don't tell her I added the glow in post.

'And look at this one, your body looks amazing.' She is pointing at a photo in which I gave myself slightly wider hips.

'Wow and look at your smile there . . . '

I snap my computer shut.

'OK, I can't do this,' I say, bluntly.

'Can't do what?' Lauren asks, nervously.

'I can't pretend that is me. I'm sitting in front of you, you can see the truth. I'm sorry, I know you have photos of yourself manipulated, and I know I'm the one who does it, but I can't do it to myself, I'm sorry.'

I get up and leave the room. I am aware she must feel uncomfortable so I am as quick as I can be. I come back in holding the shoe box.

'These are the originals.' I sit next to Lauren and open the box of photos for the first time in years. 'Look, this is what I actually looked like. Pale, gaunt, too thin, too . . . '

'Ruby, stop. You look beautiful. Look at you there, look how happy you look,' she says, picking up a photo of me taken as I walked into the wedding breakfast, holding Liam's hand. I am smiling from ear to ear, Liam too. If you focus on my happiness, you really don't notice my body.

'Who is this?' Lauren says, picking up a picture of my mother and me. She is in a wheelchair, wearing a black dress. I am standing next to her. I have managed to create a pained smile, my mother is looking off camera. The photo speaks volumes and about how I was feeling. Agonised. Hateful.

'It's my mother,' I tell Lauren. She looks at the photo for a while.

'You don't look like her,' Lauren says.

'Thank goodness,' I say.

'Yeah, she's a real minger.'

'Yeah, she really is,' I laugh. I haven't heard the word 'minger' since I was called it in school. I put all the photos back in the box and put the lid on.

'You don't need to do anything to those photos, Ruby, they're perfect as they are. They are your truth.'

'I could say the same about you,' I say. She smiles and nods, as if accepting my words.

'So have you spoken to Gavin?' I ask.

'No, not personally. Our, I mean, *his* PR wrote to me asking me to do a post. Threatening me, saying if I didn't say something myself, she would be forced to write a quote for me. Apparently, Gavin said he'd pay me three million if I said the reason for the wedding not going ahead was because I backed out due to my own "problems". She said they didn't mind what I said my problems were. I ignored her, the bitch. He can think again if I'm going to get paid off to save his reputation.'

'Good for you.'

'Unfortunately, I'm learning that I don't really exist publicly without him. Three brands have pulled out of working with me off the back of my "mental health". They say they have ceased to work with me while I work out my problems. Meanwhile Gavin continues to pull in millions and be everyone's hero and Mr Nice Guy.'

'That's really terrible. I'm so sorry it's turned out that way. What about your mum?'

'I have no plans to speak to her again. I think I've been looking for the right excuse to cut her out, and she just offered it to me on a plate.'

'It must be liberating. My mother has a hold on me like a dragnet. I've never had the confidence to cut it loose. You're being very mature about it all. I'm sure I'd be plotting some sweet revenge.'

'Oh, I would if there was a way. But what am I going to do, send him a photo of me with someone else? He wouldn't care anyway.'

An idea crosses my mind that I brush away quickly. It's a ridiculous thought. Not possible. She notices that I am thinking.

'What?'

'Oh nothing,' I say. 'Silly idea. Would never work . . . '

'Come on, what is it?' she presses.

It's ridiculous. But, if I pulled it off . . .

'You need him to stop making people think it's all your fault, right? You need some currency, basically?'

'Go on . . . '

'Beth and Risky, they saw what happened? With Gavin and your mum?'

'Yes.'

'Did your mum or Gavin see them?'

'No, not at the time. We confronted Mum later.'

'So hypothetically, could Risky or Beth have taken a photo when they saw them having sex?' Getting a little excited at the thought of this.

'God, why would they do that? That would be so weird,' Lauren says, and of course she is right.

'Yes, but it could have happened, right?' I ask, needing this to be very clear.

'Yes, I suppose so. One of them could have taken a photo if they were total perverts.'

'How damaging would it be for him and his business to know about his infidelity?' I ask, fully invested.

'Pretty bad. I mean, it would embarrass him a lot, that's for sure. He wouldn't want it.'

'OK, then I think I have an idea. Let me get you some more water, and I'll explain,' I say, disappearing into the kitchen.

I have to say, I really am a genius sometimes.

Beth

Risky and I were having a cup of tea when Lauren called.

'Beth, hi it's Lauren. You know you asked if there was anything else you could do for me? Well there is. If I come and get you in an hour, can you and Risky take the afternoon off to come and help me with something?'

I asked her what it was, but she wouldn't say. I agreed, of course, and she is due to arrive any minute. Risky and I have been speculating as to what it might be.

'Maybe she wants us to go and clear out her closets at their house?' Risky suggested, but why would she ask us that? I thought maybe she wanted us to draft a quote for the press. But she really wouldn't need to come and 'get us' for that. Risky's final idea is that she wants us to all go away for a spa break together. I warned her not to get too excited about that idea.

When Lauren comes into the office, she is accompanied by the woman who saved Lauren from her suicide attempt, whose name, I now learn, is Ruby. She's quite an intimidating looking person. Very thin, and of course I know what lies beneath her clothes.

Tommy is asleep in his bouncer. Lauren coos over him for a minute or two, before getting to business.

'We've had an idea,' she says, taking a seat. 'It will involve absolute confidentiality from you. No NDAs, just a promise. If we do this, only the four of us can ever know it happened, OK?'

Oh shit, she wants us to help her murder Gavin?

Risky just keeps nodding. She is Team Lauren all the way, and happy to throw herself into the ring, but I demand to know a little bit more. Ruby helps Lauren explain.

'Lauren tells me that you both saw Gavin and Mayra . . . at it?'

We both confirm that we did. This is such a weird conversation.

'Right, how vividly do you remember it?' she asks.

'Like it is right in front of me now,' Risky says.

'Yup, me too. Kind of hard to forget,' I add.

Lauren looks pleased. Which is strange when you think we are talking about seeing her fiancé have sex with her mother.

'OK,' continues Ruby. 'We're going to create a photograph of exactly what you saw, using photos that Rebecca took of Mayra and Gavin.'

'FUCK A DUCK!' Risky screeches, air punching and jumping for joy. 'Shit, sorry,' she says, referring to potentially waking Tommy up. Luckily she didn't. 'Brilliant. Yes, yes I'm in,' she yelps, like her favourite team just scored. Maybe they did. I take the more professional route.

'Isn't that illegal?' I ask gently, not wanting to be a party pooper.

'Yes, but also it did happen, right?' Lauren asks, looking at us and possibly thinking, *Shit, imagine if they just made this whole thing up.*

'It absolutely happened,' I tell her.

'Right then, how would Mayra or Gavin know that you didn't take a photo? You could have, couldn't you?'

'Yup, they had no idea we were there,' Risky says. I'm not going to win if I try to get out of this, I can tell that already.

'Great,' Ruby says. 'Then all we have to do is go to the venue, you show me the room and the exact spot you saw them doing it, what they were doing and how. I'll take more photos, then manipulate them together, creating a seamless image of them in all their glory.'

'Glory?' Lauren says, not liking that.

'Sorry, how about shameful glory?' Ruby says, correcting herself. Lauren seems happier.

'Do you think you can do that?' Risky asks Ruby.

'A hundred per cent, if you'll tell me what you saw. Are you in?'

Again, Risky puts up no resistance.

'I'll pay you,' Lauren says, sweetening the deal even more. 'Five grand, each, for your help. I realise this is asking a lot.'

Risky might as well lie on the floor and start masturbating. She is all over this.

Ruby has stiffened a little. 'Ten grand for me, I think, don't you? I am the artist.'

'Wow, OK. For you ten grand. I am paying for your silence. Everyone in?' Lauren asks, looking much more excited than offended.

'Well, that's way more exciting than signing more of those NDAs,' I say. 'What will you do with the picture?' I ask Lauren.

'I'll use it to get Gavin to stop making me out to be a fucking lunatic, that's what. I'll threaten him with it. Say I'll post it if he doesn't stop. His image is everything to him, he won't be able to cope with that. All I want him to do is clear my name, that's it.'

'OK, I'm in,' I say. That money will mean I can take even more time off to be with Tommy.

'Me too,' confirms Risky.

'Great, let's just get it done,' Lauren says, ordering an Uber. The four of us head back to the venue, Tommy strapped to my chest in the carrier like my little partner in crime.

Ruby

'OK, which room was it?' I ask them, as we all make our way down the corridor like the kids from *Scooby-Doo*.

'In here,' Risky says, opening a door that leads into a library-type room. 'They were over there,' she adds, and I am pleased that the table they were leaning against is in front of a window. That will allow me to use the intensity of natural light to blur the minute details of the parts of the photo that I have to create. Like Mayra's thighs, for example. I don't have any photographs of her with her trousers down, obviously. I will have to improvise.

'Right, who wants to be Gavin, and who wants to be Mayra?' I ask the group.

'I might sit this one out, if that's OK?' Lauren asks.

'But I really need either Beth or Risky to stand by the door so that they can confirm what we're creating is as realistic and close to what they saw as possible. OK? I'm sorry Lauren, but would you like to be your mother or Gavin?'

'My mother then,' she says, reluctantly.

'Great. And Beth, Risky, which one of you would like to be Gavin, and which one of you would like to help me create the scene?'

'Well, I saw it for longest,' says Risky.

'OK Beth, that means you're Gavin,' I say.

'This feels weird,' Beth says, her baby in a carrier on her chest. And she is right, it is so weird. But I am also excited to do it. This is like the ultimate assignment for what I do. Recreating the actual truth, rather than trying to create a truth that never existed in the first place, but to a standard where everyone thinks it's real. Morally this sits much more comfortably than my usual work.

Beth gives the baby to Risky, who bobs up and down with him and seems quite happy.

'OK, you bend over,' says Beth to Lauren, as they assume the position of Gavin and Mayra. Beth presses her pelvis into Lauren's bottom, and I start taking photos.

'Lift your feet slightly off the ground, Lauren,' Risky directs. 'And Beth, a straighter back.'

'Is this really necessary?' Beth asks, obviously struggling with her role.

'Yes,' I say. 'I need to capture where your bodies are in the room, so I can lay Gavin and Mayra over the top. Please, I realise this is excruciating, but bear with me. Risky, how's it looking?'

'Great, Lauren should tilt her head in this direction a bit. And Beth, put your hands on her bottom, like you're guiding it forward and back. You know? Really shagging her?'

'Simulating sex with my client in front of my baby. Winning at parenting?' she says, getting into character as much as she can.

'I won't let him see, boss. Don't worry,' Risky says, making funny faces at the baby.

Beth does as she is told and pretends to have sex with Lauren.

'How much longer?' Lauren asks. 'I haven't had this much sex in years, I might need a nap.'

'Hashtag Marriage,' Beth says, breaking the camel's back and causing us all to lose ourselves in fits of insuppressible laughter. I struggle to catch my breath, wondering if my tiny frame can even sustain this level of hilarity. It's been forever since it had to try. I hold onto a chair for support. Beth is wiping tears from her cheeks as she tries to level her breath. Lauren is slumped onto a chair, her hands on her belly, guffawing like the exact opposite to how a jilted bride should be feeling. I sense relief from her. Maybe even some hope in the solidarity of her new friends. I have to say, I feel that too.

'OK, come on. Just a few more pictures. I want to make sure I have what I need,' I say, urging my models back into position. Soon enough, I'm ready.

Beth

There was something I envied about Lauren today. Reclaiming her power. Not accepting the position Gavin had put her in. Doing what she could to put herself on top. I know there is a large question mark as to whether what we did today was OK or not. But Ruby was right, we haven't lied, we only created a visual of the truth that all we know is real.

The truth is what I have to deal with in my own life. The truth about what I did, and why I did it. A lot has become clear to me over the past week. Understanding things about myself, and the way that people behave when they are not happy. To say the words may be hard but living with them trapped inside of you is worse. I don't want to be trapped. I don't want Tommy to be raised by a domestically frustrated woman. I don't love my husband anymore. That isn't my fault. That is my truth. It's time I dealt with it.

When I get home, Michael is watching TV. Since he went back to work he has given up with the cooking. It's down to me again to make sure the fridge is full, and the meals are prepared. That Tommy is taken care of. That the household runs smoothly.

'I'm going to bath Tommy and get him down,' I tell him.

He gets up and takes Tommy from me, cuddling him and kissing him.

'Hey little man,' he says. I know he misses him now he's back at work. Maybe now he will understand how hard it was for me for the past few months. I take Tommy upstairs. I bathe him. I feed him. I kiss him and I tell him, no matter what happens, he will always be loved by both of us. I put him into his bed, and I prepare myself for the things I have to say.

'Michael, can we talk?' I sit next to him on the sofa. He turns the TV off, making the fair assumption that it's about something serious.

'Before I say what I'm going to say it's really important to me that you understand that I'm not crazy.'

'What? Who said you were crazy?'

'You, Michael. You've been trying to make me feel like I'm crazy for years.'

He shuffles and looks ready to jump onto the defence. I don't let it stop me, not this time.

'Over the course of our relationship, you've become less and less interested in sex,' I say, looking him in the eye.

'Fucking hell, Beth. This again? Really? I've been working all day . . . ' he says, standing up. Ready to make me out to be crazy, or desperate, or obsessed with some filth I should be ashamed of.

'So have I,' I remind him. 'I've been working all day, taking care of Tommy, and thinking about us. All day. Sit down.' I wait for him to oblige. 'You've become less and less interested in sex. That's OK, I somehow think that we could work that out. We could find out why it was happening and find a solution together. I'd have done whatever it took. But rather than do that, you chose to accuse me of being demented, fat, perverted. You've done what you can to make out like I'm the one with the problem, not you. You were content to masturbate to hardcore porn but made me out to be a lunatic for wanting sex with my husband. Your double standard is unbearable. Your treatment of me has been so damaging that you gave me a problem, a big one. Not about my weight, like you hoped. I am very comfortable with the way that I look. But you did make me obsessed with sex.'

He rolls his eyes. I don't care. I'm saying this.

'I became so obsessed with sex that I went looking for it. I hid behind trees in parks and watched strangers do it, I scanned the Internet looking at porn, the filthier the better.'

He stands up again. 'OK Beth, I do not need to hear this,' he says, using anger to try to silence me. A tactic I am very familiar with.

'Oh yes you do. Sit down!'

He does as he is told.

'I slept with someone else, Michael. Last week. I felt so lonely, so rejected, so unattractive and so desperate, that I slept with someone else.'

'You cheated on me?'

'Yes, I did. I cheated on you. And I'm not proud of that, but I also know exactly why I did it. And if you don't take some responsibility for it, then that's not fair.'

'Fucking hell Beth, if you were a man telling me this you'd

be a dirty cheat. Simple. You think I'm going to go easy on you because you're a woman?'

'No, I don't. I don't expect you to go easy on me at all. And so we're clear, I am not going easy on myself either. I had sex with someone else and I know I will suffer the consequences of that. I just want you to understand that you're also to blame. You know that's true.'

'You cheated on me,' he shouts, his face getting redder. I know this hurts him; he was a good husband in many ways.

'I did. But it's not about sex, it's about how you made me feel,' I say, standing firm.

'How I made you feel?'

'Yes Michael. When you slowly chip away at someone they will break. I broke, and now we are broken.'

'My mother was right, you're a slut.'

'A slut?' I say, calmly.

'Yes,' he says.

And that is that. The moment our marriage ends. I mean, it ended a long time before this, but this is the moment I fall into it. Like leaving Michael is a warm hug, and staying with him would be like sharp fingernails scratching constantly on my soul. All the names, the digs, they just fade away. I don't need to please my husband anymore. I don't need to beg him to see me. I just want to enjoy being a woman.

'Michael, I'm leaving you.'

'Oh, you are? Actually no, I'm leaving you.'

'No Michael, I am absolutely leaving you. I'm leaving you because you checked out of this relationship and married me with false promises. You have no right to deny me intimacy for my entire life, just because it's not important to you. It's important to me, and I deserve it.'

'I'll take Tommy,' he says, his chest puffing up.

'No, you won't,' I tell him. I haven't felt this calm, this right in my own skin, in my own thoughts for so many years. 'You know that isn't best for Tommy. And you know I *won't* let that happen.'

He paces more, silent now. Other than the air that he pushes through his nostrils.

'I think you should go and stay with your mum, while we work this out. You can see Tommy anytime. I'll never take him away from you. But this marriage is over.'

As if lightning strikes him, he falls to his knees. His head pressing into my lap.

'I don't know what's wrong with me,' he says, hurting my thighs in his hands as he squeezes them. I open his fingers with mine.

'Come on, get off. OFF.' I hold his face in my hands. 'You are a good man, a good dad and a good husband in many ways. And I did love you. But you know this can't carry on, don't you?'

Weeping, he nods.

'Go and get some things and go to your mum's. Don't get there too late. She'll want to bitch about me for hours and if you don't go now, she'll have you up all night. OK?'

'OK.'

He goes upstairs and appears a few minutes later with a bag.

'I'll come back tomorrow to get more things.'

DAWN O'PORTER

'OK. And we can work out a plan with Tommy.'

I open the front door and he leaves. When he's gone, I fall against it. Relief overpowering any other emotion. I did it. I got myself back.

I run upstairs and gently lift Tommy out of his cot. I lay him next to me on my bed. Me and my baby. I fall asleep next to him.

This is how it should be.

14

Ruby

It took me six hours and thirty-six minutes to get the picture just right. I couldn't be happier with it. Ten grand works out at much more than my usual hourly rate, I can't believe she agreed to it. I feel a bit weird taking the money from Lauren, but this is my job, and it means I can stop doing what I've been doing for so long. No more ruining women's lives by telling them they should look a certain way. I don't know what is next for me, but I'm done with doing that. The money gives me some breathing space.

I look at the image of Gavin and Mayra. It's truly brilliant. I broke up the pictures Rebecca took of Mayra on the wedding day and cut them together with Gavin in his suit. Luckily, apart from the top of Mayra's thighs, they were both fully clothed, so I didn't need to try to recreate their naked bodies. I used Lauren's thighs from the shots I worked on of her previously and let the light from the window blur them so no details showed. You'd never know they weren't Mayra's.

But my favourite bit is the mole that Lauren told me Mayra has on her left thigh. I lifted the one from Rebecca's face, using the photos I took of her in the room at the wedding. I cut and pasted it onto Lauren's leg, making it fit the exact description of Mayra's. It's a little touch I am very proud of. No one needs to know.

I've done a brilliant job.

I send it to the WhatsApp group we created for approval.

Risky: You're a genius. It's exactly what I saw.

Beth: Wow! WOW! Perfect. WOW.

Lauren: I don't know what to say. Thank you so much!

Ruby: You're welcome Lauren. I hope it makes things better for you. Night ladies x

Just as I am getting into bed, a text comes through from my mother.

I'm going to hang myself with your old scarf.

I can't be sure which scarf she is referring to, but my mother's texts have recently become much more specific. Usually there is a generic threat of death, now she is naming objects. Yesterday she insisted she was in the process of taking pills. The day before she was going to jump off a cliff holding her cats. This is unusual, and the frequency of the messages is increasing, giving me more cause for concern than ever before. Her suicide threats were always sporadic and bland, they are now regular and detailed. Does that mean she is getting closer to it?

I've often wished she would hurry up. Turns out I am not that relaxed about it.

I text Liam rather than call, as I know there would be a lot of questions.

Can I have Bonnie this weekend? I want to go and visit my mother.

Wow, I mean, yes obviously. Are you sure?

I'm sure. Thank you.

Call me if you need me. Or you want me to come?

I took a while to ponder that. I do want him to come, I think it would be really good for Bonnie. Especially if Mum is in a truly bad way.

No thanks, I reply, regardless. This is something I have to do on my own.

Beth

'Cheers,' I say, holding up my champagne. 'Well done, Risky. You did a brilliant job on this wedding, even if it didn't end in a marriage.'

'Cheers,' she says, raising her glass to mine. I have brought her to a fancy wine bar to celebrate the end of the job. 'Yeah, we did well. It's a shame no one got to try the cake, but hey-ho, we know it was good.'

'Oh, I never told you? I took two tiers of the cake home with me and hid them in a drawer in my bedroom. I ate them while I breast fed Tommy, Michael had no idea,' I say, feeling smug.

'Ha-ha, good one, boss,' she says, as if I am joking and that would be crazy. Maybe it was.

'Anyway, the catering staff ate well that day,' I say. 'A few guests stuck around and partied like the wedding was going ahead. I suppose they may as well have, everything was paid for.'

'God, what a massive waste of money,' Risky says, shaking her head. 'To think people are out there starving. Weddings are so stupid.'

'I'll drink to that.'

We don't have another wedding for three months, so Risky

will be manning the fort in the office while I spend most of my time at mummy-and-me baby groups, walking around the local park pushing Tommy in a buggy, enjoying living in my house without my husband tapping away at my self-esteem, and eating doughnuts while I am still breast feeding and pumping out the calories that would otherwise land on my arse. I can't wait. I shouldn't feel this happy about splitting up with Michael before our baby is even five months old, but I do. I feel like I finally get to enjoy myself.

'So how's Michael doing?' Risky asks, taking a huge sip of champagne. We got a bottle and she knows I'll only allow myself a glass, because breast milk still feels like liquid gold and I hate wasting it.

'He's OK. He's living with his mother. He's going to take Tommy for a few hours a day while I'm still breast feeding. We'll negotiate a proper plan after that.'

'What do you think he'll do?'

'Honestly, I think he'll live with his mother until she dies. He's basically in a five-star hotel, getting every meal cooked, hot baths run every night, probably a lot of foot rubs.'

'That's weird, sounds like they are a couple.'

'Yeah, well they kind of are. They can live together with their weird sex complexes. To the happy couple,' I say, raising my glass again.

'Are you OK, Beth? It can't be easy,' Risky says, her hand resting on my leg.

'Yeah, I'm OK. He wasn't who I hoped he was. I'd be way lonelier if I stayed with him than I ever could be on my own.'

'How are you ever supposed to know if it will work? It's

such a gamble,' Risky says, looking despondent. Just weeks ago heart emojis were flying out of her eyes at the very mention of love, now she's witnessed truth beyond what her own heart can handle.

'It is, but if you win, I reckon it would be the best prize in the world.'

Risky gets her phone out of her bag. She smiles as she reads a text message.

'Adam?' I ask her.

'Yeah.' She puts her phone down. 'The last few weeks have changed a lot for me too, boss. I thought you and Michael were the dream. I thought Lauren and Gavin had everything. If you lot can't work it out, what hope do I have?'

'No Risky, you mustn't think like that. Adam seems like a really nice guy.'

'He does. But he's Gavin Riley's brother. I mean, he says they haven't got on for years. That he's always had a problem with Gav's behaviour, and that he really isn't anything like him, but . . . '

'Risky, but nothing. He isn't Gavin, and there's no reason why he should act anything like he does.'

'I know, but how am I supposed to trust him? Or anyone? Either not to cheat on me or give up on me?'

I never meant to shatter a young girl's illusion of love. The idea that she will walk away, just because of the fear of it not working out is so sad. This is why parents don't let their kids watch horror movies. Unnecessary fear of a world that is probably quite safe. It's a shame Risky witnessed such disastrous examples of marriage.

'Risky, listen to me,' I say, putting two hands on her leg and looking her right in the eye. 'There are happy and successful relationships all around us. They're easy to find, and they're everything you imagine. All you have seen in the past few weeks is that when they don't work, you never, ever have to be trapped in it. Nothing bad has to be forever. OK?'

'Yes, but how would I get through it? I'm not sure I could cope.'

'You are the strongest woman I know. And you know what you do if it doesn't work out? You surround yourself with other women, because together we can get through anything.'

'We can, can't we?' she says, feeling that sistership between me and her. My unlikely friend, who has inspired me in ways I could never imagine.

'Text Adam back. Make a plan to meet up and just roll with it, OK? Don't be scared, give it what you've got, and just enjoy. Even if a relationship ends, you can't regret that it started in the first place.'

'Do you regret marrying Michael?' she says, looking at me like I have the key to happiness in my hand.

'No,' I lie.

'I know you don't have the marriage I thought you had, but you're still such an inspiration to me, Beth. The business, and Tommy. Making that work, being present for both. It's incredible. And you're a real women's woman. I don't know what I'd do without your support.'

'Thanks Risky, I feel the absolute same about you.'

365

Picking her phone back up, she does as I suggest. 'Maybe it will work out,' she says, as she texts Adam back.

'Maybe it will.'

I will always, no matter what, continue to sell the concept of love.

WhatsApp chat
Group name – Scooby-Doo

Lauren: Ladies, I did it. I sent the picture to Gavin. I said if he continued to defame me I would post it on my Instagram feed. He called me right away, the first time we've spoken since the wedding. He begged for me back. Said he was sorry. Can you believe it?

Risky: OMG, what did you say?

Lauren: I told him not in a million years. I did ask him why he did it though, why he wanted to marry me when he had no intention of being faithful. Why he slept with MY MOTHER ON MY WEDDING DAY!! You'll never guess what he said . . .

Beth: Come on, I need to hear this?

Lauren: He said fame made him feel lonely.

Risky: Oh excuse me while I puke in the bin. DIDDUMS!

Lauren: Yeah, well whatever he meant by that . . . I'm out!

Beth: Good one ;) What about your mother?

Lauren: Well, she says she will go to therapy. That she will try to work herself out. Honestly? I've made peace with her not being a part of my life anymore. I know that might sound terrible, but it's how I feel. And after all this, I want to have more trust in the way that I feel, make decisions based on my happiness, no one else's, you know?

Beth: Oh, I know.

Risky: I'm all over that! GO YOU!

Lauren: I feel like I'm finally going to break free from my past. A new era. Self-care (the real kind), friendship and honesty. Who's with me?

Beth: I'm in.

Risky: IN!

Lauren: Ruby?

Ruby: Sign me up! I'm proud of you, Lauren.

Lauren: I couldn't have done it without you all. If I ever get married again, you'll have to be my bridesmaids.

Risky: SO IN!

….Silence….

Lauren: Ruby? Beth? I'M JOKING.

Beth: Jesus, thank God, I nearly had a panic attack.

Ruby: Phew! Anything but that! See you soon, ladies x

15

Ruby

I have only been to Cornwall once since Bonnie was born. I drove there when she was five months old and she screamed the entire way. Upon arrival my mother refused to hold her and asked me to leave after just forty-five minutes. I don't know what I am expecting this time, but I am in a better place than I was. I want my mother to see that.

Bonnie is extremely excited about going on a train. I am petrified we will run out of snacks, that she will get bored and have a meltdown for the entire five-hour journey to Truro, or that we will get there and my mother will be dead, and that Bonnie will be traumatised for life. But, I am also of the mind that it is important she knows who her grandmother is. I keep having sad thoughts of one day Bonnie not wanting to see me, and her keeping her children away from me because I'm not very nice. I believe that would upset me very much. So on the off chance that is making my mother even sadder than her natural state, I am going to give this a try.

I have loaded an iPad with around a day's worth of kids' television shows, and I have an interiors magazine for myself. I love to read, but I'm not sure there is anything more glorious than daydreaming whilst looking out of the window on a train. The rolling countryside, the constant *brrr* of the engines. I am quite excited by the prospect of it.

I have a bagful of snacks for Bonnie, and a few crudités and dips for myself. I even got myself a small packet of Twiglets as a special treat.

'Can I sit by the window?' Bonnie asks me, her eyes lighting up at the prospect of it. I agree, hoping that no one comes on and takes the other two seats at the table. Bonnie chooses the backward-facing seat, and I am pleased as I am in the mood to look forward. She bounces around on her feet. I should tell her to stop, but it's very sweet to see her so excited.

'Can we go on trains more often?' she asks me, as we roll out of the station and she gazes at the tracks like she is passing over a magical land.

'Maybe,' I say, wondering where we will go.

I text my mother.

Mum, I am on my way to Cornwall and will be stopping in with Bonnie. We won't be staying, I have a hotel organised. We will be seeing you around 2pm.

I had wondered if I would tell my mother at all that we were coming, but as the train rolls on, I feel it is for the best. I'm not sure she would like to be surprised, and maybe with a little notice she will prepare herself in some way. Get dressed. Clean the litter trays. The text marks as 'read' immediately, but no reply comes through.

I found a hotel with a family room. Two rooms adjacent, connected by a bathroom. Bonnie and I have never spent a night away together before. Who knows how it will go. I rest my head against the window and watch her. Her face is squashed against the glass and I see her pupils zipping from side to side as she tries to keep up with the view.

'Mummy, Mummy, look, a cow,' she screeches in delight as she spots one in a field. 'Moooo,' she shouts in its direction, as if it might hear her. It makes me laugh. We are an hour in before she asks for either the iPad or a snack. Experience and excitement being all the entertainment she needed until then. I open my packet of Twiglets lengthways and put it onto the table. We share them. She then watches a few episodes of *Peppa Pig*. I barely take my eyes off her while she does.

'I think trains make me sleepy,' she says, rubbing her eyes. I tell her she can sleep, and after watching her not find a comfortable position, I take the aisle seat next to her, and have her lie down, resting her head on my lap. I stroke her hair until her eyes close, and she doesn't wake up again until around thirty minutes before we arrive in Cornwall. It's my favourite five hours I have ever spent with my daughter.

'Why does Granny live so far away?' Bonnie asks as we make our way out of the station. Thinking of her grandma as some mythical creature that she presumes will be like her other granny and play with her for hours and feed her endless treats. I've never told her otherwise. Her enthusiasm about this meeting is frightening me.

'Bonnie, there is something you need to know,' I say,

kneeling down to her. 'Mummy's mummy isn't like other grannies, OK? Sometimes she is very sad, and that means she might not want to play, OK?'

'She won't play with me?' she asks me, looking disappointed.

'Well she might, but if she doesn't want to then that's OK. OK? Granny June might be feeling sad because she isn't well, OK?'

I stand back up, and we wait in line for a taxi. That went OK, I think. I don't want to frighten her before she even sees my mother.

'OK,' Bonnie replies. 'A bit like you?'

'Pardon?'

'You get ill, and you don't want to play either.'

I kneel back down.

'I'm not ill, Bonnie.'

'Then why don't you ever play with me?'

I don't know if it's the sea air, the anticipation of seeing my mum, or the fact that I have realised my mistakes just in time, but I put my arms around her and start to cry.

'I love you,' I tell her. Promising myself I will do better. 'And I am sorry.'

'Where you going?' a taxi driver yells out of his window.

'Come on, Bon Bon,' I say, getting her in and doing up her seat belt. 'Let's go and see Granny June.'

I grew up in a pretty stone terrace on a nice street in Truro. Soon after I went to university in Falmouth, my mother sold it and bought a small ugly house on a dismal street about ten minutes away. People talk about living in Cornwall like it is heaven on earth, and it can be. My mother, however, chose to live in an ugly part of it even though she had the choice not to. She has always done things like that. As if it all adds to her trauma, giving herself full permission to wallow in it.

'Actually, can you take a left instead?' I say to the driver, as I give him the address of the house I used to live in. 'I want to show you something,' I tell Bonnie. She seems excited by that. I feel nervous. As we pull up, I ask the taxi driver to wait for us. He reminds me there will be a waiting charge, and I agree to whatever it is. This is important.

'Look Bonnie, that's it. That's the house I lived in when I was a little girl.'

Bonnie runs up to the gate. 'In there?' she asks for confirmation, and I nod. 'Who did you live there with?'

'My mummy and daddy of course.'

She stares at the front door. She's obviously quite confused by the concept of parts of your life happening in different places and houses. I've never really talked to her about any of this. I mean, she's three and a half, it's only in the last six months that she's truly started to grasp the English language.

'Where is your daddy?' The question I guess I should have anticipated.

'He got sick, and he died. Died means he isn't around anymore.'

'Oh. You lived with your mummy and daddy in this house?'

'Yes, that window up there was my bedroom.' That makes her smile. 'I just wanted you to see it.'

'Yellow is my favourite colour,' she says, noticing the front door. This shatters my heart into a thousand pieces. My dad painted the door yellow himself, it was my favourite colour too. By the looks of things, no one has touched it up since. To think his very hands did it makes my eyes fill up again. I miss him so much. I can just imagine me bursting out of that door, bunches in my hair, my school uniform on. Him chasing me with the car keys, ready to drive me to school. We'd sing songs all the way there, and all the way home. We were so happy. All of us, even Mum back then. Or at least she could pretend to be. I suppose you never can know what is around the corner. An illness, either mental or physical. One can strike at any time, tearing a family apart. Tearing a life apart.

'Come on, let's go. You ready?'

'Yes,' she says, happily coming back to the car with me. I look back to the house. I imagine my dad at the door. 'Bye Dad,' I say quietly. 'I love you.'

I text my mother as the taxi is pulling up.

We will be there in 2 minutes.

I give her a few moments, then it's marked as 'read'. She's still alive. The worst-case scenario will not happen, at least not today. It is safe to take Bonnie to the front door.

I knock gently but there is no answer. I knock again.

'Is Granny June not home?' Bonnie asks me.

'No, she'll be home. Maybe she's asleep.' I bang a little harder. Still nothing.

'Mum, Mum,' I shout through the letter box, a strong smell of cat piss hitting me in the face. I see through the house, and that the back door is open. I can get around the side. I'm feeling really nervous now. This seemed like such a good idea. I send another text just to be sure.

Mum, Bonnie and I are at the door can you let us in.

Again it's marked as 'read'. She's alive. We wait a few minutes, but she doesn't come.

'Come with me, Bonnie,' I say, walking to the side of the house, and down the path that leads to the back garden. It's a mess and very overgrown. There is a small fence that I lift Bonnie over. It takes a little negotiation with my dress – I wore a cotton version today, it has a small floral print. Soon we are both on the garden side. I lead the way, holding Bonnie's soft little hand.

'Is Granny June home?' Bonnie asks, nervously.

'Yes, don't worry. She's just in the garden,' I tell her reassuringly.

When we get to the garden, I tell Bonnie to stop while I peek around the corner to see what my mother is doing. She is sitting on a chair in the middle of the garden, the sun directly on her. Seeing her gives me a fright. She's never exactly looked well, but this is a lot to take in. She is enormously fat, spread over the chair with ounces of flesh hanging over each side. There is a cat on her lap, and one by her feet. Her phone is resting on her knee. In the three years since I've seen her she has at least doubled in size. She is wearing green shorts and a white t-shirt. Her hair is dirty and long, more grey than black now. Her arms are wider than my thighs. She has a thick beard.

I remind myself that her appearance is not a reason to turn away. I pick Bonnie up and approach her.

'Mum?' I say gently. Not wanting to startle her. 'Hello.'

Bonnie pushes her face into my neck as if she doesn't want to look. My mother slowly turns her head in my direction. She says nothing.

'I brought Bonnie to see you,' I say, Bonnie peeks out, but is too afraid to show her whole face. My mother stares at her. It's a little menacing.

'I don't want you here,' she says, softly but with undertones of aggression.

'OK Mum, we just wanted to make sure you were alright,' I say, gently. 'Can Bonnie see one of the cats?'

She looks at the one on her lap. I put Bonnie down. 'It's OK, go stroke the cat,' I tell her, but she is too frightened to go near my mother. I go first and stroke it. Despite hating cats only a little less than I hate rodents. Soon Bonnie finds the confidence and comes over. As she strokes it, the cat begins to purr heavily. This makes Bonnie smile.

'See, it's OK,' I say to her. 'You both love cats,' I say to my mother, wondering if this might be something they can connect with. She turns her face away and says nothing. She shuffles in her chair. Causing the cat to get off and run into the garden. Bonnie chases it.

'Mum, I know it's hard for you, but I'd really appreciate it if you could at least say something to Bonnie. She's your only granddaughter.'

'Did I ask you to have her?' she says, looking at me now. Her once pretty brown eyes now hidden with heavy lids. She turns away again, and I take her in. She is responsible for so much of my pain. So much of my anger. So much of my feeling of displacement, my inability to ask people for help, my belief that solitude is my safest place. Seeing her like this, I know she isn't well, but she was cruel before any of this. She had one job and she failed me. Why am I here? In a second so many things become clear.

'Bye Mum,' I say, boldly. Feeling like I have achieved all I need to achieve from this. 'I'm going Mum, and I'm not going to come back. My heart will always be open to you but only if yours opens to me too. If that doesn't happen, then this is the last time you will see me, or Bonnie.'

She turns her head to the centre. Still not far enough to look at me. She stares into the garden. Not in the direction of Bonnie. Her shoulders come up slowly, then she drops them down. Telling me she doesn't even care.

I lean in. She pulls her face away from me.

'I didn't ask you to come,' she says.

'No, you didn't.' I step in front of her, forcing her to look at me. 'You failed me, and I will not do the same to Bonnie.'

I give her a couple of seconds, just in case she has anything to say. Nothing.

She blows air out of her nostrils like a bull and turns her head away from me again.

'Bonnie, come on, it's time to go,' I call.

Bonnie runs over to me. 'The cat licked my arm,' she says, very happy about it. I take her hand. 'Why are we going?' she asks me.

'Because Granny June doesn't want us here,' I say, not wanting her living with any false hope about who my mother could be in her life.

'She doesn't want us here?' Bonnie asks, letting go of my hand and walking over to the chair. 'That's not very nice,' she says to my mother, but she is also ignored. 'My other granny is nicer than you. She gives me biscuits when I go to her house.'

My mother turns quickly to look at her. I wonder what she will say. She doesn't say anything. Instead, she hisses like a cat at Bonnie. It frightens her. I scoop up my little girl, and she pushes her sweet face into the nape of my neck. I remain still for a few moments, forcing my mother to acknowledge the affection that exists between me and my daughter.

'Up yours, Mum,' I say, before we leave. This time I add a finger.

Out at the front of the house, I feel an odd sense of relief. Like I closed a door, and can now keep walking down a much brighter corridor. Like the rest of my life has just started.

'Right, how about we go get fish and chips and eat them on the beach?' I say to Bonnie, wanting to distract her from what just happened.

'YES,' she screeches joyously.

As we sit at the beach, on the bench that is dedicated to my dad, Bonnie eats her fish and chips out of the paper that is resting on her lap.

'Yummy,' she says. So happy.

A text message from Liam comes in.

Just checking in, are you guys OK? I've been worried.

We're fine. It went as expected with Mum. Let's call it closure shall we?

378

I'm proud of you, Rubes.

Thanks. Hey, maybe we can have dinner Monday night, when we are back. 8pm at my house?

Sure, but isn't that a bit late for Bonnie?

Who said anything about Bonnie being there?

I put my phone on silent and drop it back into my bag.

'Do you want one of my chips, Mummy?' Bonnie asks me. I tell her no. We sit for a few moments. Her eating, me staring out to sea. The smell of the vinegar makes my tummy rumble.

'OK, maybe just one,' I say, taking a big, fat chip that is all soggy and soft.

It really is delicious.

Lauren Pearce – Instagram post
@OfficialLP

The picture is of two little girls. Both blonde. They are in a park in pretty summer dresses. Their arms wrapped around each other, they are smiling and look full of joy.

The caption reads:

Excuse my radio silence, I've had a lot on my mind ;) One is how I can get through life being more my authentic self. In the past few weeks I have read so many judgements from strangers about who I am. So little of it is true. There is something I have never shared publicly, because I have been too afraid to be identified by it. I realise now that was wrong. This picture is of me and my sister Verity. Verity died when I was five. She was two years older than me and she was the best big sister in the world. Her death was an accident and it shook my family and damaged us all in ways that may never be fixed. I've found talking about Verity impossible for my whole life. Until now. If I don't admit and accept that her death is a part of who I am then I will never be happy. I've tried to pin my identity to other things – my body, a marriage, fame. But none of that was real. What is real is that I think about her every day. I remember the way she smelt, the softness of her skin, the texture of her hair, the sound of her laugh. I remind myself so much of her that I can't cope with the way that I look. I want to be happier within myself, and that will come by accepting her death, and not trying to hide it for fear of it hurting me even more. This is the first day of my new life. A life where I accept myself for all that I am, and I don't deny myself my truth.

I am Lauren Pearce. I am sad and often afraid. I must ask for help. I am stronger than I think. I am in control of my life, and with the right people around me, I can get through anything. I miss my sister, I want to be happy. Oh, and I am single (wink wink). Who are you?

Who are you?

Acknowledgements

As always, thanks to my editor Kimberley Young and everyone at HarperCollins, for always encouraging me to push my words to the limits and being extremely patient throughout the process of giving birth to books and babies.

My agent, Adrian Sington, for always having my back and always giving me the best reviews.

Thank you to Clara Francis for helping me work Ruby out. You are a force, and our chats really helped me put her together. You narrating her part for the audiobook is even more magical. Thank you!

The Jane Club – a work space full of women where I take my baby and do a full 9–5. Why is that so unique? It shouldn't be. Thank you to all of the 'Janes' for your support and cheering on. I sat in the corner for months, barely looking up, and thrashed out this novel. Someone was always there for a chat or a cuddle when I came up for air. This place exists and that is a magical thing. Shawnta's cuddles should be sold in bottles, and everyone needs a Hailey.

To the other Janes in my life (what is it with all these Janes?): my sister and aunty. So much of you both is in me. I'm so inspired by you both every single day. I love you.

Michelle, Kelly, Mel and all your kids and husbands. My LA family. Thank goodness we have each other. Thanks for listening to me go on and on AGAIN about how hard my writing process is. Oddly, that part of the process is very helpful. Even if it's not that much fun for you guys.

Jane and Lou, my Dickheads. I MISS YOU! Louise, I write about friendship because I miss ours every day. I don't know why we live on different sides of the world, but we are nearly there with the kids being old enough for us to bugger off on a 'Mummies holiday.' See you on the beach, baby!

My Nancy Poo Poo's. You will forever be my poo, bum, willy, booby, friend. Your family is our family, we love you all so much.

Fergus, thanks for always being so generous and kind. The use of your office made great things happen over the past few years. Endlessly grateful.

Eloise, thanks for saying the first line of this novel so casually in a conversation, and basically inspiring the whole thing.

Thanks to the man who moved me off the park bench, so that he could clean it with wet wipes as it was dedicated to his daughter. I don't know you, but that moment we shared changed me forever.

Thank you, Mary Moo, for loving my babies. We will miss you so much. How will I get through writing books without you?

Thank you, Joanna, for loving my furry babies. Potato is very grateful. I think Lilu is too, but it's hard to tell.

Chris, my darling husband. We achieve a lot, and we parent well. I don't know how we do it, but we do. I wouldn't have done it with anyone else. I watch you with the boys and can't believe how lucky they are that you are their dad. We love you.

Art and Valentine, my two little guys. Thanks for the love and the material. You bring me (almost) constant joy. I love being your mum. I even like how hard you make writing. I like how motivated I have to be. I like that you distract me from total despair when I am on a deadline, even if I don't realise it at the time. My goodness, we are going to have so much fun.

Thanks to anyone I didn't mention here but should have. The rest of my family, the rest of my friends. I've been writing solidly for months, my eyes and fingers hurt. Know that if you encourage me, help me or support me in any way, I am extremely grateful.

Dawn x

If you loved the novel,
don't miss the

SO
LUCKY

podcast series

Available to download now

T FOLLOW THE H

DO READ

THE

OW

'Fearless, beyond feisty and seriously funny'
MEL GIEDROYC

'Fierce and funny'   'Wise and witty'
DAILY TELEGRAPH   DAILY MAIL

THE

COWS

[DON'T FOLLOW THE HERD]

DAWN O'PORTER

THE *SUNDAY TIMES* TOP TEN BESTSELLER

d brilliant *Sunday Times*